It struck Brianna that she could kiss him and not worry that she might draw away some of his vitality.

She leaned forward, lifting her chin, angling her mouth. His breath caught.

"It won't hurt you?" she whispered.

Travis lifted his thick brows and grinned. "Let's find out."

His broad hand went about her neck and he drew her toward him. His eyes dropped shut and he angled his head to receive her kiss. She gasped as the anticipation galloped through her.

And then his mouth found hers. The gentle pressure increasing as his fingers delved into her hair. A soft moan escaped her as her hands grasped, measuring the breadth of his chest and the round sturdy muscle of his shoulders.

Her mouth opened and Travis's tongue danced and thrust with a skill and confidence that made her go all liquid heat and pulsing need.

Books by Jenna Kernan

Harlequin Nocturne

The Vampire's Wolf #187
*Beauty's Beast #158
*Soul Whisperer #126
*Ghost Stalker #111
*Dream Stalker #78

*The Trackers

JENNA KERNAN

writes fast-paced romantic adventures set in out-of-the-way places and populated by larger-than-life characters.

Happily married to her college sweetheart, Jenna shares a love of the outdoors with her husband. The couple enjoys treasure hunting all over the country, searching for natural gold nuggets and precious and semiprecious stones.

Jenna has been nominated for two RITA® Awards for her Western romances and received the *Book Buyers Best Award* for paranormal romance in 2010. Visit Jenna at her internet home, www.jennakernan.com or at www.twitter.com/jennakernan for up-to-the-minute news.

THE VAMPIRE'S WOLF

—

JENNA KERNAN

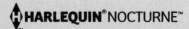

Recycling programs
for this product may
not exist in your area.

ISBN-13: 978-0-373-88599-2

THE VAMPIRE'S WOLF

Copyright © 2014 by Jeannette H. Monaco

Printed in U.S.A.

Dear Reader,

I am so pleased to introduce a new Harlequin Nocturne series featuring a fairy fleeing for her life from vampires.

My heroine, Brianna Vittori, is the daughter of a Leana-Sidhe (deadly fairy) with undiscovered abilities to drain the life force of any human lover. My hero, Travis MacConnelly (Mac), is immune to her deadly powers only because he came home from war a werewolf who can shift at will. Mac is a member of a secret force whose mission is to protect the world from vampires and knows why they will stop at nothing to capture her.

Bri recognizes that Mac is a wolf. What she doesn't know is that it is his duty to hunt, catch and kill her kind. She has run from one enemy to another. She says she's half-human. He thinks she's half-crazy. Clearly she does not know the powers she possesses. He should kill her. But like all Leana-Sidhe, Brianna is hard to resist.

Please tell me what you think of my latest story on Twitter, @jennakernan, or by writing a review on www.goodreads.com or www.amazon.com. And if you would like more about Bri and Mac, or for a sneak peek of my next story in this series, please visit my web home at www.jennakernan.com.

As always, enjoy the adventure!

Jenna Kernan

For Jim, Always.

To Mick Winjum, a former marine, for his assistance with research for this story. Any mistakes of fact or procedure are the author's. Semper Fi!

Chapter 1

Brianna Vittori peered out the windshield at the wet April snow falling so fast the wipers couldn't keep up. Any sane person would pull over. She kept going because the only thing worse than being captured by the military was being captured by the vampires.

She passed the sign announcing the distance to the Marine Mountain Training Center in the predawn gloom, driving without headlights, because for her the darkness meant only the loss of color from her vision and not the blindness humans endured. She could still see perfectly were it not for the spring storm that sent flakes splashing ice across her windshield. There had been no snow down below in Sacramento. But here in the California mountains spring acted differently. Driving conditions were so dangerous that even the plows and sanders hadn't ventured out. But then they weren't fleeing from vampires.

Was she mad to run headlong toward the only creatures that could stop them? The wolves could save her, if they didn't kill her first.

Werewolves were the vampires' natural enemy, but she

didn't know what they thought of Feylings. Her grandmother had not said. Bri thought again of the woman who had changed her world when she was only in high school. She'd told Bri that she was first generation—a Feyling. Now vampires were hunting her. She didn't know why, but they were out there right now, searching.

She might have walked right into their trap if not for her second encounter with another female of her kind. That Feyling had taken a risk to seek her out. The woman was blunt as a dull hatchet with her warning, but without her, Bri would have been caught. No doubt in her mind. They were there at the hospital.

The thermostat told her it was twenty-two degrees out there, and she was only wearing sneakers, jeans and a tight white T-shirt with short sleeves. Brianna gripped the wheel of the rental car and stared out at the night. The snow flew at her like a living thing, blasting against the windshield and exploding against the glass like drops of plasma.

She peered out at the sky, searching vainly for daylight. They didn't like daylight. She knew that much, and she knew what they wanted with her. Bri shuddered.

She glanced into the woods that lined the road, catching glimpses through the snow of something moving there. An elk, a werewolf, a vampire? It hadn't been until she was in elementary school that she discovered every child couldn't see in the dark. Now she wished that she couldn't. She shivered and fiddled with the heat, knowing the cold she felt came from inside. Better not to see what was stalking her.

She'd never run so far or so fast. But she'd outpaced the one at the hospital and the one in her apartment. It had been stupid to go back there.

She'd known she was different—"special," her grandmother had called her—but she never knew she could run like that. Perhaps you needed the devil on your heels to learn such a thing.

God, she wished she'd never found out about them. Brianna rubbed her tired eyes with her thumb and index finger as she steered with the other hand.

She passed the base entrance with all the floodlights and security. She lowered her head and continued on, anxious to get past this place. She didn't trust the military. The soldiers seemed like drones, mindless and intimidating, while their leaders were more secretive than vampires.

Something stood upright in the road. Brianna slammed on the brakes with both feet, and the car fishtailed. The man stood motionless as a ghost, his white face blotched with huge purple spots. Brianna's heart hammered in her chest as she straightened her arms and braced for the collision, no longer trying to miss him but trying to hit him, because she had realized that the being in the road was no man, but a vampire.

A moment before impact he leaped, clearing the car as her vehicle rushed beneath him. She was now sliding toward the ditch. The back end of the car hit the shallow embankment first. The car skidded sideways, tilting, and then rolled to the driver's side. She careened across loose gravel. There was a shriek of tearing metal and a crunch of collapsing plastic. The impact shattered the driver's-side window, which exploded into a million flying crystals of glass that flew at her like tiny bits of shrapnel. There was a final jolt as the car came to an abrupt halt.

Her heart slammed against her ribs, and her breathing came in puffy, white, vaporous pants of steam. Everything else was silent. Brianna unfastened her seat belt and looked about. The moment she breathed in the air, she noted the sharp scent of the werewolves. They were close.

Where was that thing that chased her? Had she hit it?

The answer arrived an instant later when the windshield exploded and the vampire reached his cadaverous hands inside the cab to haul her out.

She screamed and kicked, but he held on. He shook her to silence as another one grabbed her from behind. Brianna screamed again and the first one let go of her arm to slap her hard across the face. She'd never been struck before, and the sting and explosion of pain in her cheek and ear made her dizzy. She swayed as they dragged her to the vacant road.

Her knees wobbled but she remained standing. She was certain what would came next. Brianna recalled what that strange girl outside her high school had said. She was not to be caught by them. Not ever. For what awaited was a living death. Why did vampires capture Feylings? she had asked. The answer had turned her blood to ice. The April dawn and her panic turned her skin cold. She trembled as the first leaned in. It was the first time she had ever seen one close up, and his appearance made her flesh crawl. He stared with eyes white as milk. He seemed blind, but then she saw the perfect black pupil and realized it was only his iris that had the strange lack of pigment. His wrinkled ears and distorted head made him look as if he had some terrible genetic abnormality. But his eyes terrified her the most.

His slitted nose flared as he leaned close.

Staff Sgt. Travis "Mac" MacConnelly woke to Johnny pounding on his door and then to a female voice screaming just outside his quarters. He shook his head like a dog to clear the dreams from reality and groaned. What time was it? Oh six hundred, he realized. The pounding came again, on his window this time.

"Bloody hell. Johnny, I swear to God, I'm going to chain you up at night," Mac bellowed.

From outside the door, Johnny roared back. John Loc Lam had once been his grenadier, on his first combat assignment under a squad leader also on his first and, as it turned out, his last command. Mac scoured his face with his rough hands, trying to scrub away the grief that clung like tar.

"Fine. I'm up." Since the Marine staff sergeant no longer quartered in the barracks and he had more privacy, Mac slept in the buff. He tugged on his pants and thrust his bare feet into his boots. Then he stood, stretched and felt the familiar twinge across his torso. He glanced at the scars that crisscrossed his chest and right shoulder. There were four long slash marks from the creature's claws and then the punctures and puckered flesh where its teeth had torn open his shoulder. After four months, the battle wounds given to him by that thing had still not completely healed. Mac snatched up a shirt and thrust his arms through the sleeves, covering the worst of the scars, but he left the shirt unbuttoned as he tugged on his cap. "This better be good, Johnny."

He buckled on his holster, tapped the knife down in the sheath and checked the .45 pistol before sliding it home. Then headed out, not dressed for inspection, with his shirt-tails flapping in the wind. The first thing that hit him was the cold, the second was the unfamiliar scent. Since the attack, he could smell things, tiny insignificant things like the antacids the colonel carried in his left pocket. But now he smelled something new. Enticing. Alive. Something that did not belong in the middle of his territory. He inhaled deeply, bringing the scent to his sensitive nose. Like orchids and the ocean and exotic spices, and then he caught the smell of dank earth, rotting leaves and musty clothing. His body snapped to attention. They smelled different to everyone, they'd said, but the females' scent was universally irresistible and not like humans'. Since the attack, Mac could smell humans and differentiate between them and any other kind of animals, even from a distance. But these creatures did not smell human. They lacked the smell of meat and salt but not the scent of blood. That came through now and grew stronger by the minute.

Johnny appeared around the side of the concrete two-story enclosure that had once been a training site built to resemble the family compounds back in the Sandbox. Now it was their quarters.

John Loc Lam had once been a fine Marine. Now he was a huge wolflike creature, eight feet tall, who easily balanced on his two hind legs as he lifted massive claws and roared a warning, flashing dangerous fangs. His features were not human but neither were they wolf. Instead he combined both: small pointed ears, a long snout, wicked jaws and a face covered with glossy black hair.

"Do you smell orchids and blood?" he asked.

Johnny nodded.

Exactly what he'd been prepped to expect if he ever came upon flesh eaters. They were out late for vampires, because the sun was up. That would make it easier to spot, track and kill.

"Training exercise?" he asked.

Johnny shook his head.

Mac inhaled again. "Bloodsuckers. Males and females. Did you see them or come here first?"

Johnny gave no answer. He couldn't. He could answer only yes-or-no questions, to their continual frustration.

"I thought they avoided our kind unless provoked." He eyed his corporal. "Did you provoke them?"

Another shake of his shaggy head dismissed that line of questioning.

"Why would they come here? Can't be an accident. Got to be hunting us."

Johnny growled.

Mac drew his sidearm. He knew a bullet wouldn't stop them, but he felt better with a gun in his hands.

"Come on, then."

Johnny looked at Mac's weapon and shook his head.

"I'm going to keep it, thanks." Mac released the safety. "A couple in the head will slow them down. The bullets are steel."

Johnny groaned and thumped his chest. He wanted Mac to change.

"I'll turn when we get closer. Don't worry, I'll keep up."

Johnny nodded.

"We have to kill them." He stepped around his gunner. "Capture one if we can. The colonel's wet dream is to have one alive. Might prove we're ready for combat duty again."

Johnny nodded his agreement. He was just as tired of being a lab rat as Mac was. The two of them set off, hunting as they often did, only this time the quarry was vampire. When the scent grew strong, Mac pulled up to disrobe and stash his clothing before summoning the change.

Johnny paused to look back. Mac felt the familiar flash of guilt at his ability. He motioned Johnny on. No reason he should have to watch. Mac slipped out of his boots. Before the change gripped him in that momentary blinding bolt of agony, he issued one last order to his corporal.

"Circle behind them. If they come your way, kill them. That's an order."

Mac recovered quickly from the change, but Johnny had already gone. Mac was faster now, running on two long, powerful legs, his gray fur flashing white in the sunlight that now shone in bright rays from the east. He thought of what might have happened if the vampires had found him in his quarters asleep and wondered if they were inside or outside the perimeter of the training center.

He saw Johnny now, a black shadow running parallel to him through the trees.

Mac recalled what he'd learned in his new training. He needed to get to an artery, a big one. Femoral, brachial or carotid. *Open a vessel and hold the thing down until it bleeds out. Don't let it bite you and don't let it go.* It will regenerate any lost body part except its head. *Reopen the vessel if necessary.*

Instead of the forest, for just the smallest fraction of a second, he saw his Fire Team around him at the building they had once used for training ops before deployment. He pushed aside the tug of grief he felt at the thought of all the good men who had died in the Sandbox, his men. If he'd known what they faced, could he have kept them alive?

Decisions made in an instant now rolled through his mind with the regularity of the tides. He didn't know, but maybe.

Now he was back in the present facing more split-second decisions that he'd have to live with every damned day. If he told the doctors about the flashbacks, they'd say PTSS and he'd be sidelined for who knew how long. Maybe he and Johnny could prove their worth right here and now. But maybe he'd fuck it up again.

The changing light caused by the breaks in the clouds made it hard to see the things, but he sensed them. Could the vampires sense Mac the way he scented the bloodsuckers? Two males and a female, traveling together.

He saw Johnny drop and realized they were nearly on the intruders. He threw himself down so he could stare through the perimeter fence. He saw two male bloodsuckers dragging a female along the shoulder of the highway beside an overturned car, her feet kicking wildly, uselessly.

They seemed oblivious to their company. He glanced at Johnny who looked to him for the signal to charge.

He signaled for him to hold and glanced back to the intruders, gaping, as this was the first time he'd seen the Night Stalkers. The sight sent a shiver down his spine. There were two males and they were hideous, pale and rodentlike, just as he'd been told, with purple-skinned and misshapen heads that looked as if they'd been crushed. Their eyes were milky, and their noses, if you could call them that, were slitted as if they belonged to reptiles. And then he fixed on the woman, struggling against their grasp and making every effort to wrench herself free.

She did not seem of the same species. They'd said the females were lovely, and he was curious to see for himself.

She was tall and lithe, dressed modestly in a pair of faded blue jeans that sat low on her curvy hips. Her struggles showed him both the pink mobile phone that did not entirely fit in her back pocket and also the scrap of white lace undergarment that peeked from above her jeans. Her white T-shirt fit her like a second skin and had hiked over her flat stomach, showing a wide-open stretch of perfect skin and the dark indent of her navel. How long had she been a bloodsucker, and why was she fighting them?

The beams of sunlight chased across the yard, illuminating her to reveal that her hair was coppery red, shoulder length, and with ringlets that wound tight, curly as a corkscrew. They bounced as she tossed her head. He wanted to see her face, which was now covered by her hair.

Now what the hell did he do? He hadn't counted on killing a woman.

Not a woman, he reminded himself. A dangerous assassin. The female vamps killed by drawing energy. At least that's what the intel from the Israelis said. The Israelis had captured one but couldn't turn her, so they'd put her down.

She's not human. A killer. *A beauty,* whispered his mind.

He shook his head. This wasn't possible. Her allure didn't work on him. That was what he'd been told. But he still found he didn't have the stomach to kill her. She'd be the capture, he decided. The colonel's prize.

But first he had to get her away from those butt-ugly male bloodsuckers.

The vampire's grip bit into Brianna's wrists. She twisted and kicked, and she worried that she would simply be one more young woman who vanished without a trace.

"Look in the trunk. See if there's something to tie her hands."

The second released the latch and rummaged. "Nothing." He turned to peer at her. "Just knock her out."

"No. Not this one," said her captor, pulling her elbows so tightly that they touched behind her back. "She's special. First generation. Just smell that. I'd like a taste of her now."

Brianna stilled as the terror washed through her stomach and twisted her intestines. She felt dizzy and nauseous as his breath fanned down her neck in a hot blast.

"But you won't," said the one standing before her, just out of range of her kick. "You'll wait for orders or face his judgment."

The vampire behind her sniffed again as if she were some kind of cocaine.

"Still we did find her first. Who has to know? She's not a virgin. I can smell she's not."

"We need to get out of here before someone sees us. It's daylight, Ian. Any human could wander by."

"In this snow? Just one bite. What do you say? She'll heal before we get her to the Lord, and it will be her word against ours."

The one before her cocked his head, staring at her with those creepy white eyes, considering Ian's proposal.

There was a pounding sound, like a horse at full gallop. Both vampires turned, and the one before her shrieked as a black wolf leaped at him, carrying him backward to the ground as the great jaws closed on his neck. A second wolf, this one gray, attacked from the opposite direction, but the one behind her released his grip and vanished before the monstrous wolf got his jaws locked on him. The snapping sound came just behind Brianna's head. She crumpled to the earth as the black wolf ripped out the throat of the other vampire. So this was a werewolf, her first sighting and likely her last.

She saw that the one called Ian had run to the front of her car and then changed direction, circling the vehicle, coming back toward the gray werewolf, which now looked in the direction he had gone. She knew he couldn't see the vampire. But she could.

"To your right!" she shouted.

The wolf dropped and rolled in the direction she pointed, taking out Ian's legs.

The vampire sprawled and skidded as the gray one landed on his back, pinning him to the earth before using a hideous claw to slash at Ian's neck. The blood sprayed across the road like a fire hose turned on for just a moment. Then the blood pumped more rhythmically as the werewolf held Ian down. The vampire struggled as his neck wound sealed and healed. But the werewolf opened his neck again. Brianna held a hand over her own neck and then vomited in the snow. She would be next. Of that she had no doubt.

Ian's struggles ceased. His neck wound remained wide open and the gray wolf rose with his fellow. They turned toward her in unison.

They were huge, at least nine feet tall, and their front

forearms ended in long fingers with horrible hooked claws that dripped with blood. Neither had a tail. Their snouts were too short for wolves and too long for men, unlike any creatures she had ever seen outside of a nightmare.

Their teeth were worse than any wolf she'd ever seen, and she got a very good look as they peeled back the flesh from the long white enamel and growled at her.

Brianna scuttled backward on all fours and ran into the undercarriage of her rental. The black one snorted and stared with fixed yellow eyes, and Brianna saw her own death reflected there.

It knew what she was. She sensed that it did. A second low, rumbling growl emanated from its throat. She started to vibrate, preparing to move so fast that even a nine-foot werewolf could not catch her.

They killed the two that took her. Were there others? She glanced about and did not see any.

Brianna lifted a hand to her forehead and recalled thinking that she preferred death to the living horror that came with her capture.

Now that she looked death in the eye, she wondered if she had the courage to accept what came. They would kill her. Why wouldn't they? That was what werewolves did, all they did, if the female was to be believed. Still, she had to try. They were her only hope.

"Help me," she said, finding her voice a strangled weak representation of its former self.

The black one charged her.

"Help me," she said, huddling small and innocent as a fawn against the compact car, which was covered with so much road salt that Mac couldn't tell what color it had once been. She was an exotic bloom growing there in the snow and dirt, beautiful as dawn, as the first golden rays of morning gilded her coppery hair so it shone like flames about her pale upturned face.

Of course it was all illusion. She was as harmless as a heart attack and innocent as a brimming cup of poison. But not to him.

"Please. I have no one else."

She said it as if he were some human she could order about like a mindless slave.

And he would bet a month's pay that up until this very moment no male had ever refused her anything. Human males were easily manipulated by female vamps. Apparently she did not know that her powers didn't work on werewolves.

"They were trying to take me." She began to rise, a blooming rose reaching for the sun. He motioned her to stay down.

Why didn't she disappear, like the male?

"So I came here to find you."

She'd come on purpose into their territory? That was suicidal, he thought, or a brilliant tactic. As to which it was, that would depend on if Mac killed her or not.

Sea-green eyes, pale and lovely as glass polished in the ocean, stared up at him in wide astonishment. Her high cheeks flushed a beguiling pink, and a few freckles lay scattered across her nose, giving interest to the skin that glowed luminescent as a pearl. Yes, she was the most beautiful woman he'd ever seen. But she wasn't a woman.

She covered her face with her hands, letting her fiery hair sweep forward. *Now,* he thought.

As if reading his mind, Johnny charged her. *No,* he thought, but he couldn't order Johnny to halt. Neither could speak in werewolf form and it was too late. She must have heard Johnny for she turned, lifting her startled eyes. But instead of vanishing, she turned her head, elongated her neck, making it easier for Johnny to kill her.

This one was ready to die, prepared for just that.

Mac had just enough time to throw a shoulder into his corporal and deflect his course. Johnny crashed into the rear of the car as Mac hauled the vampire to her feet. She did not resist, as she had with the males of her species. He tugged her forward and she fell against his wide, hairy chest, looking up at him with sea-glass eyes. He had to remind himself that she couldn't affect him, because his heart obviously didn't get that message. Or his skin, for it tingled with a sexual awareness that lifted every hair.

He pinned her wrists against his chest, one in each fist. He realized her jeans and shirt were wet, and he waited for her to slip from his hold like water. But she only stared up at him with wide, frightened eyes. Next he noticed how slender the bones of her wrists were and how silky-soft her skin felt. There was an energy about her, like a static charge that made his skin tingle, as if she were stroking him. He banged her wrists on his chest, and she extended her elegant, manicured fingers so they threaded through the fur that covered his chest. Pink, he realized, like the inside of a conch shell.

Beside him, Johnny growled.

The smell of the breeze off the Gulf of Mexico surrounded Mac. So that was her game. The lure of her person. She'd counted on it to entrance him. That meant either she didn't know he was unaffected or she didn't know that it made a difference. Had she never met a man who could resist her?

Was he really immune, or had the scientists gotten that wrong, too?

If he were immune to her terrible powers, then why was he staring down at those soft green eyes, those parted pink lips? She gasped, bringing air into her lungs. She would be so easy to kill.

Johnny made a huffing sound, and Mac looked his way. The look of consternation was clear, as was the slicing motion he made across his throat. Johnny wanted her dead.

Mac shook him off and threw the vampire over his shoulder. They'd secure her for now and then call the colonel.

He easily vaulted the ten-foot security fence with the woman on his shoulder and ran with her to their quarters, trying not to notice the sweet scent of her skin or the tumble of curly red hair that cascaded over his chest like a silken waterfall. When they reached the yard he thought to wonder if her purpose was to find exactly where they lived. Would the vampires sacrifice the two males and this one to discover their position?

It was possible.

He tossed her to her feet and motioned to Johnny, keeping her wrist imprisoned in his grip. Her eyes widened as he gestured for Johnny to take charge of her. It was only when she saw him approach, teeth bared, hackles raised that she started to struggle. Her strength, though greater than what a human female would possess, was no match for a werewolf's. Johnny clasped her opposite wrist, because he did not want to give her a second to run. Not now that they had her.

How had that male disappeared? Could she do that as well, and if she could disappear, why didn't she when she had the chance?

He needed to transform if he were to interrogate her. But he wasn't about to let her see that. Standing naked and vulnerable before her held the kind of risk even he wasn't willing to take.

He gave Johnny a long look and a slow shake of his

head, waiting for the confirming nod of understanding. Johnny would not kill her, though he clearly wanted to.

Was he right?

Mac stared at the beautiful temptation and recognized that he did not want to let her go. He growled. Werewolves didn't moon after vampires. They caught them and killed them. But even as he let her go, he knew what he wanted to do with her and that troubled him.

Chapter 2

The black beast captured Brianna's other wrist as the gray werewolf withdrew, leaving her to her death. Her knees clanked together and then failed to hold her. The werewolf stared down at her with malevolent yellow eyes. She folded like a lawn chair as the black spots spun and danced, like gnats, before her eyes. Bri's head hung down, and she waited to feel the piercing pain of its bite, but it did not come. Instead, she heard the low, rumbling growl as it gave her one reckless shake before dragging her a foot along the cold earth, which smeared mud on the knees of her wet jeans.

"All right, Johnny." The voice was deep, commanding and totally unfamiliar. "Stand down."

The authority of his tone carried an absolute certainty that his orders would be followed. Instantly the punishing grip on her wrist eased, shifted as warm hands grasped her forearms just below the elbows. His hold was firm, but his fingers did not bite into her flesh as the werewolf's had done, and his index finger stroked her bare skin. She gasped at the tiny, intimate gesture.

She lifted her chin to find the black werewolf giving way to a tall, dark-haired man with a military haircut. He knelt before her half dressed in camouflage. The spots swirled into a vivid pattern of light. She closed her eyes, struggling against the darkness that threatened to consume her.

"Just breathe," he said, his words now lower, more personal, and lacking the bite of authority he used on the werewolf.

She did as he said, dragging in a lungful of air through her nose and then another. Her vision cleared and she noted his intent blue eyes pinning her, as surely as his hands that clasped her wrists. His eyes were not friendly; rather, they held caution and a glittering intensity that she could not read. He was imposing and not the least bit concerned by the giant hulking werewolf who stood panting and growling behind his left shoulder like some rabid dog. Where was the other one?

Her gaze flicked back to the soldier. The patch on his sleeve showed a chevron, but she didn't know what rank that was. His posture, his bearing, the ridged thrust of his square jaw and the fatigues all screamed soldier. Bri recalled passing the training center and the fence the gray wolf had vaulted as a child might jump a mud puddle.

The gray werewolf had brought her to this man. Who was he?

His camouflage shirt was all browns and tans, flapping open as he loomed over her to reveal a rising landscape of hardened, contracting muscle. Four long, raised scars slashed across the right side of his chest. They looked like knife wounds, except the marks were evenly spaced and puckered as if a gash, rather than an incision, had caused this damage. One scar missed his nipple by a hair's breadth.

And there was more. Peppered throughout the scars were a series of punctures. What had happened to him?

"Why did you come here?" he asked, his voice no longer holding that calming tone. Now it sounded low and deadly.

The hairs on her neck prickled. She tried to speak, but the muscles of her diaphragm seemed paralyzed.

She lifted her chin to see his pronounced Adam's apple and the dark morning stubble on his throat. The muscles at each side of his neck corded like wings. His clenched jaw looked hard as steel, except for the continuation of the beard that did not mesh with her image of the uniformly clean shave of most army men. His lips showed tight displeasure, making his generous mouth seem stingy at least for her. His long nose had a bump high on the bridge, showing an old break. It gave character to an otherwise flawless slope. His cheeks were high and smooth, above the distinct line of stubble that merged seamlessly into the sideburns of the short, bristled haircut favored by military men and athletes. Bri lifted her gaze to meet his eyes.

She saw the icy blue and decided in that instant she had made a terrible mistake. This man would not help her. He was a soldier, hardened, heartless, and she would find no pity in him.

The hairs lifted on her neck as she looked to the right and left for help. She caught movement and then the large, dark werewolf who seemed to be waiting for the order to attack. She stifled the scream rising like bile in her throat.

"What are you doing here?" barked the soldier.

"I…I'm looking for help."

His thick brows tugged together, forming a perfect bisecting line between them. She noticed another scar now, a thin white line that cut across the outer edge of his left brow, creating a thread-thin territory where no hairs grew.

His brows were deep brown. Was that what color his hair would be if he had any?

"Why would we help a thing like you?"

Bri gasped.

"That's right, sweetheart. I know what you are. Surprised?"

Her eyes rounded. "Yes. And you know about the vampires, too?"

He cocked his head as those blue eyes targeted her. Then he gave a slow nod. Maybe there was still a chance then.

"Then can you explain it to me?"

That answer made his head snap back. What had he expected her to say?

"You telling me you don't know?"

"Yes, I know. Bits and pieces. My nana knew they were after me. And a woman came last night to warn me about them." And suddenly one of the things Nana said to Bri suddenly made sense. *Stay single. Keep moving.* She understood now. Nana trying to protect her from the things that stalked her. But why hadn't Nana told her outright? Why hide the threat from her granddaughter? Nana hadn't answered any of her questions until the very end. Only when her grandmother knew she was dying had she revealed the terrible truth, and then there hadn't been enough time.

Keep your humanity, she had said. What did that even mean?

"How did you find us?"

"I can smell…" She turned to the one who waited to murder her, the scent of wet fur and wolf heavy in her nostrils. She could still scent the other, his scent closer, more earthy. She motioned with her head toward the black werewolf. "I can smell them. The werewolves. Scented them last winter and then when those things found me, I remembered what Nana said. So I came back here."

"What did she say?" he asked.

"That werewolves kill vampires."

That stopped him. He exchanged an inscrutable look with the beast and then locked back on her as if he were sighting her through a weapon.

"I hoped the werewolves might protect me from them."

He made a harsh sound in his throat that wasn't quite a laugh, for it lacked all humor. "Them? You must be crazy."

"I had no choice. They would have caught me otherwise."

The soldier leaned in, his nose nearly touching hers. "You had a choice, Princess. But you like to play the long odds. So your plan was to use the werewolves to protect you from the males that are on you like dogs after a bitch in heat?"

Her skin tingled and those gnats were back. This man frightened her again.

He moved in close, like a lover, but his expression stayed hard as iron. She could feel the warmth of his skin and the tang of his soap.

"And when the males were dead, who did you think would protect you from the werewolves?"

His shirt flapped open revealing deeper wounds on his shoulder. He saw the direction of her stare and tugged the edges of his shirt closed, leaving a long bronze strip of flesh still visible.

"I hoped to find help."

He sneered.

She held his gaze, wondering why her powers weren't working on him. By now he should have been smiling at her. But he wasn't. He was the first man who didn't get that dazed look in his face when at close range. Why didn't they work? He seemed just as cynical and suspicious as when he first set eyes on her.

She tried a gentle suggestion. "Why don't you let me go?"

He curled his lip and actually snarled. That black wolf behind him knelt at his side.

"Don't worry, Johnny. She's got nothing."

The werewolf huffed and rested his hairy knuckles on the dirt before her.

She expected the man to defend her, but he didn't. Just watched her.

Then he thumbed to his left at the black wolf. "You want help from him? He'd as soon kill you as breathe the same air."

"You can call him off," she whispered. "Please."

"It doesn't work on me, sweetheart."

How did he know that, and why didn't it work on him? She needed to understand what was happening to her. This man could give her answers. She felt it.

"Then you could protect me," she whispered.

"Not me, darling." He spun her so she rested back against the hard wall of his chest. His breath brushed her ear, his whisper like a caress. "They send me to kill things like you."

He wrapped one arm about her waist. His other hand threaded through her thick hair, drawing her head to one side, exposing her neck. She lifted her gaze to see the black werewolf snarling, long glistening teeth deadly as daggers. A whimper escaped her lips as she recalled what it had done to the vampires. So it was all for nothing. They'd kill her anyway.

Her body shook and she wished she could pass out instead of facing her death wide-eyed and trembling. Instead she seemed immobilized by the shining yellow eyes of the werewolf.

Mac tried to ignore her perfect body pressed back

against him like every man's dream. He had planned to render her unconscious so he could safely secure her without risk of her slipping through their fingers. Instead, he inhaled the sweet floral fragrance as his lips brushed the pure satin perfection of her skin. A tremor went through her.

The bellowing roar came from close by and then he realized it was him, fighting the change, the animal side beckoning, seductive as any mistress. Was that her power, working on his human half? His hands slid from her. Johnny roared and lunged. Mac saw a blur of light as his captive disappeared, then dark fur as his grenadier pursued her.

Mac sprang to his feet too late. Why had he let her go?

He could still see her, legs flashing like pistons as she leaped across the yard fast as a mustang before vanishing. A moment later she appeared on the top of the two-story concrete building.

Damn she was fast as a streak of light.

Not a woman, he reminded himself. Not human.

"Damn it!" Mac roared, knowing the escape was his own fault. Johnny had lunged only when his grip on this captive had slipped. Mac glanced up at the thing on his roof. He was tempted to get his rifle and start shooting. But that would be a waste of bullets. To capture her, he first had to catch her.

"How'd she get up there so damned fast?" he asked Johnny.

The corporal shrugged, and his silent accusation stabbed at Mac: *Why'd you let her go?*

"Did you see her move?"

Johnny never took his eyes off her as he gave one slow shake of his head.

"So how do we get her down?"

Lam gave him a baleful look and sighed. Then he drew his index finger over his own throat.

"No. We catch her and then we call the colonel."

Johnny growled.

"She used us to kill those bloodsuckers. Now she's got what she wants, she's going to fly out of here. Unless we can stop her."

His corporal lifted one brow, open to suggestions.

"I know. Maybe I should have killed her." Mac rubbed his neck, knowing that even with all his training he couldn't. "They don't affect us, right?"

Johnny gave him a long look as if he'd just shown some sign of madness.

"I know, I know. She's not some damned lost puppy. She kills guys. Guys like you and me, at least like we used to be. I get it, but…"

His silent partner stared him down.

"Damn it!" He glanced to the roof where she stood staring at them, like an angel with the sunlight pouring down on her as if the light loved her best in all the world.

Reports said they could fly, so why hadn't she?

Johnny huffed.

"They've never captured one. Never even seen one close up."

Johnny rocked from side to side in a restless gesture that told Mac he'd had enough.

"You can't kill her. That's an order. Got it?"

Johnny saluted, holding on and forcing Mac to return the damned thing. He thought they'd gotten past this, but the salute was Johnny's way of saying both *I'll do it* and *Fuck you*.

"I'm going up after her. You run a tight parameter. See if there are any more."

Johnny turned and took off at a fast run. Mac knew his

gunner could sustain a thirty-miles-an-hour speed for a considerable distance.

Mac returned his attention to the adobe building, which had been used for so many training ops that the stucco was riddled with bullet holes and much of the roof had been blown away.

"Come down," called Mac.

She turned to face him.

"Is it gone?" she called, the her voice ringing with urgency bordering on hysteria.

Mac rubbed the back of his neck and wondered if he should just let Johnny climb up there and scare her back down. But chances were good she'd disappear on him, and he wasn't sure the crumbling roof would hold Johnny.

"That roof isn't stable. Come down before you fall."

She angled her head in a way that told him she wasn't a complete fool. It was an idle threat. He didn't think she could fall, because they could fly or something damned close to it. If she really was ignorant of her powers she might not know that. But then again she might be just playing him, and she had managed to get onto the roof before he could even stand up.

"He belongs to you, doesn't he?" she asked. "He's your hound."

They were more brothers than hounds. He hoped Johnny hadn't heard that. Chances were good that he had because his hearing was excellent.

"Come down or I'll send him up."

She looked about at the crumbling roof. "Not until you promise not to let him hurt me."

"We won't kill you."

"Promise?"

What was he, twelve? He made the appropriate gesture over his bare chest. "Cross my heart."

She regarded him in silence for a moment. Why didn't she just run? They'd never catch her, even in wolf form. But perhaps there were more vampires hunting her. That would be reason to stay.

She nodded her acceptance. "All right. I'll come down."

He waited and she didn't move.

"Well?"

"How do I get down?"

"The same damn way you got up there, except in reverse."

"I don't know how I got up here."

"You flew."

"That's ridiculous."

He pointed to the ground. "Down!"

"Well I'm not doing the reverse."

"Why the hell not?"

"I'm not scared enough."

Which made no sense at all. Mac laced both hands behind his neck and stared up at her. He'd been kissing her neck when Johnny had charged her. Only that had roused him from her spell.

Maybe Johnny was right about her. She was too soft, too lost and too alluring. Everything they'd been taught said that since the attack, he couldn't be tempted by her kind. So why the hell had his body gone into a near seizure of lust when she threw herself into his arms?

Just a potent cocktail of lust and loneliness, he decided. If the colonel found out he'd let her go, he and Johnny would both be back in the brig. Johnny wouldn't give him up. That much he knew. His comrade might be pissed at him. Might disagree with him. Might even want to kill the captive on the roof, but he was first and foremost his friend. They'd walked through hell together, and that made them closer than brothers.

"Probably because you've been out here in the woods too damned long," he muttered.

"Too long for what?"

Had she heard that from way up there? Even her voice appealed to him. And her body—ivory skin, coppery hair, ocean-green eyes. Just the sight of her punched him in the guts. She looked more like a sea nymph than an assassin. He recalled those wide innocent eyes staring up at him and his gut gave another twist. Damned dangerous—very.

"There's a ladder attached to the back of the building. Use that," he called.

She glanced behind her to where he knew the ladder must be, then returned her attention to him. "Call off your hound."

Mac searched the trees, looking for vampires, because he knew Johnny wouldn't disobey a direct order. "He's gone. Come down."

She disappeared. Mac rounded the building. When he reached the base of the ladder, she was halfway down, giving him a mouthwatering view of her ass as she felt her way from one rung to the next. Lord have mercy, he certainly admired the view. It wasn't until she was nearly at ground level that he took his eyes off her backside long enough to see that she was breathing fast and seemed to be having trouble holding on to the rungs. She moved one hand to the next on the same rung, shaking her free hand, as if the ladder itself were too hot or too cold to touch. There had been a dusting of snow last night and an icy slush clung to the shady spots in the yard. He reached out to touch the metal rung, finding it cool and dry.

"What's wrong?" he asked.

"Hot. Burning," she said and shook her hand in the air as if to cool it, then lost her grip with the other.

She was fifteen feet up when she fell. He watched her

descent, expecting her to fly away or right herself like a cat, but instead she plummeted, rotating so she would land on her back. Mac raised his arms to catch her. She was small, but the momentum of her descent rocked him, nearly buckling his knees. Somehow he held on.

She gave him that wide-eyed look again. If it was an act, it was a damned good one. His body's reaction was instantaneous. Mac's skin tingled at the contact, and lower down his body went hard. He held her under the knees and behind her back. She felt just right against him. If he moved his hand a little he could feel the swell of her breast. Mac gritted his teeth and set her down.

Her kind needed sex. That was what made them so damned good at their jobs. The longer they went without sex, the more deadly they became. How long had it been for this one? Intelligence said that the vampires had kept some in isolation for years before releasing them on their targets. One night of bliss and then the payoff. A massive coronary, stroke or aneurysm. Simple, neat and undetectable.

Had she escaped them or was this a mission? Who was the target? Not him, certainly. Maybe the colonel. His commanding officer was working with werewolves. If they knew, that made Lewis a target.

"Thanks," she said.

"Anytime," Mac answered, reminding himself that the desire he felt was not caused by her magic. Couldn't be. He wasn't susceptible to her kind. But he was susceptible to this woman. Could military intelligence be wrong?

Mac held her high in his arms, becoming familiar with her weight and the long curve of her neck, the tempting hollow at its base and the riot of red curls that danced about her lovely face.

"Um, you better put me down."

Damn it, he could. Mac looked about for a place to lay

her. He was immune to her killing gift, which meant he could enjoy her charms without paying the check.

Mac stilled as their eyes met. It was the very first time since this whole fuck-up that he'd forgotten about his friend, and that was not cool. Johnny came first. Mac's job was to keep him safe and as happy as a man could be who was trapped in the body of a monster.

Now the first female who wandered into Mac's sights made him forget all of it. She wasn't an ordinary female, but still…

He released her legs so fast she startled and pressed against him. He went hard as wood; his body was still on *seek and destroy* even as his mind bugled retreat.

She pushed off his chest with her forearms and tried to step back only to be stopped by his hand, which was still pressing to the center of her back. Mac captured a wrist to prevent a second escape.

He studied her face, concentrating now on those lovely lips, pursed as if for his kiss. The woman lifted her free hand and blew on it. A shiver danced over his skin at the sensual action.

"You need to step away from me. It's not safe for you."

She was worried about him? That was a laugh. But then he realized that she must think he was human because she didn't know he was the gray wolf by the road. He maintained his grip on her and damned if he'd let go.

"Really," she insisted. "You shouldn't touch me."

"I'll take my chances."

She flexed her hands and winced. He tore his attention from her face, glancing instead at the palms of her captured hand. A cold icicle of horror slip between his shoulder blades. Red-and-pink blisters covered the pads on her hands from fingertip to heel. Some had burst and now wept clear fluid.

He clasped her other wrist and held her hand for closer inspection. "Is that from the ladder?"

"It's a burn. I'm allergic to some metals." She motioned with her head toward the ladder. "That kind, apparently."

Iron, he remembered. It was part of the folklore they had studied. But they'd been told her kind avoided only silver and that it didn't kill them, just pissed them off. It was a way to catch one, a silver pike pinning them to the earth. So that one was true, only iron worked better. Why?

He thought of the steel blade of his knife. That had iron in it, didn't it?

"I've got a med kit inside." Mac held her wrist. "You got a name, Princess?"

"Yes, it's Brianna Vittori. Bri."

His eyes narrowed. "Vittori?"

He glanced again at her milky-white skin, now taking on a luminescence in the sunlight, and that riotous red hair. She looked about as Italian as a leprechaun.

"Northern Italian on my father's side. My mother..." She trailed off.

Yes, they both knew about her mother. A seductress, just like Brianna Vittori.

"Staff Sgt. Travis Toren MacConnelly. Mac," he replied restraining himself from coming to attention though part of him already was.

"Irish?" she asked.

"American," he corrected.

"I meant the derivative of your name."

"I know what you meant."

"Sergeant? So you're an army officer?" she asked.

He winced. *"Marines.* Leatherneck, jarhead, devil dog. You're in our training center."

There were those wide eyes again. "Yes, *Marine* Mountain Training Center. I saw it early this morning."

"This way, Miss Vittori." All business now. If she affected him this way dressed in a modest T-shirt and full-length jeans, what would he do if she stripped out of those wet clothes? His pulse jumped as his heart began a useless pounding. He felt himself engorge. But he wasn't going to need that blood, thank you very much. He clearly wasn't immune to her sex appeal. He hadn't been with a woman since before he shipped out. Now that dry spell was coming back to bite him in the ass. Her fragrance drove him crazy. He exhaled and it was still there.

Wanted. Needed. Couldn't have, he reminded himself.

He'd get her inside. Call the colonel and get rid of her.

The black werewolf came back and Travis Toren Mac-Connelly sent it to clear the bodies of the vampires from the highway. The black, hulking monster trotted away with hardly a sound. MacConnelly escorted Brianna around the outside of the strange building in a grip that was more custodial than polite. She was beginning to recognize her desperate plan had some serious flaws, because though she had escaped the vampires, she was now detained by werewolves *and* Marines.

Bad plan, she thought. *Really, really bad.*

He'd said he wouldn't kill her. But neither would the vampires. It seemed she had only traded one captor for another.

The high wall around the series of buildings made it impossible for her to see more than the top of the two-story structure she'd found herself standing on. The hated iron ladder stretched up to the top. From up there she'd seen the perimeter wall and an open courtyard surrounded by one-story mud-and-brick structures that fit against the wall like the pueblos she'd seen in New Mexico. But from outside the eight-foot walls were just exposed cinder block. It didn't fit.

MacConnelly kept hold of her as she pondered how she had gotten up on that roof and why the roof seemed as if it had been the target of a mortar attack. The only solid spot was the one she had found herself on. The rest resembled Swiss cheese. She had stared right down past the collapsed timbers into the floor below.

Bri's ears prickled. She still had that feeling she was being watched.

The Marine glanced at her hands. "How long until it heals?"

So he knew about that, too, she realized. One of her earliest memories was of scraping the skin off her knee and then running to Nana, only to find the wound healed and the redness fading when she reached her. Even her broken wrist had repaired itself within minutes. She'd never been to an emergency room except with Jeffery. Her chin dropped as she thought of him, waking alone in the hospital and wondering where she was. He'd never find her. Never know the danger that pursued her and threatened him, and all because he loved the wrong woman.

He paused to check her palms. The raw skin now looked a healthy pink and the blisters no longer wept.

"You don't spend much time in hospitals, I'd imagine."

She drew back her hand, but he held on, tenacious as a terrier. "And you'd be wrong about that."

They faced off. He ground his teeth. She held his gaze and his eyes narrowed, the threat clear. She bet that was the look he gave his men. It probably sent them scrambling to follow his orders, but she only lowered her chin preparing to fight.

"You're in a restricted area. I'm placing you under arrest."

"Is there anyone else here?" she asked, ignoring that he'd just arrested her.

Mac blew out an angry blast of air. Was she so cavalier because she assumed that she could escape or charm him into doing any blasted thing she wanted? A few things came immediately to mind, and he knew he wouldn't object to her using him as her energy dumping ground for a start. He could take it. Wanted to take all she had to give.

"No one but the werewolf watching the perimeter," he said—his hound, as she'd called him. She was afraid of Johnny and that might be all that kept her here. "Why?"

"Can you speak to the werewolves for me? Tell them I'm seeking protection?"

"Why not ask for *my* protection?"

"Because you're a soldier, MacConnelly, and soldiers follow orders and kill people. I need protection from vampires. Only a werewolf can do that."

"Those things"? She had a lot of nerve.

"It's Sergeant MacConnelly, MacConnelly or Mac. I'm not a police officer."

Bri lifted her gaze to meet his. He was big and broad and tall. She could escape if he'd just let her go. She must have telegraphed her thoughts because he captured her other wrist, dragging her against him.

She made a bad showing at trying to regain custody of her wrist.

"Let me go," she insisted.

He shook his head. "The deal was not to kill you."

Then he turned and continued the way he had come, dragging her along beside him. She dug in her heels, lost her footing and stumbled, but he still kept going. *The hell with this,* she thought and sat down.

He stopped and glared but she held her position.

"You can't detain me. I'm a U.S. citizen."

She didn't like his smile. It held no humor and way too

much anticipation. "At the very least you are a trespasser. Federal offense. Now get up."

She didn't.

He stooped, using her captured hand to yank her to her feet. A moment later she was slung over his shoulder. He carried her along the wall just as the gray wolf had done.

"I'll scream."

He laughed. The world jolted as blood rushed to her head. He walked her around two corners and through an open archway to the inner courtyard she had glimpsed from above. The ground was packed earth with not a blade of grass anywhere. Along one wall she spied a huge pile of hay or straw that might have been used to bed livestock, except there was no fencing. He crossed the yard and deposited her on her feet, keeping hold of her wrist. They stood under an overhang. Three doorways lined the porch, each hung with a different color blanket suspended across the opening with a rope.

"It looks like a qala," she said. She'd seen photos in a magazine and read about the multigenerational structures created from this same reddish brick. Beside the doorway with the blue blanket lay a bullet-riddled motor scooter. She felt as if she'd stepped out of the state of California and into Afghanistan. "What is this place?"

He tugged her through the entranceway She blinked at the sudden darkness. Sunlight filtered through the blue blanket and splashed across the dirt floor. A moment later he released her. She stumbled and fell back to the packed earth.

"I assume you can't walk through walls?"

"Of course not."

"Great," he said and closed the door, leaving her in darkness save for the bright beam of light that shone beneath the door. She reached the opening in time to hear the lock click. She shook the handle and felt the burn of metal again before drawing back.

Chapter 3

Mac headed into his quarters and spent the next hour with a power drill, hacksaw and wooden planking. When he finished his work, he felt like he'd already done a day's work. He studied the results of his labors, satisfied that the barricaded window would hold her temporarily. He paused on the way through their kitchen to grab a cold bottle of water from the refrigerator, then he approached the door behind which Brianna Vittori waited. He paused, listening to her breathing—fast, because she knew he was there.

"Step to the opposite side of the room."

He heard her shuffling away. As fast as he could, he stepped inside and closed the door behind him. The closet was large, six feet by five, but he could still feel the heat of her skin. It took only a moment for his eyes to adjust to the darkness, and when he did it was to find her gaze on him.

Could she see in the dark?

He tossed the water bottle toward her middle. She lifted her hands and caught it easily, answering his question.

"Thank you," she said and released the cap before lifting the opening to her mouth.

His night vision was near perfect if only in black and white. He wondered if she could see colors as he watched her raise her chin and swallow again and again until she had drained the contents. Why did watching her drink make his mouth go dry?

When she drained the contents, she stared at him, eyes glowing slightly in the dark. "What happens now?"

"I'm moving you to my bedroom."

Her eyes went wide and he heard the sharp intake of breath. Only then did he recognize what she must be thinking. He couldn't keep the smile from twitching at his mouth. Not that he wouldn't like to, but...

"There you'll have a bathroom, shower and a bed. I'll bunk with Johnny for now."

"For how long?"

"Not sure. Right now I need to take care of the ones we killed."

Her eyes went wide, the dark pupils impossibly large in her pale irises. "What will you do with them?"

"Turn them over to our superiors."

"But not me?"

"Not yet."

"Thank you."

"Don't. I'm not doing it for you. I'm not convinced you don't pose a threat to my CO."

"What's a CO?"

"Commanding Officer."

"But I would never...not intentionally." Her gaze swept his face. "You don't believe me?"

"There a reason I should?"

Brianna swept a hand through her thick hair as she considered her captor's question. "I can't think of one."

His head gave a funny shake as if her answer was not what he expected and then she remembered. In his eyes she was a temptress, a dangerous seductress artfully using her wiles on him. But the only wiles she knew about were her power of suggestion, which did not seem to work on this Marine. Why was that? She decided to try it again. She stepped silently toward him. His eyes narrowed and went cold, as if this were what he expected. But how could he even see her in here?

"You can see in the dark, too?" she said.

In answer he made a grab for her, and she was too slow to escape. He easily caught her wrist and pulled her out into the light, blinding at first, after the cool dark of the closet.

"Come on. Let's get you to your new quarters."

She followed him at a trot to keep up watching the muscles of his shoulders bunch as he moved.

He led her down a short hall, past a kitchen that seemed strangely out of place in this believable recreation of an Afghanistan qala. Before she could ask, they had crossed a threshold and then another hallway. He paused at the third door. She stepped inside and he followed, shutting them in. He regarded Brianna as her gaze swept the interior.

The one window was covered with rough-cut boards haphazardly screwed to the wall. A full-sized bed frame dominated the adjacent wall, and the bed covers were neatly made in military fashion. There was nothing else beyond a floor lamp, an empty molded plastic chair and a closed footlocker. Draped across the bed was a muddy, wet shirt. His, she wondered, noting his bare chest. There was nothing on the walls and only a small Persian rug to cover the cold concrete.

Her gaze flicked back to the bed and then to her captor.

The Marine stood, hands on hips. Bri's skin tingled and her stomach twisted with uncertainty. He did not look like someone who cared for lost, frightened women. Instead he reminded her of every recruiting poster of a soldier she'd ever seen—rock-hard jaw and implements of killing worn as casually as a woman might wear a bangle bracelet. She suspected he wore those camouflage fatigues to make it easier to sneak up on and murder his enemies. Now *she* was his enemy. What had she gotten herself into?

Her skin flashed hot and cold as she tried vainly to disappear.

She glanced at the scars that slashed across his chest, suddenly seeing a definite pattern. This wound was not random like one made from bits of flying shrapnel. The puckered marks looked like teeth imprints. As if a bear had clamped down on his shoulder as it clawed at his torso.

"What now?"

"Still deciding." He pointed to the bed. "Sit down."

She did, rubbing her palms reflexively back and forth as she waited for what was to come.

He leaned back against the door and folded his muscular arms across his wide chest. She stared up at him, his posture now all menace and might. His eyes were cold as blue glass. A chill danced up her spine.

"How did you get away from them? And don't bullshit me."

"A woman warned me. She showed up out of the blue and told me that I was like her. The same thing the woman that came to my school my senior year said. Two different women. They looked so different in every way, completely, but there was also something akin about them, other than their stunning physical beauty. When I told Nana about her, she moved us again. And she made me promise not to tell anyone. We were always moving. She died one month ago, but before she went she told me what I am." Bri tried to remember what the woman had said, but it blurred together with her nana's warning to keep moving. But she hadn't. She'd stayed because Jeffery had asked her to stay.

"Who was the woman?" he asked.

"She said she was like me. But she'd been captured by those things."

"By the Chasers. They're the ones who track females like you."

"Yes, maybe. She said they caught her and trained her. She said years. The vampires had held her for years and would kill her if they found out she had warned me. She told me to run and I did. I ran home. But they found me there."

She'd left the strange woman at the hospital—or rather, the woman had left her. Something about her beauty and her earnest tone had terrified Brianna through and through. Her warning delivered, she had said they were coming then vanished right before Bri's eyes.

Of course Brianna had bolted. She'd hurried to the parking garage and run a red light getting home. Only home wasn't safe, either.

Brianna trembled as she told him of her return to the empty apartment. "Someone broke in."

She recalled the sound of a shatterring glass window coming from the empty bedroom across the hallway from hers. If they had entered her room instead, would she have had time to escape? She didn't think so, and the realization of how nearly she came to capture chilled her skin.

Her heart had jumped to piston-firing speed at the crunch of someone walking on a carpet of broken glass across the hall from her bedroom. She'd snatched up her shoes and thrust down until her feet her heels slipped into place. She'd headed for the window as the thing turned the knob of her bedroom door.

"It trapped me in my bedroom," she said to Mac, as she flinched at the memory of the thing hitting her bedroom door.

Bri remembered it crashing into the room. "It had glowing red eyes and a face so pale it was bluish, like skimmed milk. It opened its mouth. It had a scarlet tongue, and fangs like a lion. So I jumped. It was three floors up, but still I…"

She didn't really see the Marine anymore. Her mind had turned inward, seeing that thing charge her and feeling the air rush past as she jumped from the second-story window, screaming, into the night.

"I fell, but I didn't really. I just bounced like I was on a spring. It followed me. I saw it on the apartment roof."

Bri had jumped again, out over the parking lot, down Bell Street, past the Jack-in-the-Box and over the cars that waited at the drive-through.

"I lost him. Then I thought if I kept jumping he might see me over the buildings, so I just ran. I never ran so fast before. Didn't know I could." It wasn't her normal jogging speed. She had been as fleet as Mercury in his golden sandals, and her breathing came swift and easy as an Olympic runner. "I passed a young couple on the sidewalk, but they seemed to be standing still. Neither one even turned a head in my direction." How was any of that even possible?

"And I wasn't tired. I passed a car rental place. I got a compact car. Then I remembered what that woman had said, the one at the high school, about vampires staying clear of werewolves. At the time, I thought she was absolutely crazy. But she said they killed vampires and that I'd know if I was near one. I'd smell it. That it would raise the hairs on my neck, and then I did smell it. Before Nana died, just a few months ago when I was driving near here. I thought if I could find a werewolf before those things found me, it might kill them."

The Marine made a sound that brought her back to the here and now. He had only one arm crossed over his chest as the other cradled his opposite elbow. When had he drawn his shirt back on?

"Did it occur to you that a werewolf might kill you on sight?"

She answered with a question of her own. "Do you know what the vampires would have done to me?"

He couldn't hold her gaze. Oh, he knew all right.

"I'd rather be dead."

MacConnelly's expression changed as if he saw it coming before she did. He took a step in her direction as the tears started, rolling down her face as her breath caught and the hoarse cries came from her burning throat.

"I'd rather die than let them touch me, use me," she whispered in that little voice she hadn't heard since she was a girl standing beside her grandmother's bed begging to sleep with her after a nightmare. Her nana never let her. She'd walk her back to her own room and sit with her until she slept telling her the stories of the little folk, the Selies and the Fairy Court.

All real, according to Nana's deathbed confession. The rambling of a confused mind, the doctors had said, and she had tried so hard to believe them. But they were wrong and Nana had been right.

The sergeant moved to the bed and sat beside her. The mattress sagged. He was big and intimidating and he scared her half to death, but he didn't touch her. The only thing scarier was those things in the woods. No, the thing in the apartment. Bri trembled. Her world had suddenly become populated by walking nightmares, and Sgt. Mac MacConnelly was just one more threat.

"I'm sorry," he whispered.

Her uncertainty grew, swarming in her stomach like a hive of bees.

She didn't prevent him from dragging her to his side,

and she found she didn't want to. But she had to. If her nana was right than he must not touch her.

"Don't," she whispered, even though his arms felt so good around her. If she closed her eyes she might believe he could protect her from what chased her. But he couldn't. Only a werewolf could do that. A man, a human man, was just going to die because of her, and that would be her fault, too.

He'd been trained to fight, to mindlessly take orders, to kill innocent men and women. So why were his hands so gentle, his touch so kind?

Her shoulders shook as he held her against his chest, cradling her body to his larger one. She wanted to tell him to move back. That it wasn't safe to hold her, but the tears choked off her words.

He made a hushing sound as he stroked her head, letting his fingers tangle in her curls. The rhythmic caress and soft rumble of his voice made her tears slow, her trembling body still.

"It's all right, now. You're safe now." His voice sounded sincere. "I'll keep you safe."

Exhaustion crept through her now and settled into her joints. She ached to let him take control, and he did. His hand swept up and down her back and his strong arms enfolded her in warmth. It was almost enough for her to ignore the prickling at her neck. But it was there, the warning she'd been told to watch for and had felt last winter. The one that told her a werewolf was near.

How close?

Mac left Brianna's room sure of only one thing. He sucked at interrogation. He had turned to a big puddle of mush the minute she'd turned on the waterworks. When he held her, she had tried to warn him away. Didn't that show she didn't mean to harm him? Or did she know he was a wolf and it was all just a game? Either way he was way, way out of his league. The smart move would be to turn her over before she made him a fool.

His main objective was to get Johnny back to human form and, failing that, get them back in action before either or both of them went crazy.

Where was Johnny now? Had he finished the perimeter sweep?

Mac recognized with increasing chagrin that Brianna Vittori was very good at making people feel responsible for her, even if they were complete strangers.

He'd left the door to the head open and locked the others. If she worked fast and hard, she might pry those boards off. Depended on how strong she really was.

He should go help Johnny and he needed to move the vampire corpses, but he needed a few minutes to think, and he thought best when firing his weapon. So he headed for the narrow trench cut deep into the earth. His private firing range with an upturned stump at one end, to hold extra clips, and a target pinned to the earth at the other.

For the second time in his life, his world had tipped badly out of kilter. Decisions needed to be made, and soon. What if he made another mistake? Mac felt the panic grip his esophagus like a closing fist. The fear quickened his step. Mac walked right past the mobile phone that he should have used to call HQ and instead scooped up his ear protectors, then headed out the door. He didn't stop until he was in the pit, gun in hand. There he flipped the safety off his personal weapon, a new .45, and aimed at the square paper target mounted on the dead tree.

Should he call the colonel? His stomach tightened and he knew he wasn't ready for that. Not yet. But he no longer trusted his instincts. How could he after what had happened in the Sandbox?

He sighted his weapon and then he spotted something moving, low to the ground. *Bloodsucker,* he thought, and swung his weapon at the approaching threat. A moment later the thing dropped into his pit. Mac held fire, tipping his weapon up in a two-handed grip.

A cold finger of fear dragged down his back as he realized what he'd almost done. He tugged the ear protectors down so that they circled his neck.

"Johnny. What the fuck?" The fear now hardened into anger. "I thought you were a vampire!"

The werewolf roared and Mac flipped on the safety and holstered his weapon.

"You can't run around here on your OFP!" Perhaps a shot fired from his .45 couldn't kill Johnny, but that didn't change the fact that Lam had intentionally stepped into firing range. He recalled what they'd told him at the facility, that Johnny was becoming irrational?

Lam dropped back to all fours and growled.

"It's not funny. I could have shot you! I don't need that on my conscience."

This was met with silence.

"Did you scent anything?"

Johnny shook his head.

"Good."

The werewolf held his ground and Mac holstered his weapon.

"We need to clear the road of bodies before some damn civilians see those things."

A rumble sounded in Johnny's throat, not a growl, more an acknowledgment.

"Let me take a few shots. Then we'll go."

Johnny moved behind him.

"Johnny, I don't know what to do with the girl."

Lam cocked his head, a clear question in his expression.

"If she really needs protection, I know the colonel and the medical facility would be the best place. But they're human and, well, she could hurt them, influence them. Plus, what if she's not here for protection? What if she's here on a mission? Maybe to kill the colonel? It'd be easy. Do you think that's why she didn't fly away?"

His only answer was a shrug.

"So do we keep her out of sight for a while or turn her over?"

Johnny offered a third option, made a slicing motion across his throat. Mac felt his body tense as if preparing to defend her even from his closest friend. What was happening to him?

"Twenty-four hours," Mac said.

Johnny hesitated and then gave a slow nod. It hurt Mac every time he looked at Johnny. but he held his gaze as the guilt gurgled inside his belly like poison. It wasn't fair. Johnny was a good kid and a hell of a good Marine, or he had been. Why couldn't he change back?

Johnny had told him in sign and by scratching in the dirt that he remembered the attack. He only recalled Mac shoving him aside that night and then waking in the helo.

That much was a blessing because his own attack still filled Mac's nightmares.

"Prisoner's secure. Just let me clear my head."

Johnny sat behind the firing line.

"Probably give us a medal for catching her."

Mac realized as he said it that Johnny couldn't pin a metal on his dress blues, because since returning from Afghanistan, under heavy guard, Johnny had been just as he was today.

They'd seen action together, too much of it. His first

command ended in disaster. Three fire teams gone and only two survivors—himself and Johnny. He glanced back at Lam, wondering if either of them had really survived.

Mac would have given his life to go back to that day. But he couldn't. All he could do now was look after Johnny. And he would do that, by God, even if that meant protecting Johnny from himself.

Mac squeezed off one round after another, feeling the satisfying recoil of his pistol as the spent rounds bounced to the ground at his feet. He emptied his clip, breathing in the comforting smell of gunpowder as his wrist began the familiar aching. One clip, a second and then a third. Finally he reholstered his pistol, the warmth of the barrel immediately heating his outer thigh.

Mac turned to Johnny. "What will they do to her, do you think?" Mac asked.

Johnny lifted his eyebrows, which were two black tufts of fur with long antennalike hairs protruding from the centers.

"It's just…I don't know what to do." He looked at his gunner. "Do you really think we should kill her?"

Johnny looked away, gave a long sigh then a slow, unmistakable shake of his head.

Mac breathed away some of the tension that had collected in his diaphragm. "Should we tell the colonel or wait?"

He felt the ache settling around his heart, and he knew the answer to his own question. He didn't want to turn her in. But he had to lay it out for Johnny. "Because if we do, they might see what we can do and might give us our first assignment since…you know. Maybe back in the Sandbox. Finally get to see those motherfuckers firsthand instead of on crappy video taken through NVGs." He was referring to the werewolf that got them both, made them the monsters they now were.

Thinking of the video, shot through the night-vision goggles, made Mac queasy. The first thing Colonel Lewis had showed him was the footage of the attack recovered from the camera mounts when the first two Fire Teams went in. Both the grenadier and the rifleman wore one. HQ had six videos. Mac had seen four. Lewis had reserved the ones where Johnny and Mac were attacked, and Mac had not asked to see them.

Mac had watched their routine assignment to clear a route through a crappy little village that was so small it had been IDed only by coordinates. He saw what his teams had seen as they entered that building. Watching the footage from the first team had been hard. Watching the second, even harder. But it was just the beginning. The footage contained the only moving images of werewolves. The Afghanis called them the Devil Dogs, which Mac found ironic, since that was what Marines often called themselves.

But he and Johnny wouldn't be facing the Devil Dogs. They would be facing the werewolves' natural enemies—vampires. Up until today Mac had only seen an image of one, the first footage ever recorded. Today he and Johnny proved they could kill them.

He recalled the image he'd viewed, taken with a high-speed camera, on burst setting at the fastest shutter speed. Even so it had captured only two images, and they were blurry. The guys at MI—military intelligence—said they were moving faster than a human's ability to see them. They also said that the Taliban was using werewolves to fight U.S. troops and to protect against vampire attacks.

Vampires, they'd been told, were mercenaries, selling their allegiance to the highest bidder. Israel had at least one, and the colonel wanted a vampire of his own. He said that the U.S. needed soldiers who could keep their leaders safe, even from vampire assassins. But really, he also wanted the assassins.

Had he and Johnny been lucky today? Vampires could kill werewolves. Their fangs punctured anything, even a werewolf's hide, with the ease of a can opener puncturing a can of beans. And the poison in their fangs was deadly to any living thing, including werewolves.

Mac knew firsthand that werewolves were tough to kill, since his Fire Teams had pumped thousands of rounds into the one they faced and nothing stopped it. Mac didn't know if their skin was like Kevlar or if they just healed superfast. No one knew. But they were going to find out because Johnny's next training regime included getting shot with an M-16.

Mac's skin crawled at the thought and he met Johnny's yellow eyes, so different from the rich cocoa color they had once been. Was this why he stepped in front of Mac's practice today? Had he been trying to get a head start?

Johnny stood on his hind legs as he raised his nose and scented the air. Mac smelled the air, too, but did not find any threat.

His friend pointed to the east.

"Yeah. Let's go move those bodies." Mac removed his holster and laid it on the stump, then stripped.

Once naked, Mac summoned the change, gritting his teeth against the ripping agony that flooded his nerve endings with the upheaval within. He had become faster at changing now, and so he didn't end up on the ground panting with dry heaves.

Once in wolf form, he and Johnny bounded over the uneven ground toward the bodies.

Once at the scene they retrieved the two corpses, hastily stowed in the woods. The snow had ceased and melted, and everything was wet and cold. He could not see tire tracks on the road, so he didn't know if the accident had been seen or reported. He only knew no one had come yet.

Mac circled his hand above his head, making the signal that all Marines recognized meant helicopter. The old training pad was close and there was an associated storage shed where they could keep the bodies hidden in the short term. Johnny nodded, scooping up the closest corpse.

Twenty minutes later the two flesh eaters were packed away like the sack of blood they had always been. The cold would keep them until they could be retrieved by his superior.

They returned to their quarters together and Mac endured the change, still covered in a cold sweat as he drew on his trousers.

"You want to stay here and watch her or come in with me?"

Johnny pointed to the woods.

"Perimeter sweep again?"

He nodded and took off, leaving Mac to do the explaining. Johnny avoided the colonel whenever possible.

Mac cast one look at the makeshift home and then set off on foot to find the colonel. He wished to hell he was a better liar.

He arrived at the back door to the medical facility, the one custom-made to study and treat werewolves, so new the place still smelled of fresh paint and carpet glue. Once inside he headed to the locker room, where there was always a fresh supply of clothing to cover naked werewolves after they transformed.

A few minutes later he stood outside the colonel's office. The colonel never kept him waiting for long. He swept in with a quick stride.

The colonel still wore a jacket against the morning chill, and beads of rain showed on the shiny rim of his cap.

Mac snapped to attention and the colonel saluted without even slowing down. The eagle marking his rank shone on his sleeve as he removed his jacket, which was instantly swept away by his officious aide. From beneath the rim of his cap, Colonel Lewis's narrow blue eyes peered at Mac. His ruddy, narrow face showed his age, even if his body, still fit and trim, did not.

"MacConnelly, what's going on. They said it was urgent." He'd reached his door, opened it with a push and motioned Mac inside.

Mac stood before the desk and gave a brief version of events that did not include Brianna Vittori. An instant later Colonel Lewis was pushing intercom buttons and barking orders. Mac spent the next two hours retelling his tale, escorting the colonel to the bodies and then to the scene of the attack. Johnny's absence was noted and the colonel was pissed about it, even when Mac assured him that Johnny was checking the area for more of the bloodsuckers. Johnny had strayed off the compound a few too many times to be ignored. Where the hell was he now?

Mac waited while the techs swarmed over the wrecked rent-a-car. That crappy compact would connect Brianna to the scene. He'd just have to say it was empty when he arrived—which it was, because they were already dragging her off. She'd be reported missing and they might just assume she was a snack for the two dead bloodsuckers. All he knew was that he had to get back to her, perhaps move her to safer quarters, because he could just bet that the colonel or one of his aides would be stopping by unannounced.

Damn, he'd have to patch and cover the screw holes, take down those boards. Now Brianna faced two threats:

the colonel and the bloodsuckers. Was he willing to risk everything for her? He couldn't, he knew. He'd have to turn her in or let her go.

Chapter 4

At midafternoon, when Mac was finally dismissed and he returned to the compound, it was to find two new security cameras mounted on trees and pointing at his quarters. Damn, they had so many surveillance cameras every-frickin'-where that sometimes he felt like one of the prisoners.

He'd need to disable them both before he took Bri out. What was he doing, sticking his neck out for her? And then he recalled the smell of her neck and the soft feel of her skin. Lovesick or lonely, it amounted to the same thing. As long as protecting her didn't jeopardize Johnny, he was going forward.

He found Johnny's scent trail but opted to check on Bri first. He crossed the open ground and felt the mud sucking and tugging at his boots before he ducked inside. No need to wipe his feet, as this first room had once been part of a barn, staged for practice operations to resemble a facility to hold livestock. The back third had been walled off and given a concrete floor, converting the former barn into housing for werewolves. He stepped up onto the cold cement into the room that was a combination kitchen and living quarters with satellite TV, couch, recliner and a large futon propped against the wall for Johnny. Dirty, tattered rugs lay scattered over the concrete slab like dry leaves. Nothing but the best in military housing, he thought.

The kitchen, functional and industrial, was centered about the large freezer that held Johnny's food and his. Outside the single high window, the generator hummed, keeping the power on and the meat cold.

Mac continued through one of the stalls, pausing at the newly constructed door and the concrete addition added just for them. Unless she'd managed to get out, Brianna waited there now.

The colonel thought Johnny was scouting for more vampires and that Mac had gone to find him. Just standing here was a violation of a direct order. Or maybe not. He *had* found one, after all.

Opening the door, he surveyed the room. It looked much like a barracks with a large footlocker butted up against his bed. This queen-sized bed had been a gift from the colonel. Since space was not an issue and Mac was a big man, Lewis decided that his sergeant should have a real bed. At first he'd been pleased, but lately the larger mattress only reminded him how empty that bed felt.

He opened the door and slipped silently into her room to find her curled on her side in a ball, knees drawn up to her chest, her breathing soft and relaxed in slumber. She was beautiful as a fairy princess, he decided, recognizing that his snide nickname was actually accurate. For princess she was.

He moved closer, drawn by her unearthly beauty and the air of innocence. He's seen so much, been through so much, so to meet someone totally separate from all the horror, well, he could not resist stepping closer.

God, the smell of her. It was like a feast to a starving man. He hadn't had a woman since before he'd gone to the Sandbox. His body now reminded him of that with force. The ache settled into a solid pounding south of his belt. He'd joined the Corps, but he wasn't turning over a woman to his CO, no matter what kind of woman she was. He knew the treatment that he and Johnny had received. It wasn't always kind, but they'd volunteered. They knew what to expect, at least up until the accident. Since then things had grown more and more troublesome.

He needed to get her out of here before they found her.

Mac thought of the colonel saying that the Corps had never captured a vampire. The colonel had been pleased to have the corpses, but if Mac and Johnny could catch one alive, then they could study it. If there was a next time, the colonel had asked, could Mac try to restrain himself and bring in one still breathing? Mac thought if he and Johnny could catch one and turn it over to Lewis, they'd be heroes and still keep Bri safe, keep her out of it.

Mac pressed a knee to the bed and then stretched out beside her, carefully sliding his stomach to her back. He draped an arm over her arm and tucked her close. Bri sighed and shifted but did not wake, a testament to how exhausted she really was. He pulled Bri deeper into the hollow of his chest and arms as the need to protect her bloomed inside him like spring flowers from a dying tree. Was he keeping her safe, or keeping her only for himself?

Mac didn't know, but now he wondered what she would say and do when he told her the truth, that he was like Johnny, only unlike him—he could change back.

Immune to her kind, they'd said, but he didn't feel immune, not to her beauty or her scent or her warm, soft body. Oh, no, not immune. Instead, he felt as if she'd taken *him* prisoner.

He knew what the colonel would do to her. They'd all been through mock interrogations. She'd never make it.

He breathed in the sweet, alluring fragrance of spices and orchids and the tang of the sea.

Time to find Johnny. With a sigh, he eased away from her. She made a small sound in her throat, as if she was unhappy to see him go. If only that were true.

He crept toward the exit, afraid of what he might do if he looked back. Her sweet floral scent called to him. But he kept moving, fleeing.

He needed to be careful. If he got locked up, they'd put Johnny back in a cage.

Mac eased out of the room and shut the door, leaving it unlocked. Time to face facts. He wasn't prepared to keep her prisoner or turn her over. Johnny had wanted to kill her. He wanted to keep her. But the safest thing for Johnny was to let her go.

Mac paused outside her door. He felt a hitch in his throat.

"Bye, Bri."

Mac headed out in his human form. He wasn't as fast, but he was still as strong and had the endurance of the wolf. Plus he was carrying his pistol and phone so he could talk to Johnny once he found him. And when he found him, he'd assure him that he still had his back, would always have his back.

Johnny's scent reached him the instant he stepped into the courtyard. Lam was close and Mac had to run only a mile before coming on his friend. Johnny's wolfish head turned in his direction at Mac's approach, but he kept his back turned.

"The colonel thinks we are out looking for more vampires."

Johnny drew a suffering breath and blew it out his long snout, glancing over his shoulder at Mac.

"She says a male attacked her in Sacramento and she ran. They caught her here. She also says she can't fly, just kind of run superfast."

Johnny turned his head toward Mac, but still his ears drooped and his eyes stared vacantly at the ground.

"They have the bodies. But I didn't tell them about her."

Johnny met his gaze now, alert, waiting.

"I couldn't kill her, Johnny, and I couldn't turn her in. I'm sorry. I just couldn't."

Johnny lifted two claws before his snout and held them up like fangs.

"I know. I know she's a bloodsucker, but she's also a woman who asked for our protection, for Christ's sake. And isn't that what we do?"

It was a long time coming, but his friend finally gave one slow nod.

"Johnny, I left her door unlocked."

His gaze snapped to Mac's and his expression showed a flash of confusion. He lifted his hands in a silent question...*why?*

"I don't know. Maybe I just wanted to show her that we aren't dumb animals."

Johnny blew out a breath and gave a sad shake of his head.

"I know she'd likely kill us both if she could."

He agreed with another slow nod. Then he made a circle with his index finger.

"I don't want to catch her. I want her to go. We served our purpose. We killed her pursuers. If that's what she wanted from us than she'll disappear and good riddance. She's not our problem, is she? The colonel won't know, and we can go back to the way things were." Mac's smile faded as he held Johnny's gaze a long, silent moment. Back to living like animals in the woods and getting used as target practice as the REMF—rear-echelon motherfuckers—figured out what to do with them.

Johnny stood and offered a hand to help Mac up. His way of trying to cheer Mac up, Mac supposed. But in his heart, the wasteland stretched out like a wide, empty sea. Likely she was already gone.

"You okay with this?" asked Mac.

Johnny stilled, looked back toward the compound and then raised a hand to his eye, making a circle of his fingers and looking at Mac through the hole.

"They set up two new surveillance cameras. I knocked them out so they won't see her leave. But they'll want some answers."

Johnny pantomimed a phone at his ear.

"Good idea." Mac drew out his mobile and reported that he'd noticed a camera down. After a moment he shoved the phone back in his pocket. "They'll have someone out tomorrow to fix it. That should give her time to clear out. You want to scout for any more visitors?" Mac wanted to go back. He wanted it so badly that he knew he couldn't do it. He had to run, hunt and stay away while she cleared out. It was the only way to protect Johnny and protect the girl.

Johnny nodded and rose.

Mac removed his holster and then stripped out of his clothing, laying them in a neat pile. Then he dropped to a crouch, lowering his head to concentrate first on his sense of smell. This unfortunately brought Vittori's scent trail to his expanding nostrils.

Rage was the easiest way to summon the change. Usually he thought of the Sandbox, of that night when the last Fire Team was torn to pieces in that slaughterhouse. But not today. Today he recalled the feel of her in his arms and thought of never holding her again. The helplessness and the fury easily triggered the transformation.

The dizzy rush of power ripped through him as his body transformed. His nails turned to claws, his teeth to fangs, and his skin now sprouted the silvery fur of a wolf.

He looked at Johnny, who waited. Johnny was a bigger werewolf. But Mac was meaner and still in charge. Then they were off, searching for the scent trail of a male vampire heading through their territory at a dead run. When they reached the road, it was to find her car gone. Likely picked up by a patrol. He imagined the techies going over it, finding Brianna Vittori's name on the rental agreement. Had she been stupid enough to keep that with the car? Not doing so would buy her a little time. But not much.

Security was tight at this base, at every base. But they spent most of their energy looking outward. With luck, they wouldn't look inside the grounds for the driver of that car until she was long gone. Johnny could detect what Brianna Vittori truly was and so could he, but to the others, she would appear to be only a beautiful, alluring woman. If she really could run as fast as she said, then she might just get out of here in one piece.

Mac turned to run the perimeter of their territory, the long fence line. He would be certain that there were no other vampires here before he returned to his empty room, and the empty bed and the empty days ahead.

Mac was pretty far out when he realized that Vittori might not escape, as he'd hoped, but instead she could head right for headquarters where she would find Lewis.

That realization turned him back toward home. Not wanting to frighten Bri any more than necessary, Mac suffered the transformation before he entered the clearing surrounding the qala. He arrived at dusk and hurried into their quarters, pausing only to grab a set of fatigues from the trunk beside the door. Then he headed into their quarters to find his room empty. His gaze flicked to the window, seeing it still barred, and then glanced to the closed bathroom door. He stepped into the room and heard a soft humming coming from the bathroom, low and lyrical and so sweet it made his chest ache. So she was still here. The relief he felt took him off guard.

Why hadn't she left?

The humming stopped. Silence stretched. He hadn't made a sound, so he was quite sure she had not heard him. But what if her hearing was as acute as his? She took a shuffling step, her bare feet whispering across the tile.

"Johnny?" she called, her voice low, cautious.

And then he understood. She could smell him, scent the wolf in him.

"It's Mac," he answered.

"Mac?" The question rang clearly in her voice. "Is Johnny there, too?"

Lie or truth? He took the middle ground. "Close by, I'd imagine." Actually, he didn't know where Lam was, because he'd left him to head back here.

"My clothes are out there," said Bri.

"Yes, I see them." Anticipation curled in his belly. He wanted to see her naked; suddenly he wanted that more than anything else in the world.

He stared at the pile of clothing laying on his empty bed, which he still made each morning with sharp creased corners, though there was no one to inspect it but him. Then he glanced to the orange plastic chair set against the cinder-block walls painted sterile white and windows that were still boarded up tight. Why had he never noticed how empty this room felt?

A bare hand stretched out of the crack in the door. "May I have them please?"

He imagined the possibilities behind that door as he glanced at the pile of grime-streaked garments and then back to his target. "They're all muddy."

Frustration rang in her voice. "Well, they're all I have."

That made him smile.

"I can give you a clean T-shirt."

He waited during the long pause.

"All right."

He opened his footlocker, selecting a white one from the stack of neatly folded T-shirts, and then passed it to her before she closed the door.

"My jeans?" she asked through the closed panel.

"Those you'll have to come and get."

He sat on the bed waiting. The door cracked open and she peeked out at him. He tried to look harmless as the wolf inside him roared to life. He stared at her pretty, flushed face as their eyes met and hers grew wide.

He couldn't keep the smile from curling his lips. "I left the door unlocked." He glanced to the door and back.

She dropped her gaze. "I know."

"I thought you'd be gone."

"Where? I can't go back home. They'll be waiting there for sure."

Brianna Vittori stepped from the steamy bathroom. His T-shirt hung to her midthigh and clung in all the right places. Mac thought that scrap of cotton had never looked so good.

"Did you want me to go?"

He had. But now he was reconsidering. "It would be wise. I lied for you. Told my commanding officer that there were only two intruders."

She stepped forward, crossing the room on slim bare feet, as silent as a summer breeze.

"You have to see that staying here isn't an option."

Brianna halted a few feet away. Was she afraid to move closer or was she afraid for him, if she moved closer.

"My pants?" she asked, extending her hand.

He grasped it and tugged. She tumbled into his lap like a living dream.

"What's wrong, Princess?"

She slid off his lap, her head now hanging low as if the weight on her shoulders was too much to bear.

"Why do you call me that?"

He shrugged. "You look like one, like a princess in a fairy tale. You know, Snow White and Rose Red?"

She stared for a moment to see if he was mocking her. He wouldn't be the first to find her red hair an easy target. But she saw no malice in his pale blue eyes.

"You know that story?"

He looked away. "I have parents. They read to me."

She tried for a smile but got none in return. Instead his frown deepened. She broke eye contact and glance about the unfamiliar room.

"What time is it?" she whispered.

He glanced at his watch, a giant black scuba-style timepiece. "Eighteen hundred hours."

"What?" Briasked, not understanding. Military time, she realized. Twelve plus the other hours. Eighteen minus twelve. "What time?"

She didn't even know what day it was. She'd left the hospital on Saturday night and arrived here early Sunday morning, but then she'd slept. Was it still Sunday?

"Six in the evening," he said. "In civilian time."

"What day?"

"Sunday."

He walked to the window and tore the boards off as easily as one might draw back a curtain. Outside the daylight still clung to the barren courtyard, but the sun had set. Was Jeff eating his meal, alone in that hospital bed, wondering where she was, trying her phone and…

She scrambled in her jeans pocket and found her phone gone. Brianna drew her legs up before her and wrapped her arms about them, settling her forehead on the tops of her knees.

MacConnelly came back beside her. He sat with his feet solidly on the ground and his hands on his knees.

"You okay?"

She shook her head. "I lost my phone."

He said nothing to that.

"And I need to call someone, someone I had to leave behind."

"Jeffery Martin?"

"How did you know that?"

He reached in the pocket that sat low on his thigh and drew out her pink mobile phone. "He's left a dozen messages. Handsome guy."

"Is he all right?"

"Sounded good."

She gave an exclamation of indignation as she reached for her property. He handed over her phone.

"You can't call him or turn it on. I disabled it."

Her jaw dropped open.

He shrugged, showing no regret. "At the very least, the police will use it to find your location. But if those vamps have any kind of surveillance, they are waiting for you to call in. Get a new one."

She tucked the phone into her front pocket, wondering why she couldn't turn it on when he obviously had. He'd likely been through every contact, listened to all her messages and voice mail, checked her browser history. Why didn't she ever set that damned password?

"Can I call him on your phone?"

"And tell him what, that you are escaping from vampires? No, Princess. No calls. For now you'll stay missing."

What would Jeffery make of her vanishing?

"Is he your boyfriend?" he asked.

She thought of the image of Jeff on her phone, smiling and healthy. Then she thought of him pale and weak in his hospital bed. When she spoke her words came out in a rush, disorganized and with a breathy quality that showed upset. "Boyfriend. Nana warned me just before she died, but the doctors said her ramblings were the result of the medication. That she was delusional. I didn't know what to believe. But when Jeffery got sick, I wondered…" She raked a hand through her thick, wet hair, combing out the tangles with her fingers. "Nana knew they were hunting me and she knew it was dangerous for anyone to touch me. I mean, I knew I was different, but what she said seemed so absurd…" Her voice got small. "Why didn't I believe her?" She lifted her gaze to meet his. Her eyes were huge and round now as she grappled with her demons. "Do you think they'll hurt Jeffery?"

"No. But they might use him to try to flush you out. I would."

She gave him a look of horror. "But he's sick. He's in a hospital."

"Even better."

She pressed a hand over her mouth as the horror of this struck her. Then she slid her hand away and whispered, "I left him without a word. She said they were upstairs waiting, so I ran."

"They'll find you if you go back."

"I know. But to just leave him. It's heartless."

"Not as heartless as going back."

"Because I might lead them to Jeffery, you mean?"

His mouth went hard and grim as he slowly shook his head.

"He's very sick, and they don't really know what caused it." She didn't look at him as she spoke, and she worried her thumbnail with the pad of her opposite thumb. The shells of her ears glowed pink. "You don't think it was the vampires? They didn't bite him, did they?"

"Vampire bites don't make people sick. It's not like the movies. They rip open an artery and drink. If they're still hungry they eat. Liver, usually."

She shivered and rubbed her hands over her upper arms in a brisk stroke.

"And as for your boyfriend's illness…" Mac pointed out the elephant in the room. "He'll get better now that you're gone." She stilled and met his hard stare, her glimmering eyes a mix of hope and fear.

"Did I do something to him?"

He gave a slight inclination of his head. She bit her lower lip and braced, waiting for him to speak.

"You slept with him Friday night, right?"

Brianna's mind darted back to Friday night when her biggest worry had been whether she wanted to take her relationship with Jeffery to the next level. He was sweet and generous, and she'd been comfortable with him. Not in love but at ease, and they were like-minded on so many issues. She admired him because he helped a lot of needy people. But when he kissed her there was no spark.

Her gaze flashed to MacConnelly. The sparks were flying with him—even if she hadn't touched him. Just one shower of sparks after another. Sexual, male, with an edge of danger she didn't quite understand, Mac was one powerful source of energy. It pulsed from him like sound waves from a radio tower. Invisible, but she could feel them even from this distance and they lifted the hairs on her forearms.

Mac had guessed correctly. Friday night had been her first time with Jeffery. She'd been uncertain, and the sex had been disappointing. Her fault, she knew, because she'd held back. She told herself that it was because she still missed Matthew, but deep down she knew something was wrong and she was afraid.

MacConnelly rested a hand over hers. She glanced down at the connection, their hands sitting one upon the other on his carefully made bed, and then she looked into his eyes. She had his complete attention.

"Princess, tell me what happened."

She slipped her hand away and pressed both hands to her chest. She didn't know why he needed to know this, but she would tell him.

"We woke up together. Jeffery felt off, he said. His stomach was upset. He threw up and then the dizziness started. He wouldn't let me call an ambulance, but then he threw up his coffee, too. So I got him to my car and drove him to the emergency room. They ran tests, gave him fluids. That helped. But then he blacked out. They said he might have internal bleeding and took him to surgery, but there was nothing. Now they think there might be something wrong with his immune system. No white blood cells. That's impossible, isn't it, to be healthy one minute and so sick the next?"

He gave her a long unblinking stare. He didn't seem surprised. Her body chilled.

What if the doctors were wrong? What if everything Nana said was true? No. It's impossible. She dismissed the thought, but a tiny shard of dread remained lodged in her heart like a sliver of glass.

"Nana said I had to leave Jeffery or he'd get sick. She said Matthew had been sick because of me. But that's crazy, right?"

He didn't speak, just continued that assessing stare. Bri looked away.

She could pretend that she was normal, that everything was normal, but it wasn't. She wasn't.

Chapter 5

"Was it me?" Bri whispered. "Did I do something to him." She glanced at Mac.

His mouth was grim. A frost crept through her body. Tears leaked from the corners of her eyes.

"Been any other men in your life, Princess?"

"Yes. One. Before…" Before that woman at the high school showed up and called her sister.

"Tell me about him."

"Matt was my high school steady. We never, you know." She shrugged her shoulders and looked at her hands, now folded into one tight knot of interlaced fingers. "But senior year he proposed and I said yes. My nana was so angry. She forbade me to see him. I thought she was just being old-fashioned. During his freshman year he came home on Thanksgiving break and…" She stared at him as the panic began to rip at her with tiny, sharp claws. *Oh, God, it was her!* "Do you know why this happened?"

"Tell me the rest, Princess."

"He got sick, too. But he went back to school and he got better and then…" The unease was rising to panic. Her heart knocked against her ribs and the sound of her breathing reminded her of an asthma patient in the midst of an attack. "He came home for Christmas."

"He got sick again?"

She pounded her fists on her thighs. "No! He died. Undetected aneurysm in his brain. That's what they said." She met his steady stare. "But that wasn't it. Was it, MacConnelly?"

He cocked his head as those crystal eyes judged her. "You really didn't know, did you, Princess?"

"Know what?"

"How long between Matthew and Jeffery?"

Why? Why did he ask her this?

"I don't know...four years, I think."

MacConnelly gritted his teeth and winced. "Four? He should be dead." His gaze swept her as if searching for answers.

"What?"

"Nothing. Jeffery was lucky because you got more potent with time. Didn't you know that?"

"What are you talking about?"

"Anyone in between?"

She shook her head.

"But you lived with your grandmother. How could that be? Was she like you?"

"No, she wasn't at all like me."

"Then I don't understand. How did she live so long? I read her obit on the Internet. Eighty-eight. Died one month ago."

Brianna covered her mouth, trying to force back the grief at her grandmother's passing and the fear that threatened her sanity. "Please tell me what's happening."

She tried to remember all her nana had said. All the nonsense, the doctors called it, just the drug-induced ranting of a dying brain. But now Brianna knew better. Now she could no longer ignore her grandmother's final words.

"Did she know, Princess? She must have known to have lived with you so long. Unless you were just turned. When were you bitten?"

"Bitten? I don't understand." She stared at him in confusion. "I was never bitten. My nana said that I'm a Feyling. She said I was born of the Fey. Born, not turned."

"Feylings? I never heard that." He sat with one leg folded at the hip, half turned toward her now, the stiffness still starching his spine, as if being a Marine somehow came from the inside. "What did your grandmother tell you exactly?"

Her skin crawled at the memory and she rubbed her hands over her arms. "She said my mother was a fairy."

"A fairy?"

Brianna nodded, knowing how crazy that sounded. "That's what she said. She was a particular kind of fairy called a Leanan Sidhe. And that all fairies are real and that my mother didn't really die. She just abandoned me to return to her world with the Fey."

"Is that true?" he asked.

"I don't know. But it is what she said."

"That would make you half fairy."

That thought had occurred to her. It explained many odd things about her, things she'd tried to hide during her childhood and continued to hide now that she was an adult.

"I know," she whispered. "She said a Feyling is one born of a union of the Fey with a mortal, my father. He was a writer. A great writer."

"We've never known the origin of your kind. Fairy makes as much sense as any other crazy theory I've heard." He scrubbed his eyes with his hands and released a long breath. Then he turned his troubled gaze on her again. "But we have another name for your kind, Princess." She heard a definite note of regret in his voice.

She sat on the edge of the bed, waiting, knowing that whatever he was about to tell her, she was not going to like it.

His gaze had gone cold again. "Vampire."

Bri gasped and drew back as if he'd slapped her. "No, that's what's chasing me."

"Because you are one of them."

"But that's not possible. I don't drink blood. I'm a vegetarian, for goodness' sake. I helped build low-income housing and marched to stop the war. I'm working part-time as a social worker. I'm a good person, not a monster."

"You're one of them."

"But I don't look like them. I'm not…I'm—"

"—beautiful, like all the females. Bewitching, they say." He made it sound like a condemnation, bitten between clamped teeth. "Irresistible to mortal men."

"No," she said, gasping now, her mind screaming denial as her stomach ached like a raw, oozing wound.

He laid out the evidence. "You can fly."

"I can't."

"Well, something damn close. How'd you get up on that roof?"

"I sort of bounced." Why didn't he seem shocked? It was almost as if he expected her to say this. Bri became more certain that he knew things that she needed to know.

His brow knit together. The gesture only added to his good looks. She edged away as another truth hit her, werewolves killed vampires, and she was a vampire.

"I'm going to be sick."

She barely made it to the toilet. Mac waited in the door frame as she finished retching, then offered her a wet towel. She washed her face with the cool terry cloth. Afterward, he gave her his mouthwash and a glass. When she finished she looked at herself in the mirror and saw that her skin still looked flawless and her hair still danced merrily about her heart-shaped face. But her green eyes now looked dead.

She lowered the glass to the sink and faced the Marine sergeant who knew what she was.

"You mean that if I'd been born a boy, I'd be—"

"—like them."

She shivered, rubbing her upper arms with her hands, as if she were standing naked under a shower of ice water.

"You can self-heal, too. I'm sure you know that."

She nodded. It was one of the differences her nana had told her to keep to herself. She was never sick and never injured for long.

"And you suck the life force from any human male you sleep with. There are soul-sucking vampires, too. All female vampires are soul-suckers" He pressed an index finger to the center of her forehead as if sighting the placement of a bullet. "Like you."

She started to deny this and then hesitated. A chill broke over her and she huddled, shrugging her shoulders as the chill ate deep into her bones.

"I killed Matthew. I almost killed Jeffery."

His eyes met hers and he gave a slow nod. She saw it then, the truth. He understood her self-loathing, the disgust at what she had done. What had he done that made him understand? Something bad, it was clear in those sky-blue eyes.

"At least yours were accidents," he said.

Was that some sort of consolation prize?

"So I killed a man I loved and sent another to the hospital, but I didn't mean to hurt them, so that's supposed to make everything okay?" Her voice was nearly unrecognizable, a screeching thing, totally unfamiliar now.

"No. Not okay. It will never be okay. Just, well, we all have regrets."

"Regrets!" Her hands flew up and then dropped down limp to her sides, as she muttered, "Regrets."

"We thought vampires were made, like werewolves, from a bite. But this explains why the males have to chase the females, to hunt them, bring them in, especially if they can't make new vampires through a bite. They'd have to sleep with you."

"What!"

"I've seen the males. So have you. Would you have sex with one?"

She hugged herself. "Never."

"Then they need to catch females in order to mate. Catch them and keep them captive, at least until they deliver. And you escaped because you were warned?"

She nodded, "Twice."

He took hold of her forearm and led her back to the bed, seating her. He sat down beside her again and the bed sagged.

The lump in her throat was the size of a golf ball.

"Now about the woman. Who was she?"

"Which one? There were two."

"The one at the hospital."

Brianna thought back to the lovely woman wearing a long gray cardigan that swept the tops of her stylish boots. The black beret covered most of her strawberry blond hair, but she knew the woman was a beauty with a clear complexion, a generous mouth and startling gray eyes. She had been perfectly lovely. Too perfect, she now knew. When they'd been on the ground floor, the woman had grabbed Brianna's arm and held on until the elevator left without them.

"I'd never seen her before. She stopped me, pulled me

into the alcove before the outpatient surgery doors and told me that there were male vampires hunting me. That they couldn't track me until I was grown, but now they had and they were waiting on the fourth floor for me to show up. She told me to run."

"Why did she warn you?"

"I asked her that. She said, 'Eight years. That's how long they had me. No one warned me. No one helped me. Maybe you'll make it, because you're first generation.' But she said that will make them want me more. They won't give up. They never give up."

"What's 'first generation'?"

"I don't know, except that my mom was a fairy. That's what Nana said."

His brow wrinkled and his words seemed more for himself than her. "First generation. What difference does that make?" His gaze snapped back to her. "Then what?"

"She told me what the males had done to her. It was years of abuse. Rape. She was quick, and when she finished she vanished. I was looking at her one minute and the next she was gone. She just glanced over her shoulder and said, 'Run.' Then poof."

"So you left the hospital?"

"No. I *ran* out of the hospital. Then I went to the apartment I share, shared, with Nana. I have it until the end of the month. But they broke in while I was there, so I ran again. But it was different this time."

"Everyone slowed down?"

She fidgeted with her thumbnail. "Yes."

"Tell me about that."

She did and when she finished describing her journey he was silent for a moment as he absently rubbed his jaw. He was clean-shaven again, she realized, unlike when she'd arrived. His smooth cheeks made his jaw even more defined. She watched the rhythmic stroke of his index finger over his face and noticed how the muscles of his forearm corded with the muscles of her stomach. Just looking at him made her twitch.

"Maybe they didn't slow down. Maybe you sped up."

She paused to consider that. "How?"

"Same way you got on my roof."

It all was too much. She covered her face, hunching forward as she wept in long, wracking cries. His big, strong arm came around her, dragging her to his side as she fell against that wide chest. After a time the tears slowed. She sniffed and wiped her eyes, listening to the comforting rhythm of his heartbeat as he held her, giving comfort and asking for nothing in return.

"Nana told me some things before she died, but I didn't believe her. I didn't *want* to believe her. In my heart I knew it was true. But I thought if I just pretended hard enough, if I kept believing that I was like everyone else, I could go on as I was. But it can't ever be that way again."

She sagged against him, letting him hold her, letting him comfort her as she released some of the fear and sorrow in her heart. Then she remembered what she was.

"No!" She extended her hands, pushing with all her might.

Brianna was stronger than Mac expected. Stronger than she looked but not strong enough to escape him.

"You can't hurt me," he assured.

"Yes. I can. I will. Please, let me go." Tears streamed from her eyes as she stared up at him begging for release. "I can't. I won't do this again."

He eased his grip, letting her draw back, but not away. He wanted to tell her, if only to reassure her that whatever happened with human males, it would not happen with him. But first he'd have to tell her the truth.

"You can't hurt me, Princess. I'm like Johnny. I'm a werewolf, too."

She stilled as his confession registered. Her fingers gripped his shirt and her lovely eyes went wide. The sea-green depths, stormy as some internal turbulence made her body shudder. The flush began at her neck and then spread to make her cheeks a rosy pink.

"You're like him?"

Was that fear in her eyes or hope?

He nodded.

"I smelled it. I just thought…but if you're a wolf, then why did you keep Johnny from killing me?"

"You asked for my protection."

"But I'm your natural enemy. I thought I was influencing you, but if it's true…then what I am didn't cause your actions. Werewolves aren't drawn to vampires, except to kill them. That's what I was told."

"But I *am* drawn to you. What man wouldn't be?"

"Why don't you turn me in?"

He glared at her, angry it seemed, over her insistence to keep poking at him for answers. His jaw worked hard as if crushing something between his molars.

"Because I don't know what they would do to you."

"They wouldn't help me?"

"I doubt that very much." He filled his lungs with a great breath of air and then blew it away.

"I don't understand why you are helping me. If you are a werewolf—"

He interrupted her. "I am."

"Well, then. The woman said…she said that a were-wolf could kill vampires, but I didn't know I was a vampire then. I knew it was dangerous, but I didn't understand how dangerous."

"If you knew all that, then why'd you come?"

She dropped her chin and her hands fell to her lap. She looked small and defenseless. He kept one arm about her waist and waited. When she finally spoke, her voice was just a whisper.

"Because I'd rather die than go with them." That admission took the roses from her cheeks. She looked pale now to the point of fainting. What did they do to their women that made them ready to run into the open jaws of a werewolf? The hairs on his neck lifted at her words. Rape, she'd said. Years of it.

His CO said the males held the females for indoctrination. But that was all. Did they know what really went on?

She rested a hand on his chest. "Thank you for fighting for me, for lying for me and for sheltering me. You've done so much, but I have another favor to ask."

He lifted his brows, waiting.

"Can you call and check on Jeffery? I'm so worried about him."

His mouth when grim. "Because you love him?"

"No." She said that too quickly and realized with some guilt that it was true. She didn't love him, hadn't, even though she had tried so hard. "I don't. It's because I hurt him."

The tension in his shoulders eased and he breathed deep before answering. "I already checked. Out of the hospital. Looking for you. Back at work."

She pressed a hand to her forehead and sagged. "He'll be all right."

"If you keep clear of him."

She nodded and dropped her hand, lifting her head so

she could meet his gaze. "Thank you for telling me and also for telling me that I can't hurt you. That's a great relief."

He gave her a smile that transformed his expression. The twinkle in his eyes made her body buzz with excitement as she recognized something vital had changed between them. His hands stilled their rhythmic stroke of her upper arms and came to rest. He held her gaze.

It struck Brianna that she could kiss him and not worry that she might draw away some of his vitality. The freedom of that realization had her blinking stupidly at him.

She leaned forward, lifting her chin, angling her mouth. His breath caught.

"It won't hurt you?" she whispered.

He lifted his thick brows and grinned. "Let's find out."

His broad hand went about her neck and he drew her toward him. His eyes dropped shut and he angled his head to receive her kiss. She gasped as the anticipation galloped through her. Why hadn't she ever felt this connection with Jeffery? Why was this chemistry stronger with a stranger than with a man she respected, a man she'd almost killed?

She felt Mac's arms go around her, strong arms, capable arms. She could kiss him, hold him and nothing terrible would happen. The freedom mingled with the anticipation hovering like a hummingbird the instant before it perches.

And then his mouth found hers. The gentle pressure increasing as his fingers delved into her hair. Pleasure fizzed in her blood like the tiny rising bubbles in a glass of champagne. A soft moan escaped her as she settled against his chest, coming to rest, coming home, coming alive after a long, long sleep. Her hands grasped, measuring the breadth of his chest and the round sturdy muscle of his shoulders.

Her mouth opened, and his tongue danced and thrust with a skill and confidence that made her go all liquid heat and pulsing need. She leaned close, pressed tight, and he

captured her against his chest, the pressure a welcome relief and a tantalizing frustration.

His arms relaxed by slow degrees and still she clung.
He gently clasped her chin in one firm hand as he drew her
away with the other. She stared up at him, wanting more,
needing his touch. She blinked, recoiled at her complete
loss of control and then felt her cheeks flame.

"I'm sorry."

"Don't be."

If he'd taken her backward to the wide, inviting bed,
would she have gone? Yes, and her shame at the thought
made her blush. What about Jeffery? How could she just
forget him like that?

"My boyfriend is sick in the hospital and I'm kissing
a stranger."

"Your boyfriend is human, and he will get well if you
stay away from him. You know that, right?"

"Are you sure?"

"Positive."

She nodded. "What do I do now?"

"Working on that. My colonel would love a female vampire."

She stiffened and leaned back, her expression going
tight.

He met her troubled gaze. "And that is why he shouldn't
have one."

"I'd be a military experiment."

"Yes."

She gripped his hand. "What do they do to you?"

He shook his head, unwilling to tell her all that they'd
been through, were going through, and in that instant he
made up his mind. They weren't doing that to her. He'd
protect her if he could and help her escape if he couldn't.

He gave her hand a squeeze. "I won't let them take you."

Chapter 6

Mac headed to the lab the next day to donate more blood to their damned research. He supposed they needed it to figure out how to turn Johnny back, but lately he felt like a pincushion. Then he endured another tedious brain scan in both his forms. His mind was on Bri, alone in his quarters. He hoped that if those males showed up, he'd have time to reach her before they took her. He also worried about Johnny, who was now on the firing range getting shot. Johnny said Lewis treated him like a big dumb animal when Mac wasn't there and that worried him. Mac's request to remain with his friend had been denied because they needed more blood. When they finally dismissed him from the infirmary, he got shipped off to the obstacle course, then to the firing range to practice shooting. When they ordered him back to medical, he disobeyed and didn't go. He'd done that twice before and both times over Johnny. Mac had that feeling again, the one he got when things weren't right.

Mac needed to find Johnny, make sure he was all right and then get back to Bri. He found his friend back in the cell they held him in when Mac wasn't around. The air still held the acrid smell of gunpowder, and Mac had the sickening realization that the odor came from Johnny's fur. He scanned Lam but saw no marks on his coat and no blood on the floor. But something was wrong with his corporal; he could tell with just one look at Johnny's unfocused eyes. What had they done to him?

Lewis appeared just behind Mac. Clearly someone had alerted the commander about Mac's failure to report. Mac wondered if this was the moment he and the colonel would go at it. A face-off had been brewing for some time. Mac could take the abuse, but he couldn't stand to see Lam go through it. It was why he hadn't accepted the offer to take a leave and visit his family. He didn't trust them with Johnny.

"We wanted to give Johnny a little time before bringing you in," said Lewis.

Mac's brow furrowed and he dipped his chin, holding back but curling his hands into fist to keep the change from flashing through him like a grenade. "What's wrong with him?"

"He's fine. Just woozy from the sedative."

Mac searched Johnny's eyes, seeing instantly that Johnny was not fine. He could ask Lewis, but that meant questioning a senior officer. He could ask Johnny, but Johnny would just play stupid. His friend had made it very clear that he would not answer questions around anyone, and what first had seemed like paranoia now began to seem wise. But Johnny had made an exception for Brianna Vittori. Why did he let her see his intelligence when he would not show it to anyone at HQ? If they knew he understood, they wouldn't treat him like a dumb animal. But they'd also clam up around him, as they did with Mac.

"He wasn't cooperative when you left, so…"

Mac stepped closer. Johnny's eyelids drooped. "He's not fine."

"No injury from the bullets. We tried the armor-piercing rounds. You two *are* bulletproof. That hide wears like Kevlar. Better. We even used a grenade. No damage."

"Grenade? I didn't agree to that."

Lewis gave him a hard look. "You get a promotion I didn't hear about?"

Mac's nostrils flared as he stood between them, wanting to demand they release Johnny and knowing he trod a very fine line. Still, it took several deep breaths to keep himself from tearing at the bars with his bare hands. He and Johnny together could break through this cage. But instead of doing something so rash he just lowered his chin so the colonel couldn't see the defiance there.

"No, sir."

Lewis draped an arm around Mac's shoulders, gave him a pat and released him. "He's fine. The ME checked him. So did our vet."

"Did you give him ear protection?"

"What? I'm not...no."

Mac felt the rage building inside him like steam in a rusty pipe. Any minute he'd explode.

Lewis's jaw went hard and he made Mac wait. "His eardrums are intact. Might have some ringing for a day or so, I suppose. They said he'd be asleep, but he never went out."

Mac knew that Johnny would do everything he could not to black out while in HQ. Maybe he was right. With growing unease, Mac wondered briefly what they had just done to him when *he* was out. His unease grew, gripping his chest, making it tight and his breathing shallow. He should have been here.

He turned to his commanding officer and stood at attention. "Permission to take Johnny to quarters, sir."

Lewis made a face. "Granted. We're done here anyway. You need help carrying him? I can get a transport."

Johnny hated the transport cage. Called it his circus wagon.

Mac saluted. "I can carry him, sir. Thank you, sir."

"You want the truck or you two going to run?"

Mac motioned for Johnny to stand. He didn't. Mac's stomach twisted. Mac motioned again for Johnny to rise, which he did—then he wobbled and sat down heavily.

"The truck, sir."

Mac helped Johnny board and held on to him as they rode. Johnny couldn't hear him, that much was clear. Through sign language, he gathered that Lam had covered his ears as best he could with his hands, but that gave only minimal protection. It seemed clear to Mac that the colonel had overstepped, which brought Mac back to the same damn question: Was he going to continue to serve his country, or was he going to take Johnny and go AWOL?

A year ago he had never dreamed it possible that he would consider such a thing. But a lot could happen in a year. He'd stayed for months in hopes that the medical staff could find a way to reverse Johnny's condition. Instead they heaved grenades at him. Were they even trying to solve that problem or were they just seeing how much a werewolf could take? If they ran, Johnny would have no chance of being restored to human form. It was a terrible price to pay for insubordination. But no one would be shooting at them, either.

If they ran they'd be AWOL, and God knew the Marines would chase them relentlessly. And Mac would never be able to go home to his family, because that would be the first place they'd look. He thought of the business he planned to join with his dad. Mac's chest ached at the thought of losing so much. He pictured his mom's face as she smiled up at him and then his older sister, Bonnie, now married and expecting her first child. And Sean, who idolized him—what would he think when he heard his big brother was a coward who left his post and ran? Worst of all, he imagined the disappointment in his father's eyes when he discovered that his eldest boy had failed to serve honorably. His father was a vet, and he loved his country as much as he loved his family. His dad and mom had been so proud when he joined the Corps. God, Mac didn't want to have to break his father's heart.

He'd have to ask Johnny. They'd have to make this choice together. Mac would do whatever Johnny wanted. But God, he didn't want to lose his family. His heart ached as he thought of each person he loved and then imagined never seeing them again. It was a sacrifice he'd never considered. He knew he risked his life. But his reputation and his honor and now his family. The decisions weighed him down like stones.

If they ran, where would they go that the U.S. Marines could not find them? And, without the doctors of the Corps, how would he get Johnny back to his human form?

Mac got Johnny inside their quarters and to the futon, where Johnny collapsed, overcome by the day and the drugs they'd given him.

Mac day had been nearly as horrific, the only bright spot was finding his princess dozing on his bed. Her allure was nearly too much to bear. Only knowing Johnny was right down the hall, sick from drugs and impact injuries and possibly deaf as a result, kept Mac from approaching that bed. Instead he gave a gentle knock on the door and watched her eyes flash open. She stared up at the ceiling for a moment, her brow descending as she oriented herself and turned to face him. Her eyes were red, as if she'd been crying. He remembered their conversation, her discovery of exactly what she was, and he thought that Bri had good cause to weep.

"I fell asleep," she said.

Her warm floral scent filled the air, luring him forward, but he held the doorknob like an anchor against rough seas and remained in place. "Yes. You hungry?"

"What time is it?"

"Eighteen hundred."

She shook her head, sending her fiery curls tumbling over her shoulders. "What?"

"Supper time." He closed the door. Mac couldn't get away fast enough. Brianna Vittori was beautiful on any day, but tousled from sleeping in his bed, with her rosy cheeks and her hooded eyes, she was irresistible. But he had resisted through a strategic retreat. He double-timed it to the kitchen, surprised to find Johnny up and hunched over the open refrigerator. He knew that werewolves healed fast, but he was still surprised. The kitchen was Johnny's domain, but he'd been nearly unconscious a minute ago.

"Can you hear me?"

Johnny nodded and glanced his way, his eyes clear and his expression sullen. Well, he had cause.

"Sedative? Has it worn off?"

Another nod and Johnny returned to the open refrigerator. He lifted a packed of ground chuck and tented his eyes.

"Yeah, fine."

Johnny turned toward the counter and set aside the chuck.

"How do you feel?"

Johnny pressed a hand to his forehead and stomach simultaneously, then pantomimed being sick.

"You hungry?"

Johnny nodded.

"I'll do it."

Johnny pushed him aside and Mac let him.

He glanced back down the hall and hoped Bri didn't cook, because if there was a turf war, Johnny would win. Mac thumbed toward his bedroom.

"She was sleeping in my bed."

Johnny paused and studied him a moment then dragged the buns from the refrigerator and set them on the counter.

Mac pulled out the condiments, lettuce, onion and tomato and then turned on the oven.

"You okay with her being here?"

Johnny gave him a peeved look then gave him his back. He was definitely not fine with Bri being here.

Lam washed his hands and started making hamburger patties, way too big for the buns. Mac tore open a bag of fries and threw them in the oven to bake.

"I told her I'd protect her. You want me to put her out? I'll put her out." As Mac said it he knew he wouldn't and prayed Johnny didn't call that bluff.

Lam gave him a long look and then shook his head.

Mac breathed a sigh of relief and sagged against the counter. "Thanks."

Johnny glared and Mac met his steady stare. He stilled as he became cautious.

"You aren't going to go for her, are you?" There was still the tiniest doubt that Johnny might try to kill Bri.

Down the hall, the bedroom door opened and then closed.

Johnny froze as if suddenly made of wax. Mac went to meet Brianna, wondering if Johnny would be here when they got back.

Bri paused at the first sight of Mac and gave him a tentative smile, full of uncertainty and hope. Her eyes were still red, but it only served to make her look more tragically beautiful. Man, she was a killer in more ways than one.

"Can I meet Johnny now?"

Mac smiled. "If you still want to."

She blew out a breath and nodded. "Yes. I do."

Mac led the way down the hall to find that Johnny had vanished. "She wants to meet you. So come out. That's an order."

Johnny stepped from behind the door frame momentarily filling the space. Bri gasped at the sight of him and went rigid for a moment, but she held her ground. Now Mac could smell her fear, liquid and tart as lemon juice.

Johnny's eyes narrowed on her, sensing weakness. Mac took hold of her elbow and felt her tremors.

Mac walked her across the room and to her credit she kept her chin up and her eyes on Johnny as she moved stiffly forward. He paused to stand between them. Now what?

He cleared his throat. "Corporal John Lam, may I introduce Brianna Vittori."

Johnny continued to glare. Mac kept his eyes on the corporal.

Bri extended her trembling hand. "It's a pleasure to meet you, Corporal. May I call you John?"

Johnny did a double take, looking from her hand to her face and finally to Mac, who found he could not speak for the lump in his throat. Of all the reactions he had expected from Bri, civility was not among them.

John had been in near isolation since their return. He saw the medical staff, all male, and the colonel and Mac. That was it. When was the last time a woman was kind to him or touched him? Mac felt the tension twist his gut.

Johnny wiped his dark, leathery hand on his hairy chest, never taking his eyes off Bri. Unlike a wolf's paw, Johnny did not have pads and toes on his forelegs. His hands more resembled a gorilla's, except the claws were long, curved and deadly. Then he extended his hand to meet hers, taking it gently between his thumb and forefingers for just the briefest instant before quickly releasing her. To her credit she did not flinch or give any outward sign she was frightened or repulsed. Her bright smile held even as he rose up to his full height, now standing like the man he had once been.

She craned her neck and held her gentle smile. "Can I help with dinner?"

Johnny shook his head and pointed to a bar stool. It wasn't the warmest of welcomes, thought Mac. But he'd take it.

Brianna took a seat. "I don't want to be any trouble. Did Mr. MacConnelly tell you that he told me I could stay?"

Johnny lifted his brow and glanced to Mac, likely to see if he had any issue with being called Mister instead of Sergeant. He didn't. He was so damn thrilled that Bri was being kind to Johnny and that Johnny hadn't attacked Bri that he had a lump in his throat the size of a peach pit. He couldn't have spoken if he had tried.

Johnny nodded.

"Is it all right with you?"

He hesitated and then gave another affirmative.

"Mr. MacConnelly told me that you can't change back. This all must be very hard for you. You've made a great sacrifice serving your country, and I'm honored to know you, Mr. Lam."

When he told her what she was, she'd said she was a pacifist, likely an antiwar liberal who opposed everything that he and Johnny stood for. And still she thanked him. Mac's eyes burned. Damned if he wasn't tearing up.

She sniffed. "Is something burning?"

Johnny darted to the stove and flipped the burgers. A few minutes later Johnny had three plates. He ate standing, finishing four burgers while Brianna selected a bun, then made a salad from the lettuce and tomato to go with her fries. Johnny paused between bites to look at her plate.

"So no burger?" asked Mac.

"I don't eat meat."

"Fish?"

"No."

"Why not?"

"People can live quite happily on nuts, grains, fruits and vegetables."

"I can't."

"I'm not asking you to. But for me, it's not necessary to kill living things to survive." Her smile dropped away as she recognized the irony of what she had said. She killed things whether she meant to or not. Mac watched the pain blow over her features like an impending storm as she came to the same conclusion.

"Johnny and I need meat."

"Of course. I'm not trying to impose my beliefs on you."

They lapsed into awkward silence again. Johnny finished first and headed out. Mac was certain he'd be gone all night. He often preferred sleeping outside or in his private quarters.

"That didn't go very well," said Brianna.

"I disagree. He didn't try to kill you."

Brianna cleared the table and Mac washed dishes. Afterward, he made them coffee, and they sat on the dilapidated yellow couch that was draped in a ragged wool blanket.

She sat huddled beneath the blanket in the chilly room with her eyes wide and green as a glass bottle.

"Did you have enough to eat, Princess?"

"Why don't you call me Bri?"

"If you call me Mac."

"All right. I can do that, Mac."

"So, Bri, tell me about your mom and dad."

The smile left her face. She lowered the coffee to the low brass table and half-turned, hooking one foot behind her opposite knee. "My father was human."

"Did you know him?"

"No, he died before I was born."

They both knew why. She held his gaze a minute and then she lowered her gaze. "Shortly after meeting my mom. She was my nana's only child."

"That's tough."

"He was a brilliant musician."

"Yeah. They go for the talented ones." He realized too late that he'd said the wrong thing because of Bri's intake of breath.

"Is that so?"

"That's what our intel indicates."

"My mother, well, just before she passed, my nana said that they are called the Leanan Sidhe," she whispered. Then her eyes flashed to his. "The Fairy Mistress. Muses. I mean that's what Nana said. The men they choose live lives of brilliance."

"Short lives of brilliance?"

She glanced away. "Yes."

"Maybe the creative ones give off more juice or whatever you call the energy you drain away. Anyway, maybe your mother *was* a fairy."

"But I'm not, it that what you mean? And I'm not a Leanan Sidhe. But I'm half human, at least." Tears leaked from her eyes and she shook her head in denial. "Half human and half Leanan Sidhe?"

"Yeah, Bri. I think so."

She tried to drink a little coffee but seemed to be choking it down. He made great coffee, so he figured she was still grappling with all this shit.

"Have any other people around you gotten sick? You don't have to sleep with them, just be near them."

Now she was covering her eyes. "My college friends, yes, Gail and Kerry. They both got sick. God, that was me, too. And we moved again. Now I understand why Nana moved us around so much."

"She might have been trying to keep your friends alive."

Brianna's hand slipped from her face, and she pinned him with those lush green eyes. Her chest rose and fell, as if she were running in full gear. Then her chin started to tremble. "Why didn't she tell me long before then? Why only when she was...was dying?"

He shook his head. "Can't answer that."

Her head sunk to her knees, and her shoulders shook. He draped an arm around her shoulders and after a few minutes she lifted her gaze to meet his.

"I used to see them, when I was a child. Fairies in the woods, little ones, dancing at twilight and at night, when the fireflies came out. Nana couldn't see them and told me I was imagining things. But we moved again, and we never lived in the country after that. Fairies don't like the cities." She wiped the tears from her eyes. "I don't like them, either. The lights and the buildings give me headaches. The air smells so good here." She inhaled deeply, filling her lungs with the mountain air. "I think I belong outside."

"That's probably true."

"But Nana kept us in cities. When she was ill in the hospital, my nana told me everything she knew. I told the doctors a little of what she said and they said it was from the pain medication. Hallucinations. I tried to tell myself that was what it was. But, as you said, I can do things that aren't normal. All my life, she would tell me to shush up, not talk about it. But was she trying to protect me from them or trying to pretend I wasn't a…a vampire?"

"I don't know."

"If she was protecting me, why not tell me what I really am?"

"Perhaps she knew it would be hard."

She placed her hand in his had held tight. Her voice shook when she spoke. "She died of cancer. Do you think… did I do that to her?"

"I don't know. But she was an old woman."

"Only eighty-eight."

"She must have known some way to keep from—"

"—my energy draw? That's what you called it, right?"

"Yeah."

"She never touched me."

Mac cocked his head. "What?"

"Never. No hugs. No good-night kisses. I never crawled onto her lap or into her bed after a nightmare."

"She never touched you?" His insides felt hollow, as he imagined a child with no one to hug her or kiss away the tears.

Brianna's head hung, and her face flushed with shame at her revelation. "I thought it was me, and it was. I knew there was something wrong with me." She stared up at him, anxious to explain, to defend her grandmother. "But I know she loved me. Oh. I knew it then, too. I just never really understood why…and it was hard."

It seemed even breathing was hard for her now.

"So I'm a vampire, like the thing that broke into my apartment."

"The female version. Males drink blood. You feed on energy."

"Energy. I don't feel that. The only thing I feed on is

tofu and veggie burgers and nice green salads mixed with nuts. I've never hurt anyone. At least…I never *meant* to hurt anyone."

She met his gaze. It was hard not to look away for the pain she experienced seemed to beat in him as well.

"But I have. Haven't I?" She raked her hand through her hair. "I can't even bring myself to kill a spider in my house. But somehow I can kill people without even trying. So now and for the rest of my life, I can't be around people." She gave a harsh laugh that sounded like a cry. "A social worker who can't be around people." She laughed again and then the tears spilled from her eyes as the laughter collapsed to weeping.

He gathered her up in his arms and she nestled against him.

"But not you," she whispered. "I can't hurt you."

"That's right, Princess." He stroked her head, threading his fingers through the thick curls and angling her tear-streaked face up so he could look into those green eyes, shimmering now like faceted gemstones.

"You said there were two females. One at the hospital. Tell me about the other one."

She nodded. "She was beautiful, too. Not like that thing on the road. I was a senior in high school when she found me. She was a beautiful, strawberry blonde with blue eyes. She called me sister. She said I was a woman now, and that they'd be coming for me soon. I told my nana, and she moved us the next day."

"They'd be coming?"

"That's what she said. Nana acted weird. She wouldn't tell me what was happening. She said the woman knew my mother. I thought maybe the woman *really* was my sister, that my mother wasn't dead at all but just gone. I didn't want to leave school but Nana insisted. That was three years ago. After Nana got sick, she told me that I had to keep moving and that men would be attracted to me but I couldn't...I couldn't ever sleep with them. She said devils were chasing me. That they were pure evil."

"They're not devils. We knew the females were lovely and the males hideous. The fairy part, that's new. I'm not sure about that, but it's possible. The males are an international organization of hired killers."

She squeaked. "A what?"

"They're mercenaries. The females, too, Princess."

Chapter 7

Mercenaries. Brianna's head hung as the implication of his words ate into her bones like acid.

"Is that why they want me? To turn me into a killer?"

He didn't turn away, but continued to meet her gaze, holding it unflinching as he spoke. "They want to capture you, train you and then, yes, use you as an assassin. Human males can't resist you. You must already know that."

"I feel sick," she said, cradling her head in her hands. She glanced up, cast him a forlorn look. "I don't want to hurt anyone." Then she remembered the woman at the hospital. Maybe she hadn't wanted to hurt anyone, either, but they kept her for many years. "She said that no one had helped her. She didn't want me to get caught because she knew what they'd do and why they'd do it. They want me to be one of them." Bri grasped Mac's hand and squeezed tight. "I don't want to hurt anyone."

"But you do. You have. And you will."

"How do I stop it?" she whispered, her gaze pleading.

"You can't. It's what you are."

"But I don't want this. Can you help me?"

"No, Princess. I'm sorry."

Her red hair bounced all around her face, and she released him to push it back with both hands. When she spoke her words sounded dull and lifeless to her own ears.

"That woman, the one who warned me. She said they had her for eight years. Was that to train her?"

"We think that the females are used for breeding during their confinement."

Bri felt dizzy and dropped her chin to her chest until the spots stopped dancing around her as she thought of all the things the woman had saved her from.

My God, could all of this be real?

"My nana used to tell me tales of the fairy folk, the Fey and their court. I thought it was all just bedtime stories, but before she died she said they all exist. The doctors said it was a product of her medical condition and I should just humor her. So I did. I listened and I pretended it was all her mind coming unhinged with drugs and pain. But I knew. I knew it all the time."

Bri recalled all the bedtime stories her Italian grandmother had told her, making sure her Feyling granddaughter understood her mother's people and her roots. Now she remembered all the funny, odd and sometimes terrifying creatures that inhabited the world of Never Never.

"All true," she whispered. "All here on earth and I can see them. I *have* seen them. Now they can also see me."

Her protector fell silent. Was this too much, what she was telling him? Too much for even a werewolf to believe?

"My father died of pancreatic cancer at thirty-three. My nana said that my mother died in a boating accident off Ocracoke, North Carolina, shortly after I was born. Her kayak flipped. She had no life vest, and her body was never found. I still have the article."

"I'm sorry," said Mac.

"I used to wonder if my mother had intentionally left her infant daughter and paddled straight out to sea. It always felt like a suicide. Nana wouldn't talk about it."

"Are you sure she wasn't like you?"

"Not according to what Nana told me in the hospital."

She recalled her nana's words and she repeated them to Mac.

"She said, 'Your father, my son, Vito. He was human. He loved her and he wouldn't leave her, even when she told him the truth. He wouldn't abandon her and she couldn't walk away from him. Nothing I could do to stop them. And then he died.' I asked if my mother died, too. She said, 'Fairies don't die, Bri. I've taught you that. But it killed her heart. She loved him too much to leave him.' I said that that didn't make any sense and she said, 'Love rarely does.'"

"She couldn't leave him?" asked Mac.

"That's what she said. Nana said she begged him to leave my mother, but he told her that he'd rather be dead than live one single minute without her. It was fairy magic, but it was strong, unbreakable on both parts. Once he accepted her, she couldn't leave him unless he found another for her, but he wouldn't even though it was killing him. His death released her, and that was when she left me. It wasn't suicide. Wasn't a drowning at all. My mother is still alive, somewhere." Brianna rubbed the knuckle of her left hand absently with her thumb. "She said that my mother was a fairy, immortal, and she loved me, but I was part human. Nana said that she couldn't begin to know how to raise me. So she left me with her husband's mother and returned to the Fey."

"Do you remember her?"

"No. Not at all. Or my father. He was a composer. Successful, wildly, after he met my mother."

"The muse."

"Yes. He left it all to my nana for me. It's all mine now, or it will be when the attorneys finish settling her estate. Millions and millions, they say."

"Well, that's good."

She snorted. "If I live to spend it. Not looking good right now. I think Johnny still wants to take a bite out of me."

"He'll come around."

"And those vampires, what did you call them?"

"The Chasers. They hunt the females."

"Yes, them. They're still out there. Maybe they know by now that the ones they sent after me didn't come back."

His expression told her he had already thought of that. "Very likely."

"So what will happen?"

"They'll send more to the males' last known location and begin their search from there. If they find you, then I'll kill them, too."

"You think you can stop them." She held his gaze, her auburn brows lifted in a mixture of hope and incredulity.

"I know it."

She shook her head as if she still had any choice. "This is crazy."

"Yeah. It is."

She wondered about him, realizing all she knew about werewolves came from folklore and the movies. "What about you? Werewolves aren't born, are they?"

His eyes went cautious, hooded, and she realized that she'd broached a sensitive topic.

"Werewolves are made."

"I saw the scars. Did something bite you?"

He answered her by grabbing the sleeve of his T-shirt and tugged it over the rounded dome of his shoulder muscles. His skin was pale, taut and smooth, except for the puckered scars.

"He got me here first. Grabbed ahold with his jaws. Puncture marks," he said, pointing out the result of each long tooth.

Then he lifted his shirt from the hem and tugged it over his head. She sat up straight at the sight of so much muscular male flesh. His defined muscles contracted at his stomach and chest. Her gaze swept up at the tempting expanse of male flesh, and then her own flesh went cold as she saw again the horrible scars that laced his chest and arm. She'd seen them in the twilight when the Chasers had attacked her. Her mind cast back to that time. She realized Mac had been one of the werewolves that had attacked the vampires. Like her, Mac was more than he appeared. She understood now that he was not just a man. Johnny was the black werewolf, so he must be the gray one.

The scars looked different under the unforgiving overhead light. She took in the damage, reaching for him before she even thought of what she was doing. Her fingers grazed the raised, puckered flesh of the slashing scars that sliced across one side of his chest, measuring them with a touch. He flinched as the pads of her fingers brushed white, puckered flesh in a gentle imitation of the attack.

He held his shirt in a wadded ball before him as she circled, studying the punctures on his deltoid and the matching ones on his shoulder blade. It had clawed him and bitten him repeatedly.

"These bites are from the one that attacked you?"

"Turned me. Yes. The last scars I'll ever have. Nothing cuts my skin now."

She was behind him now, her hand caressing his shoulder, and she felt him tremble and saw the blood vessels at his throat pulse. Bri dropped a kiss on the ravaged flesh.

"Tell me about it?"

"Maybe some other time."

Her hands slid over his arms, measuring the strength of those wide shoulders. He turned and gathered her up against him.

"You shouldn't play with wolves," he cautioned. "We bite."

Mac pulled her close. His firm grip and warm hands gave the illusion of strength. Was he really strong enough for her? Would she draw away his energy just as she'd done with the others? She didn't feel anything.

But then she did. There was a tingling excitement that came from the brush of his thumbs against her bare skin of her neck. The gentle cradling of his hands about her upper arms. She could smell his aftershave now and the tang of sweat and soap.

He pulled. She resisted.

"What if you're wrong? What if I draw your energy, too?"

"You can't, Bri. I'm immune to you. That's why they send us to kill your kind."

His head dipped and his mouth pressed to her neck. Her head dropped back as a purr rumbled in her throat. His mouth was so hot, his tongue so thrilling. She turned her head.

"You could be wrong."

"It's all right, Princess. I can take it."

Her eyes narrowed at the challenge, and she tipped forward into his arms. She held on tight, reveling in the bunch and contraction of his warm muscles as he gathered her up against him, cradling her in the safe harbor of his arms.

He tipped her chin up so she could meet his gaze. "You held back with the others. I know you did."

She gasped. How could he know that?

"You don't have to do that with me. I want it all. Everything you've got and then some. I need it."

He slid his hands over her bare back, across her shoulders and down her spine. She closed her eyes, savoring the strength of those arms and the tenderness of his touch.

Excitement buzzed in her belly. She hadn't felt this way in so long. But his touch aroused more than eagerness. There was something about him that was so different from any man she'd ever known. She couldn't explain why. But she could feel the difference. The pull toward him was greater. The desire tugging at her insides was more powerful and the need that even now unfolded and grew inside her was stronger than she'd ever felt before. What if she didn't hold back? What if she released all the passion and need?

"No," she whispered. It was dangerous. Too dangerous, no matter what he said. She had to protect him, keep him safe.

"Yes," he whispered against her cheek.

You know that men can't resist you. Was he really protected, or enchanted like the others?

Fairy dust and moonbeams. Had she caught him like the Fey did, who used humans for their own amusement? Like her mother had bewitched her father?

"What if it's just the glamour?"

"Glamour?" he murmured against her ear and his breath fanned her neck.

"Enchantment. Fairy magic? What if it's like all the rest? It's not me that attracts you, just the Fey part of me."

"I want *you,* Brianna. I haven't had a woman since this happened."

"You could have any woman."

He shook his head. "No. I can't. I have to stay with

Johnny. And even if I were free, it's too risky. What if I was with a woman and I changed? What if she saw me?"

She'd never thought of that, but she knew it would be bad. She held his gaze and he went on.

"But you've seen me already. You'd understand."

Was it because she knew what he was or…a different possibility occurred to her and she shivered. "Is it because I can self-heal?"

His answer was sharp and quick. "No. I won't hurt you. I'd never hurt you, Princess, even when in wolf form, and I would never force you. But I want you like crazy."

Mac's fingers delved in her hair and he pressed her against his body, cradling her as if he were her protector instead of a man caught by her appeal. She breathed deep, taking in the newness and making it a part of her.

She believed he could protect her. If only he could also save her from this evil that lived inside her.

He leaned forward, and she let him take her weight. His mouth descended and she knew she wouldn't stop him, because she was as much in his spell as he was in hers. She read a tenderness in his expression, a delicate balance of gentleness and strength that drew her in. She yearned for him now.

This man was special. This man was right. She parted her lips, offering all.

Mac rubbed his torso against hers. Her body reacted instantly to the contact, her breasts setting off a needy ache. She gasped and her gaze shot to his. His blue eyes no longer seemed gentle or kind. Now they blazed with a flame, the hottest of all fires, the blue point of a focused flame. His jaw went hard, and his gaze flicked to her lips. The lust in his expression snapped her from the spell that had threaded between them. He was no different from any man. He was just as susceptible to her charms and just as susceptible to her deadly powers. She pushed off. He resisted a moment and then let her go.

He growled, a deep feral sound of a displeased male.

"What if you're wrong?" she asked.

"I'm not."

She drew back and he let her go. "I have a boyfriend in the hospital. I shouldn't be kissing you."

"He's human. Best thing you can do for him is leave him for good."

Her chin sunk. He was right. He lifted her chin with one finger.

"Do you love him?"

Did she?

"No," she whispered. She knew she didn't. Respected him very much. Admired him greatly. And Mac was right—if she cared at all, she'd leave him.

Some of the tension left Mac's shoulders. "You can't have him, Brianna. If you keep him, it will be just like your mother and father all over again."

He was right. She'd never have any of the things she dreamed of. She'd never delve into a community and make it her own.

"Never have a husband," she whispered. "Never have a big messy house or children."

She crumpled in the middle as if struck by a blow. He gathered her in, holding her as she shook.

"I can't. I can't have any of it. Not ever."

"You can have me."

Her gaze flashed to his and saw the raw desire burning in his eyes.

"I don't even know you."

"That's not a deal breaker."

"Mac, I'm not a one-night-stand kind of girl."

"You are. You just didn't know it because one night with you will kill most men. But not me."

She realized she was considering it. She couldn't go back to Jeffery. She couldn't turn to any friend she ever had. Her world had shrunk to two things: the vampires who wanted to capture her and this man who said he would keep her safe.

"Is that why you agreed to help me?"

His grip tightened and then he released her and stepped back, his expression grim. "No. I'll protect you either way."

Damn, why did he have to say that? It made her want him even more.

"Well, you just think on it, Vittori. We'll be great together."

The attraction between them sizzled. Her skin flushed, her lips parted and she struggled to keep from stepping into his arms. When she spoke, her voice sounded breathy and tight.

"I am grateful for all you've done, but I'm not ready for this."

"Maybe not today, Vittori. But it will happen. You know it will." He lifted a hand and used his index finger to stroke her cheek. "Go sleep in my bed, Princess, and dream of me. You tell me when. I'll be waiting."

There was a roar from directly outside the living room window. Bri jumped, finding herself in Mac's arms, gripping tight to the fabric of his shirt.

"It's Johnny. We need to run, scout the area, check for intruders. You get some rest. Sleep tight, Princess. We'll watch over you."

He kissed her on the forehead, his mouth warm and full of promise. Her body tingled all over, and she felt herself quickening with need. The pulse of wanting drummed in her chest with every heartbeat. When he drew back, her skin prickled with new awareness.

You can have me. I'll give you everything I've got.

She sighed, leaning into his embrace. The man must be part Fey himself the way he enchanted.

He pushed her gently back. "Stay inside. The surveillance cameras are back on. See you in the morning, Princess. Sweet dreams."

But she wasn't sleepy. Despite the fear and her narrow escape from the Chasers, she felt needy. And he knew it; she could see that in his sparkling eyes and the upward tilt of one side of his mouth. He wanted her to desire him, think about him and not have him.

He lifted his brows and then headed in the opposite direction.

She watched Mac stride away and followed him as far as the door, holding on to the frame to keep herself from going after him.

Chapter 8

Brianna tossed in bed, paced the cold concrete floor and finally gave up on sleep altogether. As she stared at the ceiling from the wide empty canvas of Mac's bed, she thought of Jeff and grieved over her part in Matthew's death. Then she tried to recall everything her grandmother had told her, merging that with what she had seen and what Mac had said. The headache caused her to close her eyes, and the worry finally gave way to restless slumber and dark dreams. She did not hear his approach, but something roused her from sleep as she sensed a presence in the room.

Her eyes flew open to find Mac easing to a seat at the foot of the bed. He held a steaming mug in one hand and two mugs in the other. She inhaled the aroma of coffee, the fresh tang of aftershave and soap and the scent of wolf.

"I didn't know if you liked light and sweet, light or black. So I brought one of each."

"What if I like sweet and black?"

He produced a packet of sugar and wiggled his eyebrows. "Don't add what you can't take back," he said and his boyish grin made her laugh.

"Black," she said.

"Minimalist, eh?"

He offered the mug, and when she reached to take it he said, "It's not free. Costs one kiss."

She hesitated, pushing the mop of hair back from her face and sat up, regarding him with a mixture of amusement and the slow burn of desire.

"All right. But coffee first."

"Deal."

He handed over the mug being sure their fingers brushed in the exchange. God, he was even more handsome in the bright morning light. She considered him as she sipped her coffee. He sat with a relaxed ease that she found very sexy.

"How's the coffee?"

"Strong, like you," she said.

He smiled. "We didn't find any sign of them on patrol last night or this morning.

"Well, that's good."

He watched her with hungry eyes as she drank the coffee. She felt the flush burning up her neck and face. He held her gaze, and she felt her insides heat as she imagined all the things she wanted him to do to her and all the territory she wanted to cover with her fingers and her mouth. She held out the half-finished coffee.

"Done?" he asked.

She nodded and, instead of heeding the voice of caution, crooked her finger to invite him closer.

He set her mug with the others on the wide adobe window ledge and then knelt over her with one hand on each side of the headboard.

Her heart galloped as he descended to take a long, languid kiss. The man could kiss like nobody's business, she thought, and then she stopped thinking as she wrapped one arm around that strong neck and loop the other about his broad back. She lifted herself up to press against him, gasping at the lovely pressure of his body against hers. He moved smoothly from her lips to her cheek, ear and throat. His touch stirred and coaxed until her senses blossomed into relentless need.

When she clawed at his back and made soft sounds of encouragement, he drew back and cast her a regretful look as if sorry to let her go.

"Did you dream of me, Princess?"

She nodded.

"Have you considered my offer?"

"I did and I have."

"And?"

"It's a generous offer."

"But…"

She wanted to be reckless and brave, but feared the sex appeal that oozed from him like a hive oozes honey.

"But I don't know you."

He sat back down on an empty place on the opposite side of the bed.

"What do you want to know?" he asked a note of caution in his voice.

"Where do you come from?"

"I grew up in Ann Arbor, Michigan."

"Your family is still there?"

"Yeah, Dad, Mom and an older sister and younger brother counting the days until he's old enough to join."

"Tell me about them."

Mac flinched, as if talking about his family hurt him physically.

"Dad owns a towing company. Big-rig towing. Specialized trucks, massive really. I've worked with him since I got my CDL."

"CDL?"

"Commercial driver's license, a trucker's license. I can drive a rig and can tow anything on eighteen wheels. The plan was for me to join my dad after I got my discharge. In a few years my kid brother would come on board, Mac-Connelly and sons. Once I got out of the Corps, he'd give me a share in the company. But now I'll never be out. They've already told me as much. It's going to kill Dad. But he's still got Sean. That's my kid brother. Then there's Bonnie. My older sister is married to a cop; they live in Ann Arbor, too. She's expecting their first child." He ran a hand over the stubble of his military haircut. "Shit, I won't be there for that, either. But I'll be an uncle soon."

"You can't go for a visit?"

Mac scowled at her and gave a curt shake of his head. His face showed strain and his Adam's apple bobbed.

"We've that in common, Bri. We both had plans that have turned to shit. I won't take over Dad's business. I'll never drive that rig with my name painted in gold on the door."

"I'm sorry."

"I always thought I'd have a life like Dad's. Work a little, fish a lot, find the right girl and fill up a big house with kids and dogs and rabbits and…" Mac looked away and cleared his throat.

"You can still do that."

"I hope so. But not until Johnny turns back. Until then I stay with him."

"That's very generous."

"Generosity has nothing to do with it. I owe him. I'll never be able to make up for what happened." He swallowed hard. "Things change. Plans change."

She placed a hand over his. "I'm sorry."

He stood, withdrawing as he scrubbed his face with his palms.

"It's like I died over there. You know? I went in one way and came out another." His head hung. When he looked at her again his composure had returned but his face still showed high color. "But when they figure out how to get Johnny back, I can go visit. I can see them again. Family is the most important thing. You're nothing without family."

She saw his eyes round. Had he just recalled that she no longer had family? What was most important in his life was nonexistent in hers.

"Sorry," he muttered.

"It's okay. You're lucky to have them."

"I know it. I do anything for them and I miss them." He rocked awkwardly from heel to toe as the silence stretched. Then he said, "You want chow?"

She wanted to talk to him, assure him that she understood his loss and his sorrow, how hard it was to imagine your life one way and then find out it would be another. But his expression had turned hard again. So she only nodded.

He rummaged in his footlocker and then laid out drawstring shorts and another clean T-shirt.

"It'll do for now." He spun and headed for the door. "See you in the kitchen."

She had a quick shower, dressed and headed down the hall. She swam in his clothing but the drawstring kept up the shorts, which were more capri pants on her. He drew out a chair for her at the table and brought her a plate of scrambled eggs and toast. There was peanut butter, jelly and butter all on the table before her. A feast, she thought.

"I cooked the eggs in a separate pan from my bacon."

Thoughtful, she realized. "Thank you."

He sipped his coffee as she enjoyed the breakfast he provided and then thanked him again as he cleared her dishes to the sink.

Johnny arrived, and Bri stiffened at his appearance. He

was so big and so fierce looking. It was hard not to flinch around him, hard to keep her face from showing the fear that bubbled inside her.

He slowed as she sat still as a rabbit cornered by a fox and then glanced to Mac.

"Anything?" asked Mac.

Johnny gave a shake of his head and then loaded a plate as if it were a serving platter, heaping on eggs, bacon and toast in a mound that rose like Mount Fuji. Then he signaled to Mac again.

"Her clothes are dirty," he said, as if Johnny had asked some question. "You want to sit?"

Bri tried not to look as frightened as she was and even attempted a welcoming smile but her mouth felt tight and she was sure her eyes were wide as saucers. And somewhere she'd stopped breathing.

Johnny gave her one long look and then shook his head, departing with his plate and no silverware. She blew out a breath and let her shoulders sag. When she glanced to Mac it was to find him frowning.

"He can't help the way he looks."

Guilt flooded through her. She was now certain that Johnny had left because of her cold welcome.

Mac regarded her. "He won't hurt you."

"I believe you. But he's really…"

"Ugly?"

"I was going to say terrifying." She looked to the place Johnny had disappeared. "You said werewolves can kill vampires. Can vampires also kill werewolves?"

"The males can kill anything. Their fangs are poisonous. If they inject enough venom into your bloodstream, it's fatal, that is if they don't suck you dry. The poison is some kind of anticoagulant. Keeps the blood coming."

Bri wrinkled her nose and crossed her arms over herself at the sudden chill that swept through her.

"Mostly they just tear open a vein." Mac cleared the condiments and salt and pepper from the table. She gathered up her coffee mug and followed him to the counter. He took the mug from her. Their fingers brushed. Their eyes met.

"You're cold," he said, his breath just above a whisper. The hushed intimacy of his tone raised her skin to gooseflesh.

"It's cold up here in the mountains."

"I can start a fire. It will take off the chill." He was already in motion.

The efficiency of his fire building impressed her. The smoke billowed outward for a moment and then went straight up the flue. She moved closer, kneeling next to where he squatted and extending her hands as he laid ever larger pieces of wood on the fire.

She glanced up at him and smiled. He didn't smile back. Instead he stared with an intense focus that made her skin prickle in anticipation.

She found herself wondering again what it would be like to sleep with him. Was she attracted to him because he was so different from any man she'd ever met? She didn't usually go for the warrior type. They were too demanding and too apt to make all the decisions for you. She wanted a partner, not a keeper. She realized with a jolt that she'd never have a partner, because no man could withstand her terrible powers.

"Go ahead, Princess. I can take it."

She startled. How long had she been staring at his mouth? She dropped her gaze and it fell to the white T-shirt that now stretched tight over all that muscle. Her throat went dry, making her words scratchy, as if she had some kind of a cold.

"I don't know what you mean."

"You were thinking about kissing me again. I want you to."

She met his gaze. Considered it. "That's a bad idea. Johnny might come back."

But warrior that he was, he already had his hands on her shoulders, taking what he wanted. He drew her closer slowly. Giving her time to pull back or say no. She should have done either. But she didn't. Instead, she lifted her chin and angled her mouth to accept what he offered. His lips brushed hers in a gentle exploration that set off an avalanche of desire surging through her. Her reaction was miles too strong for the simple brushing of lips. She tipped into his arms, falling like a skydiver through space. He caught her up in his arms, holding her, keeping her safe. She opened her mouth. His tongue grazed her teeth. She parted her lips, and his tongue slid against hers, bringing a sweet rush of delight and the taste of strong coffee.

Mac cradled her head as he swept an arm around her, leaning her backward as his chest brushed against hers. An electric storm of desire flashed from the point of contact, tearing through her like a tree struck by lightning. His touch scorched her to the core. A moment later her body tingled and flushed with need.

When her back contacted the rug before the fire, Bri came back to herself. She pushed with both hands. Mac lifted up on strong, muscular arms. He looked down at her, his eyes blazing with need.

"Are you certain I can't hurt you?"

He stretched out beside her. "You're worried about me again, Princess. I could get used to that."

"You're not bulletproof."

"Well, you're wrong there. I *am* bulletproof."

She sat up and he released her. Bri folded her legs, sat

and faced him. His smug smile vanished and was replaced by a haunting sadness that tugged down the corners of his mouth and dragged on his handsome features.

He pressed his lips together in a gesture that was more grimace than smile. His eyes measured hers, and she had the feeling he was deciding something important.

"They shot at me. In this form and in my other one."

"Who did?"

"The Marines at the medical facility. Just following orders."

"Why would they shoot at their own man?"

"Testing. No injuries."

"That's not possible."

"I don't believe in impossible any more. Not since I came back from the Sandbox and started sprouting fur."

He rolled to his back beside her and gazed at the ceiling. She tried not to stare at the hard definition of the muscles in his arms and failed. But his words haunted.

"It happened there?" she asked. "In the…"

"Sandbox. Afghanistan." He nodded. "Attacked by an enemy combatant who turned out to be a werewolf. Johnny and I were the only survivors."

She hugged herself tighter, wishing she could go back to the days when she was blissfully unaware of all the monsters that lurked in the dark.

"I'm so sorry." She reached out to touch his arm.

He turned his head to glare at the hand that rested on his. She drew back immediately. This man did not want her pity. That much was clear.

His eyes now looked empty. She stared at this stranger and inched back.

Just a moment ago he'd held her with such tenderness and his kiss had been lush as a rain forest. Where had that man gone?

His mouth quirked in a cavalier smile that turned her cold.

"Why don't you kiss me again?"

"You act as if I can't control myself. I can."

"But you shouldn't. The longer you go, the deadlier you get. After a while you can kill a man without even sleeping with him."

"Is that true?"

He looked deadly serious now as he nodded. "For you, more is better."

Her thoughts went to Jeffery again and the miracle that she had not killed him, too. Even before he grew ill, she had known that sleeping with him was a mistake for many reasons, not the least of which was her mixed feelings. But if she'd had known she was some kind of lethal carrier of energy she never, ever would have slept with him.

Jeffery's sudden, bizarre illness was her fault. She'd nearly killed him.

Bri turned to Mac and held his gaze. "He'll be all right now. Won't he?"

"Should be, if you keep your distance."

If she stayed away from him, he'd recover. The realization that she could never see him again didn't hurt her nearly as much as it should have. Instead her first reaction was relief. Her response surprised her so much she gasped. She had been fond of him, but now she recognized she had never loved him. He'd loved her. She knew it, and she had hoped that would be enough. It wasn't.

His insistence more than her attraction had brought her to his bed. The guilt choked her. She should have known better.

He moved closer, breathing deeply, then gave her a sensual look. The potent mixture of virile male and the edge of danger made her pulse pound. She didn't know if she should step into his arms or run.

·   "Lucky thing I'm not human. You can't make me sick."

She felt her muscles tighten and her stomach flutter. "I don't think that's lucky. More like tragic."

"You need what I can give you, Princess, and I'll admit I've been without since this happened to me. I miss having a woman."

A woman, as if any woman would do. His words made her cold and his touch made her hot. For him it was all just filling a need, his and hers.

He placed his hand over hers. She didn't draw back. Her skin began to tingle again. There was no denying the attraction that fired between them. But that was not love, either.

He used his thumb to draw small circles on the sensitive skin on the inside of her wrist.

"I don't have random sex or one-night stands. I've only had two intimate relationships and…" Her eyes flashed to his. He must have seen it, the pain that tore through her, because he opened his arms to her and she fell into them. "I killed Matthew and I put Jeffery in the hospital."

"You didn't know."

She pressed her hands over her face. "It's so terrible. I don't know what to do."

"You'll stay here until they come, and then Johnny and I will kill them. If you need a man in the meantime you take me. Do not go out and find a human. You come to me."

"Yes," she whispered. "I'll come to you."

Mac found Johnny sitting alone on a fallen log five feet off the ground, swinging his legs like a kid playing hooky from school.

"There you are." Mac leaned against the log.

Johnny smelled his nervousness in the sweat that had nothing to do with exertion. He lifted his hands palms up, silently inquiring.

Mac blew out a breath. "I've got to ask a favor. I'm... well, I'm attracted to Bri."

Johnny growled.

"I know, it's just, she's beautiful and I haven't had, well hell, Johnny, neither of us have. But I don't know if it's just that or if it's what she is."

Johnny shrugged his shoulders, unsure what Mac expected him to do about that.

"Can you get close to her, maybe smell her and touch her and see if she does anything for you. I know you don't like her. So if you're attracted it's the vampire in her, not the woman."

Johnny groaned.

"Come on, buddy," Mac urged.

His friend squeezed his eyes shut and then dropped to the ground and cleared the fallen leaves with a bare foot. Then he used a series of twigs to spell out his answer.

"Did that," Mac read.

Johnny collected the sticks and used them again.

"Still...want," Mac read.

Johnny collected and lay out his final three words.

"To...gut...her."

Mac sat back on his haunches. "Really? Well, okay. That's good I guess. But don't. Really, that's an order."

Johnny wanted to say that he didn't like her intrusion. That he wanted her dead and, barring that, he wanted her gone. They killed things like her, didn't they? Instead he nodded his compliance with the order, gave a lazy salute and motioned for them to run.

"Maybe later," said Mac, rubbing his neck and glancing

back to the compound where the flesh eater waited. Mac slapped Johnny's arm. "Thanks, buddy."

Johnny loped away. He didn't like having a female in the house. Her scent disturbed him, made him think of all the things he'd lost since the attack, like his mother and his family and his world. He understood that Mac was using her as a lure to draw more vampires, but if she was staying, at least she could be dressed. Johnny had seen her clothes yesterday. They were wrecked, stained, muddy and torn, so his sergeant had given her a T-shirt, a Marine Corps T-shirt. She did not deserve to wear a T-shirt with the Marine emblem, and he determined to do something about that today.

So he left the bounds of his larger prison, crossed into the national forest and ran until he reached the campsite.

There he staked out an RV park. Didn't take long for his recon to find a perfect target. The family had a teen daughter about Brianna's size.

The family of four finished lunch, hamburgers cooked on a gas grill and buns toasted on the charcoal. It smelled great. They ate inside at the large kitchenette, and Johnny wondered why they'd bothered to leave home for the great outdoors. Both junior and the temperamental teen ignored their parents in favor of their electronics throughout the entire meal. Johnny would have given his right paw to see his mom and dad again and to hug his little sister, but these two didn't know what they had. A lump rose in his throat. Someday, maybe. He still held hope that the doctors would figure out why he couldn't change back. It was what had kept him from ending himself. That and Mac.

His squad leader was a ballbuster in-country. But not anymore. Not since the attack. Johnny had changed on the outside, but Mac had changed on the inside.

Mac had a thick head and a warm heart and Mac had

stood by him, fought with him and lately fought *for* him getting him out of that cage. It was Mac who understood that in this form, despite the strong urges and the unfamiliar desire to hunt and run, he was the same inside. Sure he was stronger and heard a hell of a lot better, and his sense of smell was outstanding. But he was still John Loc Lam. Back in training, the guys had called him Lock and Load, because of his middle name. He'd heard worse at school in Port Chester, New York, where there weren't a lot of Asian-American kids in the sea of Latinos. But Mac had asked him what his mother had called him. At first Johnny had thought this was just another way to humiliate him, but he'd answered, and from that day forward everyone under the command of Staff Sgt. Travis Toren MacConnelly had called him Johnny or Private Lam. Mac told him later that if anyone was going to bully his men it would be him. End of story.

Johnny stared out from the trees, waiting for Junior to lumber to the car. The girl didn't seem to eat anything and was the thinnest in the group, which was good, because Brianna was a small woman, curvy but small. Of course, most everyone looked small to him now.

It wasn't until the teenager descended from the thirty-three-foot RV that Johnny got a look at her face. Her eyes were ringed in so much dark makeup she looked like a sullen raccoon dressed in black. Steampunk girl, he decided as he watched the family pile into the giant SUV and roll away.

Johnny would have preferred a night raid, but it was as Paul Cummings used to say before the werewolf tore his throat out. He galloped across the open ground, waiting for the screams that didn't come. Somehow an eight-foot werewolf had not been spotted yet. He only needed one hand to tear the door from its hinges, pealing it back like the lid on a can of tuna fish.

He was inside, pawing through drawers and making a pile in the center of the camper. Once he had what he needed he ripped open some of the food containers for show. They had frozen vegetables in neat unopened bags. He added some to the pile, then threw it in a pillowcase and took off.

His exit was not as smooth as his entrance. He nearly ran over a woman wearing boxers and a loose T-shirt who took one look at Johnny, dropped her bundle of neatly tied firewood and screamed like an actress in a slasher movie. Johnny just kept running, and he didn't stop until he got back to base.

When Mac picked up Johnny's scent, he knew he was close. Where had he been all morning? For a few minutes there, Mac feared that Johnny had gone off grounds again. It had been hell to get him the small amount of liberty they now enjoyed. But Johnny still wasn't predictable.

Mac wasn't sure if it was the wolf or post-traumatic stress syndrome. Maybe it was both. God knew, Mac still had nightmares.

Mac admitted to himself that he'd been preoccupied with Bri and turned his gunner down when he'd asked him to run.

Johnny was fast on all fours, but he ran only when Mac was also in wolf form. Now he strode into the yard like a nine-foot shadow monster.

"Where you been?"

Johnny lifted the pink pillowcase and dropped it at Mac's feet.

"What's this?" Mac peered within and scowled. He reached inside and drew out a half-thawed bag of soybeans in the pod and a skimpy pink scrap of silken fabric which now dangled from his index finger. "Johnny! What the hell is this? Holy shit! Did anyone see you take these?" Mac now shook a fist full of brightly colored underwear at him.

Johnny looked away.

"She's not going to wear other women's underwear." He tossed the scraps of silk into the trash.

Mac continued to rummage through the sack. Women's clothing.

"These are good," he said and tossed them into a pile. Next he discovered several small plastic bags of vegetables. All for Brianna, he realized. Johnny had known she had little clothing to wear and little to eat, since both he and Johnny preferred meat, lots of it, and rarer was better. Mac faced his friend and released his anger. "That was a nice thing to do."

Johnny snorted and Mac wondered at his motives. If he didn't do it from kindness, than what?

"How did you know she's a vegetarian?" But he knew the answer the moment he said it because he knew as well. "Smelled it, right? She's sweeter, somehow. Must be the grains." Or the fact that she was irresistible to men.

Johnny nodded.

"If anyone saw you, then we are in deep shit. Did they?"

Johnny shrugged, then motioned his head toward the compound.

"You want to give them to her?" he asked.

Johnny bared his teeth.

"Fine. I'll do it. But don't run off." Mac retreated, stopping briefly in the kitchen to toss six bags of frozen vegetables and one box of veggie burgers into the freezer. Then he returned to the kitchen but heard her down the hall in his room. What was that she was humming? "Werewolves of London," he realized and gave a single sound of mirth. The woman had a sense of humor.

He knocked on the open door, pausing to see her bent over his bed tugging at the sheet. She startled and then straightened as she turned to face him.

"You are so quiet. I never heard you and I hear everything."

"Habit," he said. "What are you doing?"

"Trying to make the bed, but I can't do it like you."

He took in the draped blanket instead of the crisp corners of a tight bunk. Then recalled her bending over and felt his body harden. He lifted the sack. "I've got clothes. Johnny's doing."

She was looking up at him with rapt interest. Her gaze fell to his mouth and his skin burned. He waited and she glanced away. She wasn't ready for what he offered, but she was considering it. He could tell by the pink color of her ears and the sound of her heartbeat, audible to him even from where he stood.

"Johnny and I have to report to headquarters. Stay inside or my command will see you on camera."

"Yes. I'll stay inside. When will you be back?"

"After dark. Eat what you like in the meantime. There's a TV, books and video games, though you don't look like a gamer."

"I'm not. But I do read a great deal."

"Soldier of Fortune?"

Her brow wrinkled, and then she realized he was joking and cast him a dazzling smile. He knew he was outmatched and retreated down the hall.

Back outside he discussed their situation with Johnny. Both agreed that the compound was the most defensible position available. Mac still wanted to keep her appearance secret, and he had no way to explain Johnny's panty raid if that came to light.

Mac made suggestions; Johnny listened, giving his opinion about what to do with their uninvited guest. If more male vampires did follow her, they would have an opportunity to capture one and be heroes. The colonel would see that they were ready to return to combat duty, and that might get them both the hell out of this glorified prison. He was sick of being a fucking lab rat.

Johnny reminded him that they had already captured one.

"I'm not turning her over."

Johnny glared and looked away.

"So I'm leaving you today. You sure?"

Johnny nodded, agreeing to do the training alone so Mac could quit early and watch over Bri. Mac felt pulled in two directions. Because Bri had now become his responsibility.

Chapter 9

The morning at the medical center stretched to afternoon before Mac and Johnny were finally dismissed. Mac paused some distance from their quarters as he smelled lilies where there were none. There were deeper fragrances, cinnamon, soap and the alluring scent of a female's most secret places. He growled at the unwelcome flash of desire as his body reacted before his mind could even process what was happening.

"You scent her?" asked Mac.

His comrade nodded his head. He looked glum after spending an afternoon as a living target. Mac had wanted to leave him, and that was exactly why he hadn't. Instead he'd stayed and watched Johnny suffer from the rounds that bounced off his hide like bullets off Superman's chest and worried about Bri, alone in their quarters.

"Me, too. And I kept thinking about those lacy, silky things you stole and how they'd look stretched—"

Johnny sighed and Mac stopped talking. At least *he* could have a woman. Mac glanced from Johnny to the path leading to Bri.

"So if I can scent her and nothing else, I guess she's all right. What do I cook for the vegetarian?"

They reached the courtyard and then the inner chambers that led to their living quarters to find Brianna standing in the kitchen, a glass of water poised at her mouth. Her skin glowed with good health and the turquoise tee and black yoga pants hugged her curves like nobody's business. Part of the wardrobe Johnny had provided her, he realized. She lowered the glass and cast them a tentative smile.

"Welcome back, Mr. MacConnelly. Good evening, Mr. Lam," she said and stopped to glance from one motionless male to the next. "Did I do something wrong?"

Johnny shook his head, but Mac thought he was smiling. Had he changed his mind about having her here?

"I would have cooked something, but I didn't know when to expect you."

Mac and Johnny managed to chase her out of their kitchen and got her parked on a stool when they cooked steaks and fries for them and macaroni and cheese for her. His gunner was grace in motion but clumsy as a cook, so Mac cooked and Johnny set the table and did KP.

Johnny pushed the salt and pepper closer to the second chair Mac had added and placed a paper napkin where Bri could reach it, folding it once. Then quickly drew back his hand. Now Mac stared at Johnny who gave him a casual shrug. He didn't know his gunner knew how to use a napkin, let alone fold one. Johnny sat on a cushion on the ground and still reached the surface of their table. Mac slid two large steaks onto Johnny's plate and then heaped on the French fries before making himself a similar plate.

Brianna took her seat and gave Johnny, seated adjacent to her, an anxious glance before returning her attention to Mac who carried over a bowl of macaroni and cheese for her to eat. Johnny remained motionless as a dog with a biscuit on his nose awaiting the command for release. Mac stood in confusion. He had never seen Johnny wait before a full plate of food. Was he waiting for their guest? He turned back to the stove to retrieve his portion.

Mac sat and stared at Johnny, who glanced at Brianna.

"This looks delicious." She lifted her fork, grimaced and took the tiniest of bites, then winced.

"Something wrong with the grub?" asked Mac.

She startled and then poked at her pasta, making a show of taking a bite. "No, they're delicious." Her smile faded and she lay aside her fork. "I don't have much of an appetite. I feel a little sick to my stomach."

Mac looked at the metal fork and the aluminum bowl. Was that making her sick?

He took her portion and returned a moment later with a fresh helping on a paper plate. He offered her a plastic fork. She tried them and smiled.

"These taste so much better."

"It's the metal."

She nodded. "Yes. I didn't want to be a bother."

An elephant trumpeting in the room would be less disruptive than having her seated at their table, but he managed a smile. His reward and punishment was that she reached out and squeezed his hand, right there beside his fork. The buzz of sexual energy started in his ears and plunged downward to the usual places. He glanced at Johnny who just gaped at him from over the fork full of meat he'd been about to swallow whole.

"Thank you for helping me," she said.

Oh, he would have liked to do a lot more than help. He managed a civil response. "No problem."

"But I need to get back to my life."

Johnny's fork paused again and he turned from Mac to her and then back to Mac. Did Johnny want him to cut her loose? He felt the tug of uncertainty as he realized he wasn't letting her go regardless of what Johnny wanted and then felt the familiar kick of guilt, low and sharp in his gut. He lifted his brow at Johnny who looked up and to the left as he lifted his tufted brows. Johnny was deferring to him, thank God. Mac looked back to Bri's lovely upturned face.

"You're on their list now, Princess. They know your name and where you live."

She tried to keep her chin up but he noticed a slight tremor there. "I won't go home."

"Or the hospital."

Bri slumped. "But what about Jeffery?"

"That life is over, sweetheart. Gone for good and all."

Mac found himself curious about a man who could keep the likes of Bri without gaining her love, for truthfully, that was just what he wanted. Sex. No strings. That was the perfect relationship. Besides, you didn't bring a vampire home to meet the folks.

"Will they hurt him?" she asked.

"Doubtful. He doesn't know where you are, so they have no business with him. They might stake out the hospital. Hoping you'll turn up. You aren't going to."

Johnny resumed eating like a teenager anxious to get away from his arguing parents.

"Right now the authorities are searching for you. Eventually you'll be added to a list, one of many young women who've vanished and were never found."

She blinked at him and for a moment neither spoke.

"I don't want to disappear," she finally said.

"You don't have much choice. The vampires are searching. And they won't give up. You either join them or you run and hide. There's no middle ground. The males are stronger and faster, and so the females do what they say. As far as we know, none of the female soul…" His words dropped off, but she knew he was about to say *soul suckers*. "What did you call them?"

"Leanan Sidhe. But those are fairies. Full fairies like my mom is supposed to be. I'm half human."

"Maybe all the others are half human, too. Maybe all vampires are descended from fairies."

"From Leanan Sidhe, you mean. Most fairies can't kill people. Except for the Banshee, of course."

He stilled, his gaze flicking to Johnny who lowered his fork to his empty plate and shrugged.

Mac returned his focus to Brianna. "What the hell is a Band-She?"

"It's a fairy that kills by touch. To the heart for death. To the head for madness. It's just folklore. One of the stories my nana told me. A way to explain mental illness, I suppose."

"Or those fucking things are real, too."

Johnny threw up his arms.

"What?"

He spelled out the curse word Mac had used.

"Oh for Christ's…" He met Johnny's scowl and let his words trail off. "What? I can't swear now?"

Johnny inclined his head toward Brianna. Apparently Johnny didn't swear in front of ladies, even ones with powers that could shrivel a man's heart like a prune.

"Well I never heard of those things, but I suppose werewolves can kill them, too."

She drew in a breath and looked at him as if he were her knight in shining armor. Mac held her gaze, wanting that to be the case so much that it hurt.

"How?" she whispered.

"By hunting and killing them, like we hunted ECs."

"I don't understand." she said.

"Enemy combatants."

She didn't raise any objections. Seemed killing farm animals and killing vampires did not fall into the same class for her, which was fine with Mac. He could hear her blood thumping through her veins as she sat perfectly still. Bri lifted a hand to her throat and spoke in a whisper. "Go on."

"Bullets don't kill vampires because they heal too damned fast. If you get lucky and hit one, the holes just heal up. You can spike them with silver, but the minute that silver is removed, zip-zap, they're whole again. Decapitation works, if you use a silver sword and you are damned quick. But if a werewolf tears out their throat or rips open a major artery, it doesn't heal and they bleed out."

"I think iron is more damaging than silver," she said. "It bothers me much more."

Why would she tell him her weakness? Unless it was because it was also the weakness of her enemies. Was she beginning to trust him? He hoped so.

"That's helpful, thanks."

She cast him a wary smile and then glanced to Johnny whose fixed stare was often unnerving.

"So that's what you and Johnny do? You are training to kill vampires?" She was clutching her throat as she waited for the answer.

Johnny held her gaze and nodded.

"That's terrible."

"You'd rather have them out there assassinating world leaders? Because they're killers, Bri. Drink blood, collect millions and kill human targets."

"But they can't come out in the daylight."

He shook his head. "Myth. Most of the stuff out there is wrong. Except the silver part. It's not the cross that deters, its the silver, and if you have a gold crucifix you are shit out of luck. They tolerate gold, I think." He waited for confirmation.

She nodded. "Pure gold, yes."

"Holy water doesn't work. Same for wooden spikes, sunshine, holy ground and coffins. And they don't need to travel with dirt. That's just weird. They mostly go out at night because they are butt-ugly and they can see so much better than humans in the dark."

She shivered, recalling the one she had seen. "That makes a lot of sense. But they have white eyes, like a blind man."

"And purplish skin mostly. It is pinkish after they feed."

Bri pushed her cold meal about with her plastic fork. Finally she lifted her head to meet Mac's stare.

"I don't want to endanger either of you. This is *my* problem."

Mac grinned and met Johnny's eye. "We're Marines, Vittori. Problems are what we do."

"I don't want you to have to face those things because of me."

"That's not up to you. You might not understand this, Princess. Marines don't just kill things. We protect things. Roads. Towns, positions. Lines in the damned sand. Convoys, cities, countries and people. And as of today, we also protect one female vampire."

"I've never needed protecting before."

"You've been protected your entire life. Otherwise you wouldn't be here."

Her face went pale as that arrow struck home.

"You needed it then and you sure as hell need it now."

Her eyes glittered with tears. "My nana was human and she knew, and *still* she kept me safe."

"She loved you."

Bri nodded, the tears slipping in silver trails down her pale cheeks.

Johnny started signing. Bri watched and Mac put the letters together.

"What is he saying?"

"He's reminding me that you're one of them. But I'll protect her as long as I can." This last part he directed at Johnny who then glared at Bri. Did he have to protect her from Johnny as well? He didn't want to have to choose.

That night Mac and Johnny ran as usual, only they had a purpose—search for sign of intrusion by male vampires. Mac's needs had changed when he had. He needed more food and less sleep, and he needed to run. That was one of the reasons he had to get Johnny out of lockup at the medical facility. He worried that his gunner's trip off grounds yesterday was going to bite them both in their big hairy asses.

After the moon rose they returned to the compound where he could hear Bri's breathing. He took first watch and Johnny relieved him three hours later.

It was a quiet night, except for his thoughts, which kept creeping down the hallway to his bedroom where Bri slept alone. He woke the instant she rose from his bed, hearing her breathing change and the whisper of sheets as she slipped to the floor and crossed on bare feet to the bathroom that had been installed for him. A moment later the shower spray began.

He imagined her bright red hair, now wet and turning a deep shade of auburn while a mass of ringlets danced about her head. Her face would be covered with beaded droplets that would run down her bare shoulder in rivulets. He released his breath into the sofa pillow and crept into his room, moving silently to the bed where he leaned down and inhaled her scent on the sheets. The shower ceased and Mac retreated out of doors to find Johnny sitting watch.

"You still okay with this?"

Johnny gave a reluctant sigh and then a slow nod. Not enthusiastic but he'd take it.

"Thanks, Lam. I want you to know that I still have your back. Nothing has changed there."

His gunner gave his shoulder a quick squeeze then headed inside. They had breakfast before Bri arrived.

"Do you think she'll eat oatmeal?" asked Mac.

Johnny shrugged and Mac heated the water. He added raisins and had the gooey mess ready when she appeared, scrubbed and dressed in tight jeans and a tighter T-shirt. Mac gawked and then glared at Johnny, who grimaced and then covered his eyes.

"Good morning," she piped.

Her hair was indeed a deep auburn when wet, just as he had imagined. But her skin was now glowing pink and fresh as dew.

"I made oatmeal," he said, extending a bowl.

"I love oatmeal." She grinned as she accepted it and paused there, staring up at him as her smile faded and the buzz of sexual energy began again between them.

Mac needed her to get away from him, because he was contemplating marching her back down the hall to that bed. Instead he cleared his throat. "Sugar's on the table."

Mac's phone roared like a Harley motorcycle. It was the ring tone he'd chosen for his commanding officer, Colonel Lewis, and both Johnny and Mac jumped every time they heard it.

Lewis had been in charge of his squad in Afghanistan. The colonel had surprised Mac by leaving his combat assignment to follow him and Johnny to the Marine Mountain Training Center. It showed the kind of concern for his men that Mac had stopped expecting from rear-echelon motherfuckers. Johnny still didn't like Lewis, but he never said why. Just the mention of Lewis made Johnny's hackles lift.

Mac took the call and the order for him to report ASAP.

Mac hesitated before leaving Brianna with Johnny. But he couldn't bring her with him, and they both knew he had to report.

"You'll be all right?" he asked Johnny.

His gunner took his sweet time nodding his acceptance of his new position as babysitter and showed his fangs as a measure of his displeasure.

"Thanks," said Mac.

Mac again felt that pull to be in two places at once, and Bri's assurance that she would be fine did nothing to relieve his mind.

He left Bri reluctantly, lingering for one long look and to give final instructions to stay inside to keep her from revealing herself to the newly repaired Marine Corp surveillance cameras and to trust Johnny if anything happened. All the way to the facility he second-guessed his decision to leave her. Damn, he knew this would blow up in their faces. Only question was when.

At HQ, he reported to his commander's office and to his assistant, who pressed the intercom button at his appearance. He paced, but that made his agitation too obvious. So obvious even an officer might notice it so he stopped, fixing his feet to the floor as if glued there.

Mac didn't like the uncertainty swimming around in his belly like a hungry shark. He knew it was his duty to tell the colonel about Bri. But he knew what would happen if they found her. The possibilities kept him mute. When had he started picking and choosing which orders to take?

Colonel Lewis's assistant opened the door and then stepped aside. Mac removed his hat and entered. He stood at attention, holding is salute.

"Staff Sergeant MacConnelly, sir," announced the colonel's aide.

Lewis stood behind Captain Steward, staring at the computer monitor over the computer tech's shoulder. He glanced up at Mac, frowned and snapped a quick salute. Mac dropped his arm to his side before the colonel's index finger had left his forehead.

Lewis stared at Mac. "You want to tell me anything?"

Mac swallowed but remained at attention, feeling his weight on the balls of his feet as he resisted the urge to change into his wolf form. When unsure, Mac generally feigned ignorance. He held his blank expression, perfected in basic training.

"Sir?"

The colonel didn't know about her. He couldn't. Could he? Still Mac felt the sweat break out on his forehead. If anything happened to Johnny because of this, Mac would never forgive himself.

Lewis spoke to the captain but kept his gaze directly on Mac. "Run it again, Steward."

Captain Steward clicked away at the computer keyboard. The man sat erect with a serious expression that gave the impression of disapproval. He glanced at Mac then back to the screen. Was this about Johnny going off base?

Mac stood motionless until the colonel waved him forward. Mac had the feeling he didn't want to see what was on that screen. Colonel Lewis pointed at the monitor and Mac followed the direction he indicated.

"Our camera caught this on Sunday at zero six thirty. Can you tell me what it is?"

Mac's skin began to crawl as he stared at the blurry, frozen image on the monitor. The shape was unrecognizable.

"I'm increasing the resolution and slowing it down as much as possible," said Steward.

The colonel barked at Steward, "Run it again."

Steward's movements were as crisp and mechanical as any Marine's. He didn't look at Mac as he set to work. Mac's stomach dropped as he saw the image was from the back of his compound. Something swept up the wall, something wispy and white. It showed for an instant and then shot up toward the rooftop and out of frame. The captain clicked a few keys, and a still image of the effusion filled the screen. Mac knew what it was. It was Brianna leaving the compound the first time she'd seen Johnny. She'd moved too fast for him to see, but not too fast for the camera, apparently. Johnny had missed one. Mac calculated the angle and realized the camera was in the woods, pointed at his bedroom window. *Son of a bitch.* His jaw tightened. The surveillance was not for them, but also *of* them.

"You want to tell me what the hell this is?" The colonel pointed at the screen.

Mac moved closer, checked the time stamp to confirm his suspicion and shook his head. "It looks like wood smoke."

"Smoke can't change direction," said Steward, never taking his eyes from the screen. "This thing is moving so fast the naked eye wouldn't see it."

Lewis lifted his busy eyebrows at Mac. "Steward here thinks you're hiding something."

The shark in Mac's stomach swirled in a circle and took a bite of the lining of his stomach. They might be searching the compound right now. No, they weren't. Johnny wouldn't let them in. He knew that, but still his pulse raced.

"He thinks Johnny knocked out those cameras on purpose."

Mac glanced at the captain, who narrowed his gaze. Then he cleared his throat. "If he were hiding something, sir, I'd know."

That much was true.

The corner of the colonel's mouth ticked upward for an instant. He held Mac's stare long enough to make him uncomfortable.

"I told him you are a good soldier and you follow orders. I vouched for you, son. I've given you a lot of leeway with Corporal Lam. That kind of special treatment comes with strings. I thought you understood that."

Mac's hands began to sweat. He gripped them into fists.

"But Steward here thinks that Johnny can understand things. He thinks he saw him writing something in the dirt. You see anything like that, Sergeant?"

"No, Colonel, sir." His throat went dry.

"We'd want to know if Johnny is showing signs that he remembers who and what he was. You got that, Mac-Connelly?"

"Sir, yes, sir."

"You see anything, you tell me ASAP. That's an order."

"He wouldn't be able to see this, Colonel," said Steward, eyes still glued to the screen.

"That would explain why the sergeant didn't report anything," Lewis said to the captain, but then added. "Doesn't explain the cameras though." He rubbed his prominent jaw and exhaled through his broken nose. "Maybe we need to bring you two in. Our intel suggests that vampires can fly. If those vamps are hunting you, you'll need backup."

"Sir, request permission to remain in our compound, sir."

Lewis pressed his lips into a thin line. "I don't want you hurt, Mac. And I don't want Johnny hurt any worse than he already is. I feel responsible for you both."

Mac understood that feeling and the weight of duty that he lifted each morning where Johnny was concerned.

"Yes, sir. We appreciate it."

Lewis gave him a winning smile. "You do, but as for Johnny, he still growls if I get too close to him."

"He doesn't mean anything by that, sir." Mac needed to speak to Johnny about that, but not near the compound. Too many eyes there. Did they have microphones, too? He recalled his conversations with Brianna this morning and his stomach heaved.

"I expect you two will be fighting vamps in the future. But sometimes the enemy comes to you. You did well against those two, Mac. But it was even odds, and they might have been scouts."

"If there were more, sir, we'd scent them. They can't just sneak in and out of our territory."

"Who the hell knows what they'd do? They are fast, smart and unlikely to come at you head-on. They have a better chance of killing you if you don't see them coming."

"Those two didn't take us, sir." But one nearly had. It was only Bri's warning that told him which way the attack had come. "I haven't seen any evidence of any more bloodsuckers. No scent, no trace. Nothing, sir."

"All right. But eyes open and stay alert. You catch their scent and you haul ass here. You got that?"

"Yes, sir."

"Good. Now report to the lab for testing."

He wanted to go check on Bri and tell Johnny what had happened. Instead he saluted and was dismissed.

They'd caught Bri on video. Maybe the colonel was better equipped to protect her, but then who would protect her from the colonel? Not only that, who would protect the colonel from *her*?

Mac spun and crossed to the exit in two long strides, then looked back at Lewis.

The colonel was still human. Being around Bri might

kill him, and if she learned how to use her gifts she could make him dance like an organ grinder's monkey.

But that was not why Mac was keeping his mouth shut. Not for Lewis and not for Johnny. It was that damned kiss. She'd turned him inside out. God damn, he was defying orders.

Mac made it to the door and had his hand on the knob when the colonel called him back.

"Oh, and Mac, remember, Johnny is only out on a trial bases. If I find out he's screwing up he's back in lockdown."

Mac thought of the woman's clothing Johnny had mustered and flinched.

"Yes, sir."

Chapter 10

After three nights here, Bri still jumped at every unfamiliar sound. During the long, lonely afternoons, when Mac was away, Johnny guarded the compound but stayed out of doors, so it wasn't clear to Bri if he was keeping intruders out or her in. Possibly he was just avoiding her. Today, she was more nervous than usual because both Mac and Johnny were gone and all she had for protection was a radio.

She stayed clear of the windows, because Mac said cameras could detect changes in light even though the blinds were drawn. She listened to the rain hit the glass and wondered if it was changing to snow. He'd left on the TV but she was afraid to change the channel and afraid to add wood to the fire. What if the cameras saw smoke from the chimney hours after Mac and Johnny had gone?

When she heard the truck engine, she hid in the bedroom, as Mac had instructed. Finally, she heard him calling for her to come out. She darted from the room but her smile died as she saw him, supporting the eight-foot werewolf who wobbled on legs that seemed unable to support him.

"What happened?" she cried, rushing forward and taking a position flanking Johnny's opposite side without even thinking what she was doing.

"Don't know yet." Mac steered them to the futon in the living room. They almost made it when Johnny groaned and collapsed, taking Bri with him to the ground. She landed under Johnny's massive arm with her chest and head on the futon. That thick pad kept her from any serious injury. But according to Mac, she could heal from all such injuries anyway.

Mac lifted Johnny's inert arm and together the rolled his big body onto the mattress.

"Is he hurt?"

"Drugged. Has to be oral, since they can't get a needle into him. They just snap off."

"Gas would work, or what about his gums? They could inject him there."

He stared at her a minute and then drew back the loose skin of Johnny's upper lip, revealing his fangs and the black gums that matched his skin. Sure enough, there was an abrasion and a small circular bruise around the needle puncture. Someone had done a sloppy job because Johnny's tongue had been lacerated, as if someone had sliced through it with a knife. It was a nasty gash, deep and raw. "Probably used a pole because he won't sit still for doctors or medical techs, and he hates the veterinarians."

"Veterinarians? You can't be serious. He's a soldier, not an animal."

"When you arrived you thought those were the same things."

"Well, I've reconsidered. I never really met an enlisted man before. I thought people who joined up were underprivileged or…" She let her words trail off.

"Or what?"

She looked uncomfortable but she spit it out. "Delusional."

"And now?"

"Well, it's not a job I'd want. But you two aren't what I expected."

That made Mac give a harsh laugh. "I'd imagine not."

She studied Johnny, who was sprawled on the mattress, his head lolling and his eyes rolling back in his head. He looked dead, Mac realized, and he immediately checked Johnny's breathing to find it shallow but easy to discern.

"I think they used him for target practice again."

"Let's make him more comfortable." Bri headed for the kitchen and returned with a moistened dish towel. Then she brought it back and tried to bathe Johnny's face.

Mac held her back. "Wait over there," he said motioning to the far side of the room. "He can be hard to control when he comes out of anesthesia."

She stared up at him, and he thought she might turn tail, but instead she just handed over the cloth and moved where he indicated.

Mac washed the blood from Johnny's snout and then laid the folded towel over his open eyes. A few minutes later, Johnny started to growl. Mac stood between Johnny and Bri. Next his friend roared and bolted to his feet, running blindly into a wall and then scrambling up.

Mac usually met Johnny in his wolf form, but he hadn't wanted Bri to see him for what he now was. Now he recognized his mistake, because his gunner had the advantage of size.

He inhaled, caught the scent of a vampire, turned to Bri and charged.

Johnny barreled toward her, teeth snapping, blood dripping from his jaws as the wound on his tongue broke open again. Mac met Johnny's charge. Together they tumbled and hit the opposite wall.

Johnny rolled from his grip. Mac's heart stopped and an instant later a pulsing burst of fear flooded through his veins. If he bit her, she'd turn or she'd die. Mac called the change, allowing the fury to fill him, take him. As the pain tore through him, the fear beat in his heart. What if during that split-second transformation, Johnny got a hold of Bri?

Johnny wobbled, unsteady as he charged Bri and Mac leaped, catching Johnny before he reached her. She stood frozen in terror. Mac knew he'd never forget the horror etched on her face. As he carried Johnny to the ground, Mac noticed a vibration about her, as if she stood in her own private earthquake. For a moment he thought it a trick of the light, but in the next instant she vanished.

"No," Mac said but the word came out as a roar. But she was gone.

Mac and Johnny crashed to the floor. He held Johnny down as his gunner dropped his head back and groaned. Mac held on as Johnny went slack, coming to his senses Mac hoped.

If Johnny had hurt Bri, Mac didn't know what he would have done. One more mistake to live with. One more responsibility to hold in his heart. Johnny struggled, but Mac held on, waiting for him to come to his right mind. This was the drug, not Johnny.

He knew when Johnny was back, because of the regret he saw shining in his friends clear yellow eyes.

Mac swung his gaze from his gunner and scanned the room, roaring. Where was she? He couldn't call out to her, not in this form. Was she outside again? Was she on camera right now?

Mac rolled to his feet. Johnny followed, looking about and then made a whining sound that Mac had never heard before. He ran to the window, but when he tried for the kitchen, Mac strong-armed him. He wasn't 100 percent sure that Johnny was back from the sedation and damned if he'd let him near Bri until he was certain.

Johnny scented the air and a moment later crawled out the kitchen window. Mac followed. If she'd gone this way they'd have caught her on the surveillance cameras. He glanced up, noting that the cameras were now housed in a protective cage. It seemed the colonel didn't want any more "windstorms" causing breaks in their surveillance.

They made it to the exterior wall, where her scent trail went straight up. Neither could follow it, so they headed toward the compound exit at a run and ran through the gate as the colonel's jeep arrived.

He couldn't have seen the footage so fast. Could he?

Lewis swung from his seat and marched toward Mac, his tight jaw a ready indicator that they were about to get their butts handed to them.

Lewis aimed a finger at Mac. "Change back, now, Sergeant!"

Mac retreated to the compound with Johnny at his heels. Mac returned less than a minute later, hastily tucking in his shirt while Johnny hung back.

"You said you'd watch him," snapped the colonel.

"Sir?"

The colonel barked at his driver, who hustled around the jeep, jogging as he booted up a laptop, which he offered to the colonel.

"You do it," he growled, and then to Mac, "Look at this."

The driver set the laptop on the hood of the jeep. Mac watched the blurry image that he thought might be Bri. But then he recognized Johnny running for the woods on all fours, a pink pillowcase clutched in his jaws. He actually breathed a sigh of relief until he met the colonel's narrowing gaze.

"Damn clusterfuck. It's already on YouTube. Calling it a Bigfoot sighting!"

Mac glanced at the screen, saw an RV flash by and understood. It was the panty raid he'd gone on for Bri.

"You want to tell me what you are doing while Corporal Fido is stealing…" He looked to his driver who began to rifle off a list ending with "six thongs of various colors and four bags of frozen vegetables."

The colonel removed his hat. Rubbed the bristle on his head and then jerked his hat back in place.

"If you can't keep him in bounds, he goes back with us."

"Yes, sir. It won't happen again, sir."

"Your ass if it does."

Mac watched the colonel stride angrily away, forcing his driver to jog back to the driver's side to keep pace. Once inside Lewis banged the top of the vehicle with his open hand as a signal to start, and the jeep lurched away.

Mac scraped his knuckles over the bristle on his jaw and turned in a full circle. The colonel hadn't seen Bri's exit. Or at least he hadn't seen it *yet*. The home movie had been taken several days ago but apparently just hit the Internet or just reached the Colonel's attention. As for the surveillance, Lewis appeared to be about twenty-four hours behind. That gave Mac a few hours to move Bri. But first he had to find her.

Mac felt his world collapsing around him, and all he could think to do was run. He knew it was a mistake to take her in. Because of her, they might lose everything.

Mac turned to discover Johnny already searching for a scent trail. He followed, letting Johnny track, staying in his human form, telling himself it was so he could communicate with Bri. The colonel hadn't yet seen Bri's latest on-screen appearance. What would happen when he did?

Together they raced through the pine, jumping over gullies and dashing up inclines. All the while Bri's scent trail grew stronger. Mac told Johnny that he wanted to move Bri somewhere beyond the surveillance.

A few minutes later Johnny stilled, sighted her first. She sat on a large gray boulder, knees drawn to her chest, forehead on her knees. She was as still as the rock that grounded her. The breeze ruffled her hair and the sleeve of her pink T-shirt.

Johnny pointed.

"Yeah. I see her." He cast his friend a long look. "You coming?"

Johnny shook his head and looked at the ground.

"It wasn't your fault. You were drugged. You'd never hurt her if you weren't coming out of that stuff they gave you."

Johnny looked away. They both knew that he had tried to hurt her the night they'd found her and that he wasn't pleased at Mac's decision to protect her. Mac rubbed his neck.

"Nothing happened. She's fine."

Johnny pointed and then pretended to wipe his eyes. Mac looked at her again and had to agree with Johnny. She didn't look fine. She looked like she was crying.

"Shit," he breathed, his insides already rigging up as he prepared to face this woman in tears. Mac drew a long breath. "Well, what should I do with her? Can't bring her back to our compound. Can't turn her over." Mac raked a hand over his hair. "Shit."

Johnny scratched something in the dirt. Mac tried to read it, but the ground was uneven and Johnny's handwriting sucked.

"What's My Bacc?"

Johnny tried again.

"My *Place?* You have a place?"

He nodded.

"Where?"

Johnny pointed.

"Cameras?"

Johnny said no.

"All right. We'll move her location. Too much surveillance here anyway. You lead the way. I'll follow your trail."

Mac left Johnny and stepped from cover. If she heard him she gave no sign, just sat dejected with her head bowed and her shoulders hunched. He stood beneath the rock, looking up at her. He could have jumped but he didn't want to startle her.

"Bri?"

She tightened her arms about her knees. He waited and after a few more moment she lifted her head. Mac's stomach squeezed at the sight of her tear-streaked cheeks and red-rimmed eyes.

"I'm sorry we scared you. Johnny's sorry, too. He didn't know what he was doing."

She unfolded her arms and then she pushed off from her stone island and landed beside him. He didn't think, just enfolded her in his arms. She buried her face against his chest.

"He'd never hurt you."

She nodded her understanding then met his gaze. "What about you?"

"He can't hurt me. I'm already bit, already a wolf." He looked away. "I'm sorry you had to see that."

"What I saw was you protecting me from Johnny. But it wouldn't have happened if I wasn't here. My presence is making it hard for you to care for Johnny."

He couldn't deny it. His life had become infinitely more difficult since her arrival, but he knew that she was also the first good thing to come his way since returning from deployment.

"Maybe he needs your full attention."

"You want to leave?"

"No. But I can't stay hidden in your bedroom forever."

"If you go back to Sacramento, the vamps will catch you."

"I'm not going back. I'll just do what my nana taught me. I'll keep moving. I'll stay away from people."

"That won't work anymore. They are hunting you now and they will find you. If they take you, you'll be their prisoner, underground for years while they use you, brainwash you until you'll do anything they tell you. Your only hope is that *when* they find you, Johnny and I are there."

He guided her back the way they had come using a hand behind her back as he tucked her against his side. She felt natural there, as if that was exactly where she belonged. *Don't get used to it,* he warned himself. He couldn't have her. If he tried, the flesh eaters would just keep coming, tracking her for her entire lifetime or until they killed him.

But he didn't want to let her go. Even if it risked his neck and Johnny's. He wouldn't. But then he thought what choosing her would really mean, and his breath stopped. He couldn't bring her home to meet the folks. She couldn't go out on a double date with his high school buddies. Bringing her into their lives would be like bringing the plague. To choose Brianna was to give up every human connection he had. To protect her and to protect his loved ones, he'd have to choose: Bri or his family.

His breath left him in a whoosh, as if he'd been sucker punched, for in fact, he had.

Was any woman worth that? No. She wasn't. He had to

figure out how to protect her and then teach her to protect herself. And then he'd need to let her go.

"You shouldn't have to risk your lives for me."

"Marines are used to risking their lives." He didn't want her to know how important she was becoming. Didn't want to admit it to himself. So he retreated. "Besides, it's not for you. My colonel wants to catch a vamp. You're the bait."

She paused and stiffened. He watched the hurt break across her face.

"I see."

He wished he'd told her the truth. That he wanted her safe and happy, but most of all he wanted her here with him. He thought of his parents and felt guilty for his need for this woman.

She moved away and he let her stray a few steps before pursuing her. He wished he could lift that sadness that hung on her like a cloak.

"What now?" she asked.

"My commander saw you on surveillance cameras a few days ago."

Her hands shot to her cheeks and her face went pale so fast, Mac grabbed her elbow to steady her.

"Just a wisp of smoke. But he's suspicious. And there is a good chance they caught your exit today."

"Oh, no!" She wrung her hands and glanced about as if expecting tanks to come barreling through the forest at them. She started to vibrate again, and he saw the distortion of light that had preceded her last disappearance. He grabbed her arm and held on.

"Wait. Don't run."

She looked back at him, her green eyes huge and round but she nodded and the vibrations ceased.

"Listen now. There are more cameras up. We can't go back there. But Johnny says he has a place where you can hide. We're going there now." Mac followed Johnny's scent trail, catching a glimpse or two of him. Johnny had kept just ahead of them and out of Bri's sight.

Mac and Bri walked together in the quiet woods. When he was with her, it was hard to remember that this was a training facility. That just a few miles away from them, men were crawling under barbed wire and practicing various assaults.

Chapter 11

It was twilight by the time they came to Johnny's place, as he had called it. Mac recognized it as a supply drop used in winter maneuvers. Now, in early April, it was all but abandoned and as far as Mac could tell from his recon there were no cameras in the vicinity. Johnny had torn off the lock and gathered supplies, much of the supplies that the colonel insisted that Johnny had been stealing from various outfits and of which Mac had denied having any knowledge. Johnny had sleeping bags and blankets and mattresses and crates of food padded with more mattresses to make a raised seating area. His gunner had made his own man cave. *Or wolf cave,* Mac thought.

"It's nice in here," said Bri. Then she turned to the woods. "Thank you, Johnny."

He must have heard her, but he did not appear. Mac and Bri moved outside. Bri sat on a crate while Mac got a fire started in the fire pit before venturing into the woods to find Johnny, but his gunner could not be convinced to join them. He indicated he wanted to run. Mac warned him to stay in bounds this time, and he nodded his understanding before departing at a lope.

Mac returned to find Bri warming her hands. The evening air held a chill as the temperature began to dip with the approaching night. Bri untied the hoodie from her waist and slipped into the tight-fitting sweatshirt as he rummaged through the crates for MREs, meals ready to eat, choosing the mac and cheese for her because it was vegetarian and not as terrible as some of the others. For himself, he chose the beef stew, which was pretty bad, but he was hungry enough that it wouldn't matter. He heated them in a pail of water from the stream, keeping the little packets sealed as the water came to a rolling boil.

Bri divided her time between watching him work and watching the woods. "What if they come when you aren't here?"

The vampires or the Marines? he wanted to ask. But instead he told her that he'd get the radio but he feared that he'd never get back here before they took her. She seemed to know it as well, for she held his gaze for a long moment and then nodded, flicking her gaze to the fire.

"I can run. I outran them once." She glanced to him. "You really think you can stop them?"

"Bloodsuckers? Already did. Do it again, with pleasure."

"Then what?"

He met her gaze. "Then I catch them if I can and kill them if I can't."

"After that?"

"I'm going to teach you to defend yourself. Teach you how to kill them."

She hugged her knees tighter and glanced away. "I'm not a killer. I might run, but I don't think—"

"You'd be defending yourself. There is no moral dilemma."

"Maybe not for you."

"You'd rather be captured?"

She rested her chin on her folded arms. "I'd rather be human and still unaware that monsters are real."

"That's not going to happen for either of us."

She met his gaze. "Yes. I know. But even if I do survive this, I will never be free." She watched the sky now. Did she see the stars beginning to twinkle to life, visible as the daylight released the earth to darkness? "It's strange to have your whole life seem like one thing, and then it tips on its axis and you get a new perspective, and you realize it was something altogether different all the time. I thought I was helping people. I thought I was a good person. I thought my nana was just very stern and the fairy tales were just stories. But I'm not good and she wasn't cold and it's all real. I'm like Typhoid Mary. Everyone I touch gets sick."

He moved closer, forcing her to shove over on the crate. "Not everyone."

"What will Jeffery think when I just disappear?"

"He'll look for you, I suppose. But he'll get better and he'll move on. There's no other way, Bri."

She blew out another breath. "He's a chemical engineer and has been working on some big research project. They've been stuck for months. But the team he's heading just had some big breakthrough. He was so happy. Management made him their golden boy, and he said I was his lucky charm. But I'm not."

Mac's ears pricked up. Maybe she was. He thought of what she had said about her father: a brilliant musician, famous, wealthy. How often did that happen? What had the website called her—a muse? A suspicion began to form in his mind.

"What did the other one do?"

She stared at him. "What other one? Do you mean Matthew? He was a writer. Mostly freelance for various magazines. He wrote feature stories."

"Did that change when you two met?"

"Yes." She paused and her brow furrowed. "He took out the novel he'd written in college and completely rewrote it. I read it. It was marvelous. He got an agent, and then two publishers bid on it. It will be published soon." She dropped her head and her shoulders rounded.

"So it's true then."

She stared at him, her face golden now in the firelight and her hair blazing more brightly than the flames.

"I looked up that fairy name, Leanan Sidhe. It says that they're a fairy muse. That when she chooses a man, she kind of makes his energy burn faster or more brightly. I don't really know which. She is like fuel to his talents, feeding them."

"While killing him."

"The price, yes. The site said that their chosen ones lived brilliant lives, but short ones."

"But I'm not a Leanan Sidhe. My mother was. I'm a soul sucker. Isn't that right?" She lifted her trembling chin.

"Maybe you don't draw energy. Maybe you make a man's life run faster. Make his brain run faster, too."

She shivered at this, and he wrapped an arm around her. "I don't know why you agreed to help me."

"You can't hurt me, Princess. That's what they tell me. It's why we can get up close and personal with bloodsu... vampires."

He realized that he wanted to help her, he *could* help her. She was not like his squad, now planted in Arlington. Bri was alive and in danger. It gave him hope again, because unlike Johnny's issues, she had a problem that he might actually be able to solve. Up until this very minute he never realized how much he needed that hope.

"But Johnny needs you, too," she said.

He let his arm slip from her shoulder and moved to

check their meals. She was right about that. And his family—what about them? Was he prepared to drop off the planet for this woman? She was beautiful and alluring, but really she was just a woman.

"It's hot." He tore open one of the packets and offered it to her. "Just wait until it cools and then tip it up, like you would if you were drinking out of a milk carton." He handed her a bottle of water from Johnny's larder and a tube of crackers.

She did as he instructed and for the next few minutes they ate in silence. When they had finished, he burned the containers, watching the plastic twist and shrivel on the logs, writhing like a living thing.

Bri cleared her throat and then spoke. "Do you have a sweetheart, Mac?"

He wondered why she cared. Was she considering his offer? His body twisted like the collapsing plastic on the flames.

"No. Had one. Cut her loose when I signed up. She's engaged now to someone who will stay put."

"I'm sorry."

"My choice."

She nodded. "Have you had contact with your family since…?"

His smile turned to a grimace. "They think I'm still in-country. Made a few video calls. My dad had some trouble with his heart. Seems okay now. But…" He shrugged and then went cold as he thought of what meeting Bri might do to his father's narrowing arteries.

"They must worry."

He rubbed his jaw. "Yeah."

"And you must miss them."

"Well, I can see them online, call them every week,

but…" He glanced toward the scent trail that threaded through the dark woods. "I have responsibilities."

"Johnny." She squeezed his hand. "Will you tell them what happened?"

"Can't. Top secret."

She took the hand that rested on his knee. "Then will you tell me how it happened?"

For just a moment he thought that her appearance and the vampires' attack were all just a setup to learn about how he became a werewolf. But then he remembered the intel they got from Israel. The vampires knew how to kill werewolves. But they preferred to run rather than face the chance of dying. That made them as smart as they were ugly.

He poked at the fire with a stick, recalling the night he turned and not wanting to go back to that dark place in his mind.

"Mac, I'm half fairy and I'm some kind of a monster. Surely if anyone can understand what you are going through, it would be me."

"It's rough," he warned.

She nodded her acceptance of that.

He sat across from her, fixing his gaze on the flames as he traveled back to the Sandbox in his mind and recalling the distress call he'd received from his second Fire Team. Sometime in the remembering he began to speak. He described the mission, to clear the road and perimeter so they could use the route for transport to the combat outpost. The COP had been cut off by heavy engagement, and they were low on everything. They'd pushed their enemy back, but not before the retreating force had littered their escape route with improvised explosive devices. The IEDs and mines were being handled, but in the meantime a new road was going in and the buildings along the way needed to be cleared of the enemy. They could permit no snipers on the rooftops taking shots at their guys.

Staff Sgt. Travis MacConnelly stared through his infrared goggles at the ground before them. The lifting of his forearm and the closing of his fingers signaled his men to halt. No light spilled across the small courtyard inside the enclosure on the moonless night. But he could see everything clearly in green and black. Kabul, Afghanistan, at zero three hundred, and nothing stirred not even the hot wind that deviled them, blowing sand into all their gear. But appearances were deceiving, because his first two Fire Teams were already in positioned, one clearing the building and one standing by.

Mac waited with the men of the third and final Fire Team for the agreed-upon time. His heart jackhammered in his chest as the silence seemed to collapse in on him. Too damned quiet. His first command since his promotion to staff sergeant, and now the responsibility of all twelve souls in this squad rested with him. They were good Marines, and he was proud of them already.

His watch ticked off the seconds.

At zero two fifty-six his sharpshooters neutralized the watchmen on the roof, and his teams moved in. His first Fire Team used silenced .22s to take out the guards at the front entrance, the only noises their footsteps and the next round being chambered.

His team moved inside the wall. He watched the first team enter the building in tight formation. Now the way was clear for his third team. Their grenadier was a corporal named Lam. Hell of a name for a Marine, but his team respected him, and from what Mac had seen he was more lion than lamb.

His Fire Team leader checked his watch and then

glanced to Mac, who nodded. He signaled his men and they ran the distance to the entrance.

Lam was the first man in. By the time Mac cleared the archway, Lam was dropping a body on the foyer. The man's blood made a dark pool against the pale tile floor. The first team had missed him, so he wasn't here when they came through. Mac signaled for them to check the ground level, knowing the first and second team had the higher two floors.

Systematically they searched each room and then hit the corridor still in formation, his men searching for targets as they climbed the narrow stairs. A shooting gallery for anyone above. The quiet was deafening. Where were the gunshots? With three guards so far, there had to be more.

From above them came the first report of gunfire, a spray of bullets and then the shouting of his men. More gunfire and shouts followed. Then high-pitched screaming echoed down the narrow stairs with frantic shouts to pull back. Fire Team One requested backup, and Mac sent them the second team. They could then hear the second team charging up the stairs ahead of them.

An instant later, the howl of agony seemed to vibrate from the walls. Why weren't they firing?

The screaming diminished and then stopped. Lam looked back to Mac, and he gave the order he would live to regret.

"Double time," he yelled, and his men responded, eager to come to the aid of the first two teams.

They reached the west wing and met with silence and an open door. Lam stepped into the room first followed by his team: the rifleman, Towsen; the assistant light machine gunner, Barbari; and the light machine gunner, Gonzalez. They fanned out, backs to the wall, as Mac cleared the door and stepped into the large room. For a moment, he made a perfect target against the opening. Something streaked forward. Robert Townsen, Lam's point man, managed to squeeze the trigger of his M-4 before something tore him off his feet. His scream came a moment later and died in a liquid gurgle.

"Get down," called Gonzales as something clasped his ankle and dragged him off his feet.

Mac swept the room and his heart went cold. Bodies littered the floor like trash bags. His first two Fire Teams, he realized as the bile rose up in his throat. What the hell was going on?

There was something here, something big as a bear. What was this, a half-assed zoo?

A creature ran straight at them on all fours.

"Fire," Mac yelled.

Barbari and Lam both opened up, and they continued firing but the thing kept coming— slashing at Gonzalez and tearing his innards out despite his Kevlar vest and body armor. Then it turned toward him. Lam stepped in front of Mac, swinging his weapon at the beast's head as Mac drew his knife.

That wasn't a bear, he realized, but he'd never seen anything like it. Huge, with massive forearms and claws that still dripped blood from its attack on Gonzales.

"Kill it," shouted Lam, striking the thing in the forehead with the butt of his weapon. Mac raised his knife as Lam was tossed across the room.

Mac aimed for the jugular and sliced across the creature's neck. Nothing happened. No laceration. No blood. The thing stared at him, seeming to grin. Had this one thing killed his first two teams? In that instant, looking into those yellow eyes, he knew that it had.

Mac fired his personal weapon until it was spent, and

the monster just stood, as unaffected as a tank being struck by rocks. What the hell was this thing?

Johnny came back, charging the monster like a lineman on Friday night. The creature turned.

"No!" Mac shouted. He couldn't watch another man killed by that animal. Mac moved to intercept Lam, shoving hard, knocking him off balance as he took the hit intended for Johnny. Fangs punctured Mac's shoulder. Top and bottom jaws clamped on to him as the creature tore him from his feet. His weapon clattered to the ground as he lost control of his arm. Pain seared through him, and his stomach heaved. As abruptly as it grabbed him, the monster let go, using its claws to flip him and then toss him. Mac sailed across the room and crashed into a concrete wall. He lost his goggles and with them his sight. Now he was blind in the dark, seeing the world only in short blasts of machine gunfire.

Towsen, he realized. Where was Barbari? Was he alive? Was Lam?

"Fall back," Mac ordered. "Fall back, damn you. Get the hell out of here." The smell of blood filled his nostrils and he slipped on the viscous fluid, unable to regain his footing. "Get out and call it in."

His shouting brought the thing in his direction as he'd intended. It grabbed him again and shook him like a terrier with a snake. Mac's arms flailed, his jaw snapped on his tongue and his vision blurred. It shook so hard Mac thought he'd lose his arm, but instead he'd only lost his humanity. He hadn't understood at the time, but that was the moment when everything had changed.

Mac blinked until he could see the fire again and Bri seated beyond, still and pale as carved ivory.

"I told him to fall back," Mac whispered.

She'd wrapped her arms about herself, though whether from the cold or the horror he could not tell.

"I woke up in a medevac. Johnny was there with me, right beside my stretcher. My memory is bad here, because I remember him telling me to hold on, but he couldn't have, because they said he was in worse shape than I was. I think he was in wolf form before we touched down." Mac pushed the guilt down deep and rubbed his hairline, feeling the raised scars that threaded over his head. "It also tore my scalp. They said it was flapping like a toupee. Collapsed a lung here." He hiked his shirt to show her the puncture mark in his ribs. Mac pointed at the scars as if displaying a road map. "I have these because I was still human. Nothing scars my skin now. It's better than Kevlar."

Bri nodded, having seen the scars before; he was still impressed that she didn't look away.

"They must have hurt."

Not as badly as how much he hurt inside. At the time they were a welcome distraction from his anguish. The pain and the pain pills both gave him the only respite he knew from the haunting memories. When he closed his eyes he still heard those screams. Marines, screaming like animals in a slaughterhouse, for they were.

"They shipped us both stateside. But not to a hospital. They sent us here. When I was allowed out of bed, I went to see Johnny. He was all that was left of the team. They'd already buried the rest." Mac felt the air leave him as he recalled writing a letter to each family.

He pulled a stick from the fire and used it to poke at the dirt until the flaming tip extinguished. Then he threw the stick, watching the glowing ember spiral until it hit with a tiny explosion of sparks.

"They said he was…like he is, because he'd been attacked by two of those things. They knew because of the separate bite marks. The shape of the canines were different."

"There were two?" Bri asked.

He shook his head, not trusting his voice to hold steady. Mac clamped his hand over his mouth as if that could hold back the self-loathing. For just a moment he thought he was going to puke.

He was supposed to protect his men. He was supposed to keep them safe, for Christ's sake. He damned sure wasn't supposed to attack them.

"Mac?"

He dragged his hand from his mouth and held up one finger. "Just the one that attacked us and then me. *I* attacked Johnny. They said the teeth marks matched. Lam did his best to protect me and I turned on my own man. I don't know how many I killed. Which ones. I don't remember. Towsen, probably, and maybe Barbari, too. They wouldn't show me those videos and I didn't ask. But they said nobody else got out. Me and Johnny were the only survivors." Though part of him had died with them. The best part. He kept going to see Johnny through this nightmare. After that…he didn't know.

He wanted to go home to his family. Pretend none of this ever happened, lock it down so deep and so tight that he forgot everything. But he already knew that wouldn't happen because of the nightmares. They just kept coming.

He pressed the heels of both hands into the sockets of his eyes. And then she was there before him, kneeling at his feet, her slim arms slipping about his middle and her soft breasts pressing against him as she held on tight.

"Did you hear me?" he whispered.

"I heard."

"My own men."

"Shhh, now," she cooed.

"You should be running the other way."

"No. I'm staying."

"Might turn on you, too."

"I don't believe that."

"I'm dangerous."

"Yes. And so am I. Maybe that's why we are together."

Mac looked into her eyes and saw understanding. It drew him in, captured him more surely than any magic spell she might be able to cast over human males. But this was stronger, this bond they shared, this parallel of being different, being dangerous and hurting those you cared about.

"We have that in common," she whispered. "You and I are not human. Before she died, my nana told me she wanted me to hold on to my humanity. I think I understand now what she meant. She wanted me to be like my father, passionate and full of life. But I've been like my mother, attracted to those who have that life instead of generating my own. When I'm with you I feel alive inside, Mac. Sometimes I'm afraid and confused, but always very alive."

He felt that, too, not the mindless infatuation he'd heard described in a briefing of the only known survivor of a female vampire attack. The victim was saved by werewolf bodyguards, who recognized the female before she got too close. Even after he knew what she was, he was ordering off his bodyguards, who ignored him, of course.

Mac's attraction to Brianna was also physical, but there was more. So much more he didn't want to dwell on it. But he knew that she did understand his sorrow and the loss of so much of his life. She knew what it was to be other among your own friends and family and to have hurt those she loved.

"With anyone else I have to live with the knowledge that whether I draw their life away or make them burn it up like gasoline, I don't bring my own flame. It's different with you. I feel my own passion burning now. When I'm with you, I feel my own life force instead of yours."

"Because I block your powers."

"And you are certain that it's safe for me to let go. I never have. Even before Nana told me, I knew deep down it was dangerous."

"It's not with me." He ran a hand up the long muscles of her back and then wrapped his fingers about her slender neck, controlling her. "You can't draw my power. We're opposites, I think, or perhaps we are just the same."

"Are you sure that I can't hurt you?"

"Not in the way you mean. Not physically." But she could do a job on him emotionally if he let her get too close. This had to be just physical. It was his only protection from the inevitable loss. Once Johnny was human again, Mac could leave here and return home, at least to visit. He might always be a Devil Dog, but he could reclaim some of what he lost, unless he chose this woman. He couldn't do that, not without losing everything and everyone else. But he could have this moment.

Bri still looked unconvinced. "How do you know I can't hurt you?"

"Lewis told me. For years the Israelis have had werewolves acting as bodyguards for political officials. Recently they added a female vampire. She works in their intelligence operations. They've done studies. Placed the male werewolves in close quarters with her. They found that werewolves are on a different frequency or something. I don't understand it exactly, but my brain doesn't respond to your mojo."

"This werewolf was all right?"

"Even after he slept with her. They checked cell growth and division. All normal. They said that vampire-werewolf teams were safe and that werewolves would make natural colleagues for working agents, as the vampires wouldn't have to worry about killing their partners."

She stared in silence as the ramifications of what he told her sunk in. Could it be true? Hope fluttered in her chest but she held it in—afraid to accept the possibilities he dangled before her.

"He wasn't attracted to this woman?"

He shook his head. "He reported he was no more attracted to her than he would be to any beautiful woman, and all her attempts at persuasion failed."

Bri tried to say something, but her heart was pounding so hard in her chest that it hurt her ribs. He wasn't drawn to her.

"Bri, do you understand what this means? It's safe. Lewis showed me the report. I read it. Female vampires emit power is a high-frequency electrical wave that increases brain activity in humans. It stimulates the, oh shit, I forgot the name." He lifted his hand and scratched his head. "It's the part of the brain that is responsible for creative thinking. It also damages growing tissue and interferes with cell replication."

She understood what that meant. "Cancers."

"Yes and bruising and nosebleeds and loss of hair. Damage to reproductive organs. It's like radiation, sort of, or that's how they explained it to me. Your body gives off this energy all the time, but on occasion, the emission is much higher. High enough to kill." He held her gaze as her cheeks burned. They both knew what kind of occasion caused this high emission, as he dubbed it.

"But you are part human."

"So are you. Now come here."

She closed her eyes as he tipped her head and lowered his mouth to hers. The first kiss came sweet as cane sugar.

His warm mouth pressed to hers, filling her with a honeyed lethargy. He used gentle pressure to encourage her to open her lips for him and stroked her tongue with his own. The contact set off electric charges of excitement through her body. She leaned against him, and he took her back to the earth, pinning her with one strong leg as he sucked her tongue. She gave herself willingly, knowing that with this man she could burn away her passion without stealing his. She had always been afraid of what would happen if she ever allowed herself that ultimate release. It had been a sore spot with Matthew, and since she had been with Jeffery only that one time, she didn't think he realized she had not reached her own fulfillment. Both men thought she was reserved, shy. But she was none of that. Instinctively she had felt the danger and had kept her response tamped down deep inside herself.

Mac pulled back and gazed down at her. "You taste so sweet," he whispered. "I want to taste you all over."

She closed her eyes and made a sound that most resembled a purr of anticipation. Yes, she wanted that, too. She wanted all of it. She wanted to plunge into passion and open wide to all he offered.

Bri stretched out beside the fire, the flames warming one side of her as the night air cooled the other. Above her, Mac stared down, his face half gilded and half in shadow. Just like the man, he was half apparent and half mystery. But she felt she knew him better now, understood how he became what he was.

Bri pushed off the ground and lifted the hem of her T-shirt and outer sweatshirt, drawing them both away in one graceful sweep. His eyes went to her breasts first, made more tempting, she knew, by the turquoise push-up bra that Johnny had collected. The A cup did not quite fit her, and so she spilled over the top. Mac used a thumb to brush her exposed top of one breast and Bri trembled. Ah, yes, she thought, this was what she'd longed for and never had—until now. Mac offered himself like a banquet to a starving woman. She wanted to touch every square inch of him and take everything he had to give.

She captured his big, warm hand against her breast, savoring the sweet aching pressure at his touch.

"Now you," she whispered, releasing him.

He reached up behind his neck, grasping the T-shirt with one hand and yanking it with a violent tug that made her stomach flutter. He was her warrior, violent and dangerous. He was also part wolf, feral, driven by instinct. And now his only ambition was to have her. Her gaze devoured him, both the hard muscles and the raised white scars that had made him what he was—hers.

The edge of danger that clung to him aroused her in ways she did not want to consider. She let her eyes gobble him up, rising to explore the hard planes of his muscular chest. Was this what they meant by body armor? He certainly had muscle to spare, hard, defined, ripped. Her fingers swept up his torso, and he inhaled sharply through his nose. The pads of her fingers registered the change in texture from the satin of his skin to the puckering nubs of his nipples and then the leathery white scars where the werewolf had torn him open.

"I haven't had a woman in a long time," he said.

"Dry spell's over," she whispered and kissed his chest.

Bri patted the place beside her, and he rolled onto his back, wrapped an arm possessively around her hips and brought her flush against him.

She wiggled away, feeling the need to go exploring. Bri leaned forward to kiss those scars. She let her tongue follow them like a river, down to his nipple, where she sucked. He gasped, clasping the back of her head and holding her there. She didn't mind. She used her tongue to flick over his taunt nipple, feeling her heartbeat quicken in anticipation.

His fingertips danced over her shoulders and down her spine, raising a tingling awareness and stoking her internal furnace. He held still for her exploration, but she felt what his stillness cost him in the tightly coiling muscles. He did not grab at her or hurry her, as Jeffery had done. He let her do as she liked, letting his body be her playground. The sense of power elated her. She knew that he was the stronger, but for this moment she held the power. Bri glanced up at him and saw her intuition was right. His stillness was a thin facade. He watched her like prey, his mouth grim and his eyes blazing with emotion. He was waiting for her to finish, waiting for the signal to advance. He held her gaze and his mouth quirked as his eyes issued a challenge.

"Go for it," he whispered.

"You think you can take it?"

"Oh, yeah. Take it all."

Her fingers danced down his ribbed abdomen but she paused when she grazed the top of his fatigues and found his erection there beneath the wide waistband.

She gasped in surprise at the length of him. He took the opportunity to sweep down and capture another kiss. This was no gentle caressing or quiet exploration. He plundered as he brought her head back, his fingers grazing her neck as his tongue invaded her mouth. She gasped at the thrill of desire bolting through her middle and streaking down to her core, and felt herself go hot and wet. He moved from her mouth, the stubble of his cheek grazing her sensitive skin as he took her earlobe between his teeth and bit down with just enough force to make her startle in excitement. Mac pushed the straps of her bra down until the lacy undergarment encircled her waist. His hot tongue stroked the ridge of her ear before dipping inside. She trembled and clung to him as excitement shuddered through her. With each kiss and caress she grew wet until she shifted her hips impatiently. She wanted out of these clothes.

"Take off your jeans," he said as his gaze roved over the long length of her.

He must have read her mind.

Her fingers trembled as she released the rivet fastening of the adolescent, straight-legged, low-riding jeans and sat back to peel them off, turning them inside out in the process. He shook out his T-shirt and laid it down for her and then lifted her onto it with frightening ease. He smiled at her surprise.

"I'm stronger than I look."

"Apparently."

"It's part of the whole wolf-thing. I'm just as strong in either form."

"Good to know."

"I keep the strength, hearing and sense of smell while in human form. You smell delicious, by the way, all musk and smoke. I can't wait to taste you."

Was he talking about her…? Bri flushed with embarrassment and anticipation. She met his steady stare, swallowing as a trickle of fear rose up inside her. In many ways he was still a stranger, and she was about to place herself in the most intimate of all vulnerable positions. But that wasn't what gave her pause. What if this was as good as she hoped? What then?

"You're looking at me like I'm the big bad wolf," he said and smiled, showing straight white teeth.

"Aren't you?"

He dropped his smile. "No. Not with you. I'll only bring you pleasure, and I'll stop when you say. For me it's just about the sex. You good with that?"

It sounded good, so good her body vibrated from a deep internal need that rose up like an orchestra crescendo.

"Yes," she whispered, taking what he offered with both hands, greedy as a hungry child.

He had her permission to do as he liked, and she had his permission not to hold back. She held his gaze as his sensual smile made her stomach flutter. He still frightened her, but not because of what he might do. He frightened her because of what he made her feel.

Just sex, she repeated, knowing it was a lie.

Chapter 12

Bri sucked in a breath of air at the first contact of his tongue to her abdomen. He licked and stroked, using his mouth and his hands with feathery-light touches that brought all her senses buzzing to dizzying arousal. She shifted beneath him, anxious for more.

"Are you sure you're safe?" she whispered, some remnant of her thinking brain still fighting for control above the flood of sensation, still afraid to allow her release.

"Yes, Princess." This time when he used that nickname, it was like a caress. "Relax. It's safe. And good," he whispered. His tongue dipped into her navel. "So good."

His voice went all gravel, the male equivalent of a purr, she thought and let her head drop back to the earth as she lifted her hips to meet his descending mouth. He stroked the sensitive skin of her inner thighs, moving ever closer to her most needy places. She could have him, enjoy him, let him enjoy her, and there would be no price to pay.

There's always a price, came the voice in her head.

She pushed it aside. No, his touch was magic. He was so good at this. A gasp escaped her as his fingers delved into her tight curls. She glanced down, aroused by the picture he made, his short, dark hair contrasting against the white of her thigh, and his long, tanned fingers laced into the thick orange hair as he separated the folds of flesh to reach her clitoris. His mouth descended, her eyes fluttered shut and she arched at the first contact. His tongue swirled and he sucked. The tension built inside her, jumping and climbing to heights that made her dizzy. She lifted her hips and he clasped her bottom in his strong hands, bringing her to him again and again.

Sharp threads of tension, pulled tight within her, taut now to the point of breaking. And still he kissed and sucked and caressed. The threads vibrated as a web of nerves fired all at once. Bliss.

The contractions surged outward with her cry. He didn't stop. His fingers delved inside her, prolonging her first orgasm. The echoes of pleasure retreated like a sound wave, leaving her body relaxed and weak. And sated. She'd never felt so perfectly at peace. She gave no resistance as he continued to kiss and stroke, moving up her hips with slow progress, as if bent on kissing every inch of her. The floating sensation of peace ebbed, replaced by the rising need to have him inside her. She groaned as her body begged for opposing needs.

He lay at her side and then pulled her over himself, so that her head lay on his shoulder and her back was pressed to his stomach. His erection now slid between her legs and along the slick folds of her cleft. He used it to stroke her without entering her. The sensation made her shudder. She now lay open to him like a banquet. He stroked the soft outer mounds of her breasts and then worked toward the peaks that budded at his touch. A gentle tug and squeeze sent pleasure rippling to her core, and she shifted as the arousal grew, building with each skilled stroke. He kissed her ear and neck, whispering of her beauty and the exotic taste of her. She lifted her hips, clamping her legs about his arousal and stroking the long, tempting length of him. When she tried to take him inside her, he stopped her. One moment she was lying across him and the next he had spun her so that she straddled his thighs. His erection stood at stiff attention before her. She glanced at him to see his knowing smile and the invitation in his eyes.

"I'm all yours," he whispered.

"Permission to come aboard," she said.

He laughed. "Navy talk. Granted. Marines don't ask permission. We just take the ship." He reached for his trousers, retrieved his wallet and then came away with a condom in a small green packet.

"Always prepared," she said, lifting a brow.

"That's the Boy Scouts."

She plucked the foil packet from his fingers and took her time as she slipped the thin sheath over his magnificent erection.

She rose to her knees and admired the view of Staff Sgt. Travis MacConnelly stretched out before her, willing and able. She took hold of his erection in one hand and guided him into her soft, wet folds. He rolled his hips, and she sank down upon him inch by inch, savoring the friction and slick slide as he filled her. She straddled his hips and he smiled up at her.

"You're a wonder," she whispered.

And he was so. She lifted up. His hands settled on her hips, guiding her but not allowing her to break this new connection. With downward pressure he sped her descent. The glide of his erect flesh on her yielding folds was magic. She wanted to move faster, but he kept her from galloping along. One hand left her hips, and he moved to finger her again, his stroking only hurrying her ascent and increasing the urged to move.

"Faster," she said.

The muscles at his jaw bulged. "Just a few more minutes."

She threw her head back and tried to hold on, but the tension inside her built and she felt her control slipping, allowed it to slip, because she could trust him to survive her need.

"Now," she cried. "Please, now."

She was on her back an instant later and Mac was over her, his eyes glittering with passion as he drove into her with strong, smooth strokes. Each one bringing her closer. He moved fast, so fast, a steady marvelous pounding that shook her deep inside and brought her second orgasm.

Bri cried out his name, "Travis! Oh, yes. So good!"

He never slowed as her contractions broke, rolling outward to her fingers and toes. She was dying, the pleasure making her weak. And then she felt his control break with the last great thrust. His cry mingled with hers as another orgasm swept through her, milking his erection as he began to slip from inside her.

"Look at you," he whispered.

She opened her eyes and saw a shimmering sheen of gold, like a heat mirage, only this came from her skin.

"What is that?" she asked.

"Damned if I know. But it's beautiful. *You're* beautiful."

He straightened his arms, drawing back to watch the shimmer.

"Do you feel all right?" she asked.

He grinned. "Spectacular. Don't worry, Bri. I'm fine." Slowly the glimmer faded, like a lamp turned low.

Mac fell back to his elbows, grasped Bri and rolled until

he lay on his back and she rested in his embrace. "Does it happen every time you come?"

"I don't know."

He lifted his head to give her an incredulous look. "What do you mean, you don't know?"

"I never…I didn't…I never looked for it."

He tipped his head. She looked away but still felt his stare.

"That's not what you were going to say." There was a pause. She kept her eyes down. "You were going to say that you never…Bri?"

Her skin went hot and her ears tingled.

"You've been engaged and you have a boyfriend or had one. This wasn't your first rodeo. But…was that your first orgasm?"

Bri went slack against him and nodded, feeling somehow ashamed and inadequate.

He stroked her head. "Why?"

She swallowed, trying to regain her voice past the fingers that seemed to now grip her larynx. "I was close a few times but I got scared. I don't know why. Or I didn't know why at the time. But I felt it was dangerous. My nana said I shouldn't ever sleep with a man. I thought she was just being old-fashioned. But it wasn't only her warning that stopped me. I felt something inside myself, something dark."

His hold tightened. "It's not dark."

"Dangerous, then." She found the courage to look up at him, and when she did Bri was relieved to find his expression held no condemnation, but rather gave an impression of sympathy.

He stroked her cheek. "You were trying to protect them."

She nodded. "But it didn't matter. I still made Jeffrey sick, and Matthew. I killed my fiancé."

"It wasn't your fault."

She pushed off him, coming to a seated position beside him. "It was *completely* my fault! Why didn't my nana come out and say it until her death bed?"

He met her glare with an open gaze. "Maybe she hoped your human side was stronger than the other part."

"The female vampires you are supposed to hunt and kill. That's what you said. Mercenaries. Assassins. That's what you said. And you are supposed to capture one."

"No. Capture and kill."

She inched away. "So you've captured me. Why haven't you turned me in?"

He dragged a hand over the bristle that was his hair and pushed up to his elbows. The position was so enticing she gave a quick sweep of his body, tucking the memory away for later consideration.

"I guess it's the same reason you haven't run away. I know you could. And I could track you but I doubt very much that I could catch you."

They sat in silence for a few moments, he with his thoughts and she with hers.

"What's going to happen now?"

"What do you mean?" he asked.

"Well I can't stay hidden here forever. Your commander will surely find out."

"I'm working on it. For now, I keep you out of sight and I keep Johnny out of trouble."

She wrapped her arms about her knees and rested her chin on her folded wrists. She liked Mac, and she wanted to help him and Johnny. They were the first people she'd ever met who understood what was happening to her, and they were different, just as she was. What would he do if she told him that she didn't want to leave them even if they did kill the vampires? His words came back to her: *just sex.*

She closed her eyes and groaned. How could she be so stupid?

Mac eyed her cautiously. "You okay?"

She forced a smile and nodded. "Perfect."

"How long have you been able to go into supersonic speed?"

Bri gathered her panties and gave them a shake, then slipped into them. "I only did it once when I was a girl. I got called to the office and they told me my grandmother was sick. That they took her to the hospital and that I would be going to stay with a neighbor. The next thing I knew I was at the hospital. The school was searching for me for hours but I found my grandmother. She had an intestinal blockage and had to have surgery. But she was fine afterward." She wound a lock of hair around her index finger and then let it slide away. She thought of something she hadn't before. "Do you think I caused the blockage?"

"I don't know."

Honesty, she realized. She appreciated that.

They stared at each other in silence as each wrestled with their demons. Hers were too dark, so she turned to his.

"When did you find out what happened to you back there?" she asked.

Mac drew on his boxers and trousers and sat up. "A few weeks later, maybe."

She nodded her acceptance of this and motioned for him to go on.

He rubbed his temples, and when he spoke his voice carried a weariness unfamiliar to her. "I was pretty chewed up. I don't remember much of evac or the hospital over there. Maybe I was sedated. They said my lung collapsed and I lost so much blood that I flatlined. When I finally came around I had healed, so I thought I'd been out a long time and that I'd been hallucinating. But then the memories started, first in my dreams and then when I was awake. I started asking questions. They showed me Johnny." He pressed the pads of his fingers into his eyes as if trying to keep himself from seeing.

Bri rested a hand on his leg. He lowered his hands and she caught a glimpse of the unfathomable sadness that hung heavy inside him.

"They had him in a cage. Like the kind they keep tigers in at the circus. I didn't recognize him. I thought it was the thing that attacked us." He shook his head at the memory. "I tried to kill it. My brain stopped working and I tried to kill it with my bare hands. Only they weren't my hands. They were dark with long claws and gray fur. I started screaming but it was just a howl. That was the first time I changed. They used a tranquilizer dart on me. Had to hit me in the mouth to break the skin. When I came around they told me what happened back there and that it was Johnny and he couldn't change back."

Bri rubbed his shoulder.

"I'd do anything to change him back," he whispered.

From somewhere far off a wolf howled. Mac straightened and his muscles grew tense.

Bri rested a hand on his shoulder.

"He's out there all alone," she whispered.

"Running the perimeter to keep you safe." Mac stood and dusted off his backside. He glanced toward the dark woods and then back to where she sat huddled beside the fire.

"Go on," she said.

And in a moment he was gone.

The instant Mac left Bri, he broke into a run. The howl came again. Johnny needed him. He glanced behind him at the retreating campfire. Bri needed him. He wished he could cut himself in two.

He and Brianna had been so good together. He'd been with women, more than a few. But never had he felt so in sync and so moved by sex. Because it wasn't sex. It was making love. Now he understood the difference. And on some deep level that he did not quite understand, he knew that it was the woman that drew him, not the part of her that was fairy. Finally, he realized he was in way over his head.

He was deep in the pines before he realized that he was heading back toward Bri instead of tracking Johnny. He scented the air for signs of threat and found nothing but the sweet smell of the damp earth and the alluring fragrance of her skin.

Mac shook himself like a wet dog and turned to search for Johnny's scent, hurrying now with this task that now seemed a burden. He wanted to get back to Bri, back to her warmth and her smile and her sorrow. Back to the welcome of her arms.

Damn it. Before her arrival he knew his duty. It was to his country and his family and to Johnny. But now…

He concentrated on his fury, letting the emotion break through him with the wave of pain, tearing him apart from the inside. He endured it, dropping to his knees briefly before rising in his wolf form to follow his gunner. He could change quickly now, in the blink of an eye. But it still hurt like hell. He ran Johnny down, finding him on the east side of their territory. His friend heard him coming, because he was waiting, tongue lolling, as Mac loped up to him.

Mac suffered the transition back to human form. Naked now, he dropped to his haunches, covering his privates as best he could. After three months, he and Johnny had few secrets.

"Why were you howling?"

Johnny roared and swung an open hand through the air. His claws made a whistling sound as they lashed out.

Had Johnny seen him with Bri? Mac stilled at the possibility, knowing instinctively that his friend would be pissed. Now he wished he had bathed. Bri's scent was heavy on his skin along with the aroma of sex.

Mac stayed downwind as Johnny motioned to the east and then signaled him to follow.

"Wolf or man?" asked Mac.

Johnny used his fingers to simulate upright walking and Mac followed at a jog.

After a few minutes Johnny pointed to a tree. Mounted on the trunk was a surveillance camera.

"Son of a bitch," said Mac.

Johnny sighed.

"Any near your place?

His gunner shook his head.

"Do you think they caught us moving her?"

Johnny shrugged.

"Bri can't come back to the compound. She has to stay at your place."

Johnny nodded.

"No more writing in the dirt. No more sign language around the compound. Only out here."

Johnny nodded his agreement and looked about as if searching for more surveillance cameras.

"How long do you think we can keep her secret?" Mac asked.

His friend gave a slow shake of his head and then breathed a deep sigh.

"We can't leave her unguarded. One of us needs to be with her from now on."

Johnny used an open hand on his chest. He'd take the first watch.

"Twelve hours each?"

Johnny nodded and set off toward his secret hideaway.

"I'll see you at noon. Do you think I should go explain it to her?"

Johnny huffed and kept going. Mac wondered what Bri would think of her new guardian sleeping opposite her at the campfire.

The two male vampires finished checking the apartment where the female and her grandmother lived before the old woman's death and Vittori's escape. They found nothing to indicate where she might have gone and no trace of the two sent to apprehend her. The elder, Burne Farrell, stood on the balcony looking out at the empty street below. The hours between two and four in the morning were usually quiet in human neighborhoods, and he felt at his best then. His lavender skin held no purplish cast because of his recent meal, but the artificial lights made his veins prominent. He stared at his hands, seeing the twisted bluish ropes beneath his transparent skin. Beside him stood one of his best Chasers, Hagan Dowling, flipping through the loose paper in a file folder. Beneath one arm he clamped a battered red leather journal. A younger vampire by two decades, Hagan's skin remained the unnatural cadaver white of his birth, but that would change in time as his veins bled through. Eventually they all ended up looking like ripe plums.

Hagan had scored a hit, one of the females that had eluded them for a decade. Unfortunately he had sent two of his less experienced men to retrieve her and they had failed. Vanished, really. No report, no location. Just gone. It made Burne angry, for he expected better from his Chasers. They had better both be dead, because if not, he'd kill them for disobedience.

Now he understood why this female had been so successful at remaining loose.

"She had a protector," said Burne.

"Yes. Her grandmother knew what she was and she knew exactly how we check each quadrant. Her moves were methodical, from one cleared territory to the next. It was almost as if she was chasing us."

"How did she know?"

Burne lifted his gaze from his hands to look at his Chaser. Hagan's lips were the color of blood and his fangs had grown so long that they no longer fit in his mouth. The faded color of his irises made his eyes look milky, instead of gray, as if he were staring at a corpse. The effect was deceptive because their vision was perfect, far better than the humans.

"According to this, the human learned of our methods from a Leanan Sidhe. The female we seek is the human's granddaughter, Brianna. She's not like us. She's first generation."

"First?" Burne blinked. "Are you sure?" The most pure vampires he knew were fifth generation. Many were tenth or more. To capture a first-generation vampire might change everything. They might even have children by her that were not so abhorrent. He might even have a son who could walk among humans.

"Her father was human. Her mother was a true Leanna Sidhe."

"How do you know?"

He held up a battered journal. "The old woman kept a record of everything. Where they were, where they should go next. Instructions dictated to her by Brianna's mother. Photos of her mother." He flipped open the journal and withdrew a snapshot, handing it to Burne.

He stared down at the face that could have been an angel's, she was so lovely. Flowing red hair, crystal-blue eyes and skin smooth and pale as cream. Burne felt his heart pitch and his loins tingle. "Where is her mother now?"

"The best I can piece together is that after Brianna's birth, she returned to the Fey."

"She was afraid her power might kill her child." Burne stared out into the night. "Does her daughter look like this?"

Hagan handed over another photo. Brianna's eyes were leafy green, and her skin was more pink than ivory. But in all other regards she resembled her mother. Hagan held out his hand for the photo. Burne tucked it in his vest pocket.

"Do you think that is why your man failed? Is she more powerful than our females?"

"She might be very fast and her draw stronger than our females, but she has no training. We could give her that. I volunteer, sir, to train this one."

Burne snorted. Of course he did. Anything to get close to a first-generation vampire. Perhaps impregnate her in the process. "First we catch her. Then we worry about the rest." He forced a smile for Hagan's benefit, felt the sharp tips of his fangs graze his lower lip.

"Yes, sir."

"I want three Chasers on this. The first is to return to the area we just swept and begin again. If she follows her grandmother's pattern, we will find her there. The second is to begin a search of increasing circumference from this spot."

"And the third?"

"Follow the direction of your men's last check-in. All teams are to contact me at any sign of our target. I want this one, Hagan. Bring her to me."

Chapter 13

After Mac left her, Bri spent an unpleasant night tending the fire and jumping at every rustling sound from the forest. She could see past the orange flames of the campfire, and though the light gave her a certain comfort, it also made her very easy to find. It was for this reason that she left the fire and moved deeper into the darkness. At first she thought her perception was a trick of the night. But the longer she sat away from the flames, the greater her visual acuity became. She could see everything down to the creases in the bark and the tight new pinecones clinging to the upper branches. Her vision wasn't that funny green night-goggle thing, either. It was a perfect gray, like a black-and-white movie. Why couldn't she do this before?

She thought back and could not recall one single time in her life when she was away from streetlights, away from a city. She breathed deeply.

Another rustle brought her head swiveling about, and she spotted a small rodent, a mole or vole, perhaps, scuttling along in the pine needles and sounding like an elephant. Bri sighed and rubbed her tired eyes. How long until Mac came back for her?

She settled against a pine and drew her knees up for warmth and comfort. Her head rested against the trunk of the tree, and she rubbed her legs to try and sweep away the gooseflesh there. Bri caught some movement out of the corner of her vision. She turned in that direction and saw something big moving between the trees. She gasped as she came to her feet, then covered her mouth as a tiny squeak emerged from her throat.

Vampires!

The rush of energy surged through her and she bounded away, seeing the tops of the trees before coming back to earth. She looked back and saw the creature running toward her. She jumped again but this time she heard a howl. Bri froze. She knew that howl.

"Johnny?" she whispered.

There was a huffing sound and then she saw him clearly. He stood on his hind legs, arms at his sides, the long claws curled slightly as if he cupped something in his palms. His shoulders sagged and he lifted his furry, dotlike eyebrows as he met her stare. He made a whining sound and then a huff.

She didn't know what to do. Mac trusted Johnny, but she'd never been alone with him in the woods. On those few occasions when he guarded the compound he had never approached her. And she knew he had been against Mac taking her in. Then there was his recent attack on her. Mac said it was the drugs. Was it?

Suddenly a more frightening thought struck her. What if something had happened to Mac? What if he couldn't come back? Her worry for Mac overcame her fear and she hurried toward Johnny.

"Is Mac all right?"

He nodded and then motioned back to the supply depot she had left.

"Is it safe?"

Another nod. She hesitated only a moment and then joined him. They walked back side by side. He was so tall that her head only reached his elbow. She could feel the impact of his footsteps on the earth as they continued along. When they reached Johnny's personal hideaway, he added more wood to the fire and then dragged a rug from inside for her to sit upon. Through a series of questions and Johnny's scratching words in the sand, she discovered that she must stay here for the time being and that he and Mac would take turns as her bodyguards.

He held her gaze until she stopped shaking and gave him a nervous nod. Then he continued his slow scrawl in the sand. More cameras had been found in the woods; plus, they had replaced the cameras at their quarters and added new ones. Bri felt cold right through to the core at this revelation, and her inclination was to run again. Johnny must have sensed her need for flight because he gripped her at the elbow. She trembled and he gave her arm a squeeze before releasing her.

Bri thought about the risk that Johnny and Mac took for her, a stranger, an enemy, a defenseless, soul-sucking vampire. Her chin sunk to her chest with shame.

"Maybe I should go before you get into more trouble."

Johnny growled. He clearly didn't like that idea. Bri nodded her understanding, and Johnny motioned to the rug, lifting a blanket and pillow. She accepted the offer and nodded off to sleep with her werewolf bodyguard keeping watch.

Bri's life fell into a pattern from then on. Johnny watched her during the day and Mac returned at night. The only deviation was when Headquarters wanted Johnny for tests. On only one occasion was she alone. Since this supply depot was her home for the foreseeable future, she gained Johnny's permission to do some decorating. She arranged the oriental rugs and ammo crates and the low Moorish furniture into a living area inside the concrete shelter. Mac brought her a mattress, bed frame and bedding, helped her fix meals using the MRE packets and stocked the firewood. She felt like Rose Red living in the woods. At least here there were no cameras. And though the shelter was less comfortable than the qala, that Mac and Johnny that used as their quarters, she still preferred it because even though it had no electricity and no kitchen, it also had no surveillance. So she had the freedom to walk in the woods here, as long as she didn't wander too far. Johnny accompanied her on daily walks during his shift. Mac kept her distracted with stories about basic training, but he never spoke of his squad again. After supper they retired to the compound, where she fell easily into Mac's arms. He was a gifted and generous lover—inventive, playful and intense. She'd often fall asleep in his arms, but he never slept, at least not in her bed. He was holding back, she knew. Keeping their relationship sexual. But sometimes she caught him staring at her and felt the longing in his eyes echoing in her soul.

Tonight, after making love, Mac sat on a folding chair, drawing on his boots while she remained in bed, now dressed in his long T-shirt, which she used as a nightshirt. Johnny would be here soon, with the changing of the guards at midnight.

"When do you think they will come?" she asked.

"I don't know. I expected them to have tracked you already. Seems they didn't know your pursuers' exact location. They're backtracking, circling until they find your trail. That rental, for instance."

Bri tried to push back her anxiety and pretend she was safe, and that Mac's protection came from something more than keeping the only known she-vampire safe and sound.

The nights they spent together were magic, but knowing that this was a "no strings" relationship poisoned the sweetness of their joining. She knew that when they parted she'd miss Mac. Chances were good she'd never meet another man who could resist her energy draw, and so she faced a terrible choice. Spend her life alone or kill the one she cared for. It was no choice at all, really. She'd have to remain celibate, but that would make her more dangerous to be near, if Mac's information was accurate. So even if she didn't sleep with a man, just being near a human—any human, male or female— would be toxic.

Bri had once thought to have a family, settle in one place and be like other people with a job and a mortgage and toys underfoot. She'd lost all that when she'd discovered what she was. She couldn't love a man without risking his life. *Except one man.* But he didn't want strings.

Mac was an escape clause in a life sentence of solitary confinement. She still held stupidly to the hope that he might find her more than physically attractive. But Mac was a Marine. He had a mission—to look after Johnny— and he wanted an active combat assignment. Beyond that he wanted what she could never give him: a house filled up with kids and dogs and rabbits. Bri stifled a sob and covered her mouth with her hand as she ached for that life.

He'd be a fool to choose her, though he was opportunist enough to take advantage of the situation at hand. And what more could she expect? He protected her and satisfied her and then left her at midnight like some male Cinderella, reverting back to a soldier.

And what did that make her? Bri sighed miserably and

hugged herself, sitting up on the single bed that Mac had provided her. She hated these nightly partings. His arrival at midday was always joyous, and the afternoon would fly by. Then they would have sex, and he would leave her like a married man hurrying home to the wife and kids. Bri wondered if they were protecting her or just using her as bait. Perhaps she was naïve. Perhaps Mac wasn't keeping her safe but just keeping her. If she tried to leave, would he let her, or was she more prisoner than guest? After they caught a male vampire, if they could catch one, what was to stop him from turning her over to his supervisors? Wouldn't it be better to bring in a male *and* female?

That evening she asked him about her situation again.

"Even if you catch the ones that are tracking me, there are more of them. Aren't there?"

His silence was answer enough.

"You can't hide me in the woods forever." But a small part of her wanted just that. "How will I keep them from finding me, Mac, after you have your prize?"

He leaned forward, elbows on knees, hands relaxed with fingers before him. "We have to teach you to use your powers. Tactics, hand to hand combat. Practice. Just like basic training, so that you'll be ready if they find you and ready when the time comes to defend yourself."

And there it was. The implication in his words. *I need to defend myself so I can survive after he leaves me.*

She nodded woodenly. He was right. Her nana had protected her without her even knowing. Mac and Johnny protected her now. In their way, both Matthew and Jeff had tried to protect her. She'd allowed others to jeopardize their lives to guard hers. It was too much. She needed to start taking care of herself.

"Yes. I want to learn."

* * *

Bri spent the next week practicing her bounding. At first she was clumsy, faltering between her human speed and her vampire one. It was difficult to summon her power when she was not frightened out of her wits. At first, Johnny provided the scare, leaping out at her unexpectedly. One day it just clicked. She switched to her vampire speed without being afraid and bounded away so fast that even Mac, in werewolf form, couldn't keep up. She shot straight up to the top of a pine tree and watched him run in circles trying to find her. Unfortunately her laugh gave her away. Then she found she couldn't get down. That scared her so much that she gained her power again and made the jump to ground.

"It just keeps cutting in and out like a bad wireless signal. Like dropping a call. One minute I have four bars and the next, nothing."

Mac gave her shoulder a squeeze.

She looped her arms about his neck and smiled up at him, then gave him a quick kiss on his furry snout. "You're right. I'm getting better."

She let her hand slide off Mac's hairy shoulders. He captured one hand and held it for a moment longer. She looked up at him. "What?"

His fingers dropped away and he sighed.

She wanted him to change so she could make love to him right here in broad daylight. Then at least she wouldn't see the shimmer. She and Mac didn't talk about it since that first time. But they often saw the golden glow, the wispy tendrils that emanated from her skin when she found her pleasure. Neither knew what it was.

"Phew! I'm tired. All this running and jumping. I feel like I'm in boot camp."

Mac grinned showing rows of sharp white teeth. Then he scooped her off her feet so fast it made her head spin.

She shrieked and laughed as he set off at a run, carrying her in his arms as they returned to her new home. His jarring gate forcing Bri to wrap her arms about his neck.

"Mac! Put me down. I'm not that tired!"

He sped up and she laughed again as the wind whistled past them. Mac skidded to a halt. Bri turned to see what had stopped him and found Johnny.

Mac released her legs and she swung down to his side, her arms slipping from his neck as she reached the ground. Mac kept one hand on the center of her back. Bri stepped away. Johnny's dark expression and ridged posture made her cautious. He stood with hands on hips glowering at them both and finally fixing his glare on Mac.

Johnny growled.

"I said I was tired and Mac just…"

Mac had taken a defensive pose. He'd lowered his head and bared his teeth.

"No," she said, stepping between them. "It was just a joke. We were laughing and—"

Johnny lifted a finger to his lips and pointed towards their new quarters. Brianna went still. Was someone here? Had they come at last?

"Vampires?" she whispered.

Johnny shook his head and then patted his ears.

"Too loud?"

He nodded.

"I'm sorry," she said. "It won't happen again." He turned to Mac. Her silliness had put them both at risk. Thank God it was only Johnny that heard. "Thank you, Mac, for helping me down from that tree." She addressed Johnny. "I'm getting better, but I poop out sometimes."

Johnny gave them one last look of censure and then disappeared back the way he had come.

Mac took her back to the compound, his mood no longer

light. Once there he left her, going into Johnny's refuge to change shape and dress. She didn't have long to wait before he returned, in wrinkled khakis and a rumbled olive-green T-shirt. Mac's shoulders slumped and his chin dipped. For just a moment he looked defeated.

"What's wrong?"

When he spoke his voice held a deep sorrow that struck Bri like a blow. "You made me forget."

"Forget? Forget what?"

"Everything. This place, the danger we're in, your attackers, Johnny…my duty." He stared down at her with blue eyes that glittered with emotion. "And I can't forget. Not any of it."

She nodded her understanding. "You have a duty."

"Yes." He scrubbed his face with one hand. "I have to stay. The colonel and the med techs are working to bring Johnny back. Trying to find a way to make him human again. It's terrible, but they need my blood and they need more time."

"I understand."

He glanced at her. "All I can do is follow orders and pray they figure out how to bring Johnny back soon." He took hold of her shoulders and drew her in front of him. "I need Johnny's cooperation and I need him not to give up."

"And you've been neglecting him because of me."

"Yes. But I think he enjoys spending time with you, too."

"I'm asleep most of it."

"He says you talk to him at breakfast."

She smiled. "Yes. Sometimes I sing. He likes that too, I think."

Mac nodded. "He misses his mom and his sister."

"I didn't know he had…" She stopped. Had she really been about to say that she didn't know he had a mother?

Or family? She realized she just never thought about who Johnny was before. "They must miss him terribly."

"They think he's MIA. They don't even know he's alive."

She gasped, pressing a hand to her chest. "That's terrible."

"For them and for him. It eats at him. But he can't visit or call or write. He can barely hold a pen."

"I could write it for him."

"No. No contact. They can't know. Not ever. It's for their protection as much as his."

She held his gaze and then recognized the truth. "You're hoping that they fix this and he can reappear."

He didn't deny it.

"But what if that doesn't happen?"

"It's a military secret either way. But if he can't change, he stays missing." Mac rubbed the back of his neck. "Anyway. He says you remind him of his sister."

"What's her name?"

"Joon—Julia, they call her."

"I'm making things harder for you both."

"Yes. And easier. We both miss home."

How was Mac's family? Had he been in contact with them, made his video calls when he wasn't in her bed? "How is your sister?"

"Bonnie? She's good. Getting big. She says it's a boy."

He rubbed the back of his neck and glanced away, as if anxious to be rid of her. She sensed that he didn't want his world and that one colliding and why would he? She could kill them all by just spending the weekend.

He'd mentioned his father; heart trouble, she recalled. She briefly considered what her appearance might do to him.

"How is your dad?"

Mac actually flinched. "On a new diet and grumbling about it." He forced a smile.

Bri felt the sorrow well up inside her like floodwater. She missed her nana. Johnny missed his loved ones. Mac couldn't see his family except on a computer screen. Suddenly it all seemed too much. She wanted to be independent, but instead she'd let Mac and Johnny risk their lives for hers. "Maybe I should just go."

"You aren't ready to defend yourself. Though you are a damned good runner."

"Are they close to a cure for Johnny?" she whispered.

"Damned if I know. All I can do now is hold on and hope. But it's hard. Really hard."

Mac started a fire in the brazier after supper. He was damned tired of sitting on the ground in these freaking qalas. He wanted to go fishing in his bass boat or sit in a recliner, preferably with a beer and a remote. He wanted to watch a Detroit Tigers game with his dad while his mother made pot roast and Yorkshire puddings.

He wanted to go to a bar with his squad and laugh and tell lies. But his squad was buried under the sod at Arlington, and he couldn't leave Johnny or Bri to visit his family. Mac jabbed at the embers and watched the sparks fly into the metal pan. He readjusted the pillow behind his back and sighed.

Bri appeared from inside Johnny's storage depot carrying two mugs. The aroma of coffee reached him an instant before the intoxicating scent of orchids. She gave him a smile, and he knew she was worth all the trouble. Bri didn't make demands. She accepted that their relationship was physical. The problem was, he was having trouble accepting it. This attraction between them only seemed to grow with each passing minute he spent with her. And he liked her. He enjoyed talking to her nearly as much as sleeping with her. That had never happened before.

He'd told her that when she could defend herself, he'd let her go. But now he saw two problems with that. First, she might not ever be ready to defeat a pack of hunting male vampires. And secondly, he didn't want to let her go. But how could he keep her? The woman killed people just by showing up.

"Here you are." She passed him one of the mugs.

He took a sip. She made damned good coffee. She also managed to spruce up those MREs with the fresh vegetables he brought her to make some really good grub. He was getting used to having her around, and that was a problem.

Why couldn't Bri have had a difficult mother or a brother in prison or a kid or some shameful secret in her past like other women? Why did he have to go for a fucking vampire?

Mac raised his nose to inhale the scents on the breeze. Her coffee came to him first. But then he scented the rain, coming from the west. There had been no sign of vampires. MI said that they smelled like blood, which was true, but they also smelled like rot. Apparently they didn't just drink blood; they cannibalized their victims. Unlike the myths, being bitten by a vampire did not insure immortality—but death.

Mac sipped his coffee and stared at the fire. It kept him from looking at Bri, which was what he wanted to do. He failed to keep his attention on the flames and glanced her way.

She wore a white T-shirt. The stretchy cotton molded over her breasts revealing the shocking turquoise lace bra beneath. None of her clothes fit her, since they weren't her clothes. He wondered what she wore before coming here.

Likely not skintight blue jeans, extrashort shorts or tops that was gauzy and as transparent as a bridal veil.

Their usual routine was to finish their coffee, move inside and make love, sometimes more than once. Then Bri would fall asleep, and he would move outside to await the dawn and Johnny's appearance to relieve him. The physical intimacy sated his body, but he wanted more. He wanted to know everything about her. He'd been trying to resist, instinctively fearing the intimacy while craving it.

"What did you do back there before this happened?" he asked.

She paused with the edge of the mug against her full lips and then lowered the coffee. She brushed the hair back from her face. Her eyes sparkled when she talked, and her nose moved when she smiled. He felt a tug of desire and pushed it aside.

"I just finished my bachelor's degree. It took me five years, because we moved around a lot and because I was working to pay for it. I just started at Social Services in Sacramento. Nana didn't like it. She said social work was for saps. We argued about it. She was getting ready to leave again, and I was planning to stay put. She hadn't told me yet and…"

Mac held her gaze. Bri looked away.

"That's how they found me, isn't it? Because I wouldn't leave when she told me to."

"Do you think your grandmother knew how to stay out of their way?"

"She must have. I never saw one until after her death."

He drummed his fingers on the mug, wanting to know how to keep her safe. Needing the knowledge that her grandmother had. "But she never spoke about them or how to keep away from them?"

"Not until she knew she was dying. She kept a journal,

but it's still at my apartment. It was as if she thought keeping her secrets would keep me safe. But I knew I was different. Like when I'd ask about my mother, Nana would just say she was a bad mother, abandoning her child. I didn't think she died on purpose, but Nana would get angry, so I just stopped asking."

"Did your grandmother ever see you run?"

"No, but she knew about my metal allergy. She made sure the bathtub was fiberglass in the apartments so I didn't get a rash, and she used ceramic knives. She mostly cooked casseroles in Pyrex. We ate with plastic cutlery."

"Metal just makes you itch?"

"Break out, itch, a nasty allergic rash. I get headaches, symptoms of an allergies, runny nose. Only we both knew it wasn't pollen. I'm a mess. I get carsick even when I'm driving and airplanes…" She shuddered. "The worst migraines ever. But now that I'm away from the wires and cars and well everything, I feel so much better. Stronger. And I can see more clearly, especially at night."

She described her new night vision which was much the same as his own. "Sense of smell?"

"Yes, always better than…humans."

"And you don't know how to intentionally draw energy?"

"No!" She turned back to the fire and her mug of coffee. Her posture told him she was upset.

"You don't want to learn how to use that power?"

"Only if I can learn how to shut it off." She stared at him, her eyes luminous and shimmering.

"It might save your life."

"I don't want to hurt anyone. I'm a pacifist. I'm a good person…or I thought I was. Now I discover I'm—I'm this." She swept a hand over herself. "Mac, if we get through this and you catch your vampire and, we part ways…well, I'm not really free to go anywhere, am I?"

He inclined his head. "What do you mean?"

"I can't go back among them. Humans, I mean. Not knowing what I can do to them. I can never do that again. So where will I go?"

He was silent as he considered that problem.

"I've spent my whole life trying to help people. I've put my energy into social causes. I've marched, petitioned, rallied, worked in the trenches. Well, not the kind of trenches that Marines work in, but I've tried very hard to make this world a better place. But I haven't. I'm a fraud. I'm not a good person. I'm a killer like you."

"No. All my kills were intentional." The instant he said it he knew it wasn't true. He still didn't know if he'd killed any of his own men, because he couldn't remember what happened after the werewolf attacked him. He'd tried several times, but there was nothing. But Lewis told him he'd attacked Lam.

She lowered her gaze to the flames and her words came at a whisper. "Mine wasn't."

Her fiancé, he recalled. His obituary said it was leukemia. That was a hard thing. He knew something about living with regret.

"You can't change it by reliving it. Going over it and over it will just drive you crazy."

She stared at him a long moment, those lovely green eyes shimmering. She looked at the contents of her half-empty mug. "But if my grandmother had explained it to me earlier—"

"Would you have believed her? If you didn't see that vampire coming for you, if you didn't jump out of that window, would you have believed any of this?"

She sniffed, and the tears that had hovered on her lower

lids splashed down her face. Damn, she was even beautiful when she wept. "I don't want to believe it now."

"We are what we are. All the tears in the world won't wash that away."

"You're the only one I can't make sick."

Her glamour didn't work on him. He knew it. So why then did the thought of letting her go fill him with a kind of creeping panic? The only thing more frightening was losing his family. He ground his teeth together and met her gaze. "Me or another werewolf."

She set aside her mug and clasped her arms around her knees. She looked small and helpless. An illusion, he knew. She was powerful, more powerful than she knew. If he were not able to tolerate her, would he be able to resist her? He didn't think so.

But he knew that Bri was getting faster each day. Fast enough to outrun them, he believed. After he caught his vampire, he'd have to let her go, because he knew he was growing too attached to her. He felt it, those tendrils that bound him more tightly to her. The intimate moments and the realization that each day he wanted her more, instead of less. This had never happened before. He wasn't bored, distracted, restless. The only restlessness he felt came from thoughts of their parting.

But he'd have to let her go soon. He'd send her on her way for her own good as much as his. He and Johnny could go back to the way they had been. The med techs could find a cure for Johnny. Then maybe he could visit Mac's family, see with his own eyes that his dad was all right. Hold his nephew. Oh, damn.

What if they didn't find a cure, and what if they couldn't go back to the way they had been?

Her chances were worse without him. He knew it.

But she was safe now. He'd put himself against any

vampire to protect her; he relished the thought. He anticipated the encounter more than he should have, and that made him think he was in the right profession. He wanted to fight. Needed to.

Bri sniffed, and he found that her suffering cut him as deeply as his own. He reached out to her, wrapping an arm about her shoulders. She sagged against his side, molding to him as he stroked her back.

"Come here," he said and turned her so he could brush away the tears that now glistened on her cheeks. "There have to be others like you. Ones the males haven't found yet."

"I could join them."

He nodded, but he didn't want her to join them. He wanted her to stay here with him forever.

He kept thinking what it would be like to have her in his life. It wasn't a pretty picture. To have Brianna, he'd have to give up his commission, possibly go on the run, because he just couldn't picture military intelligence letting one of their two werewolves and the only one who could change shape, just waltz out into the general public. So he'd be a wanted man. They'd be coming after him and Johnny, because he wasn't leaving his friend behind.

Even if they did remain free, Mac would have to be on constant guard for the vampires who hunted her.

Then there was his family. He couldn't introduce Brianna to his mother or his father. His sister was pregnant. Mac thought what horrors Brianna could bring to a fetus or newborn, and winced. And while he was on that topic, what about kids? He wanted them, a pile of them. Her children would be vampires, and his…

He lifted one hand and used his thumb and forefingers to rub his tired eyes.

He couldn't have the life he led or the one he imagined and have Bri. He would have to choose.

Chapter 14

Mac watched her as she left the brazier's warmth and swept inside toward the room they had arranged for her to sleep in. He let her have a few moments' privacy, but the pull was there, urging him to follow her. His skin itched and he could no longer sit still. He poked at the fire. He paced. Still the need built inside him. He could hear her removing her clothing. Here the whisper of sheets as she pulled back the covers. Her scent lingered in the air, growing weaker by the second.

He needed that scent, needed to touch her soft skin. He balled up his fist and pressed it to his forehead. Mac didn't remember leaving the fire or walking across the clearing. Instead he just found himself at her door.

The door she had left open.

To him.

He drew himself up, tightened the muscles of his shoulders and torso. Even if he went in there it would change nothing. She wasn't his. Couldn't be. He could sleep with her, but eventually he'd have to let her go.

Her scent came to him with the rustling sound. His body went cold, then hot, then ready.

The flickering light told him she'd lit a candle again, instead of the kerosene lantern. She said she preferred the soft illumination, and the lantern was mostly metal. Likely it burned her to turn the knob.

Did she know how lovely she was by candlelight, her hair all ablaze and her skin gilded?

He stepped into the doorway. She stood beside the bed straightening to stillness at his arrival. The tension between them tugged like a rope stretched to its limit.

The bed stood between them with the covers turned back so that the top sheet lay half over the blankets. She'd centered the two pillows, one at the headboard and one where her hips would be when he kissed her there. He lifted his gaze to Bri, seeing first her long, taut legs and the scrap of blue lace that hugged her like a second skin. Her wide hips narrowed at her bare waist, and he studied her belly button, the small, enticing indenture. She didn't wear a bra or tank this evening. Her lovely, full breasts hung like ripe fruit, soft, perfumed and inviting. Her large rosy nipples tightened under his scrutiny. He took a step closer. She lifted a hand to her throat, her fingers splayed. He watched her hand slide down to cup one breast.

He closed his eyes and listened to her approach. He heard everything she did, whether it was brushing her hair or rubbing on moisturizer. She glided across the room on bare feet, pausing so close that he could feel the heat of her skin in the cold room.

"What's wrong?" she asked.

He shook his head. How could he explain that even with her right in front of him, he already missed her, grieved their parting as if it had already come? Dreaded it as one dreads the phone call from the doctor with the test results.

His mind scrambled to find a way. How could he keep her and not lose everything and everyone else?

Mac reached for her, letting his hands slide from her waist to the enticing curve of her hips. Then he tugged, bringing her against him. He'd take her again, knowing that each time he did he only wanted her more. He wasn't immune to this woman, because it wasn't her vampire gifts that drew him. It wasn't just her scent and her lush body. It was her kind heart and her brave spirit. She was too idealistic. Too gullible and too trusting for this world. She was his opposite, his perfect fit. She needed him. He needed her.

He could protect her, satisfy her. He wished he could offer more.

Her hands slipped under his shirt. Fingernails raked his back as she removed the garment and then lifted her chin, silently demanding a kiss.

He swept in, the passion rising in his blood, in the melting of their bodies. She stroked his neck, and one hand caressed his head, but his hair was too short for her to find any purchase there, so she wrapped her arms about his neck and clung as he walked to the inviting bed. She fell backward and he landed on top of her, taking enough of his weight on his arms that he did not hurt her, but not so much that she was not pinned beneath him. He relished the contact of their mouths and the pressing of his hips to hers.

She made a sound deep in her throat. He loved that sound. It held anticipation and pleasure, the cry a sweet blending of need and the purr of contentment. She wrapped her long legs about his hips and locked her ankles, pressing against the ridge of engorged flesh as she rocked. Mac released his breath in a whoosh. He'd wanted to go slow, but she was giving all the signals of needing a more aggressive engagement.

He drew back, arching up onto his extended arms. "What have you got in mind tonight, Princess?"

In answer she clamped her long legs about him. She lifted up again, bouncing against him and then falling back on the bed.

"I want what you always give me."

"And what's that?"

"Mind-blowing orgasms and…" Her words drifted off.

He lifted his chin, urging her to go on.

She bit her lower lip. He watched the plump pink tissue slide between white teeth and felt his mouth go dry as hunger surged and thundered inside him like an avalanche.

"When you're here with me, I'm not scared anymore. I forget what's out there hunting me. That's the best part. I make it through the day knowing that you'll be here with me at night."

He wished he could be there forever. His smile faltered. When had he stopped wishing to go back to that day, the moment before he'd ordered his men into that building, and started wanting Bri? There was so much he wanted to forget. So much he needed to remember, and Bri was confusing him. His hands stilled.

"Mac? Did I say something wrong?"

"No. Nothing." He slipped out of his trousers and Skivvies, dropping them on the floor. Then he stretched out beside her.

That was when he realized that she did the same thing for him. When he was with her, he wasn't back there reliving that night, fighting against his guilt and anguish. She freed him from that pain.

He rested on his hip to stroke her side, starting at the soft junction of her arm and torso down to the scrap of lace that didn't quite hide her charms. Expertly he swept it down her slim legs and tossed her panties to the ground.

She settled back on the bedding, sliding one hand behind her head and smiling up at him. She was letting him decide. He liked calling the shots.

He started at her wrist and worked to her neck. All the while the scent of orchids and musk surrounded him. She was so sweet, he wanted to take a bite. Mac let his teeth score the skin of her collarbone. She gasped, and her fingers danced over his shoulders, kneading his tired muscles and scoring his skin with her sharp nails. By the time he reached her breasts she glowed from within, that strange, alluring golden shimmer that he was now certain was not a trick of the flame but just her reaction to arousal. The skin of her stomach was the softest, softer even than her full breasts. Here he had to pull back and take a breath. Her arousal fired his own, and the need became nearly too sharp.

She was close. He could see it in the moisture on her skin, read it in the shimmering color of her green eyes and hear it in the soft, needy sounds vibrating in her throat.

He stroked her most sensitive flesh and sucked in a breath through his teeth. She was so damned wet and ready. He'd bring her to orgasm and then come with her on the second round.

Then she did something new, sliding two fingers inside her cleft. He watched her move her hand in and out. He stopped breathing. Then she reached with her wet fingers until she had a hold of him. Her hand was slick as she moved her palm along his shaft. He closed his eyes and rocked to his back. Sensing his momentary confusion, Bri pursued like any good warrior, lifting a leg and throwing it across his hips. She straddled him and brought his erect flesh to her slippery folds. Then she dropped down on him until her hips collided with his. He groaned at the rush of pleasure that shot through his abdomen.

No you don't, he thought. *Hold on, soldier. You are not coming. Not yet.*

He gritted his teeth and glanced up at her. She sensed victory, because her eyes widened and glittered dangerously.

Oh, the hell with this.

He rolled her to her back and thrust. This time she gasped, her eyes rounding.

"You want it like this?"

She nodded and rocked her hips. He slipped farther inside her. His eyes closed as he grappled for control.

"Faster," she whispered. "I'm so close, Travis. Please. Faster."

Orders received.

He slipped out and then came back hard. She arched, lifting to meet each thrust. He forgot to breathe as she made her final climb. Wisps of golden mist rose from her heated flesh. He felt her so close in the tightness of her passage and the frantic thrusts that met each long descent. Her breathing changed. She cried out once and then again.

"Travis! Oh, God, yes!"

He loved the sound of his name on her lips. Her contractions gripped him and he relinquished control. The came together for the first time. She threw back her head and then felt his last thrust. She opened her eyes and stared up at him, her face flushed and her expression filled with wonder. He watched the pleasure roll through her as it fired along every nerve ending in his body.

Her eyes drifted shut as he fell beside her. Their bodies came to rest. Breathing fast, they lay inert.

His limbs now heavy and clumsy. God, he'd never felt anything like that and knew he never would again. He didn't deserve her.

He closed his eyes and his body went slack. He didn't deserve this peace. Not after what he'd done.

How fast the guilt closed in. He squeezed his eyes shut as the faces of his men rose up to haunt him.

He could hear their voices calling to him for orders, and then the sound of gunshots and the cries of agony. When his first two teams went silent, why had he sent in the third? He was like those miners in West Virginia running into a mine shaft filled with methane trying to save their fellows and ending up just as dead.

They'd all run in. Every damned one of them. And they'd all died. All but him and Johnny.

Why had he sent in the second team and then the third? If he'd waited, they'd all be alive. Nothing could have saved his first Fire Team. He accepted that. But he should have held at least one team back. Any squad leader worth his salt would have done so. But not him.

His first command. His last command.

Mac bolted up. Bri groaned and then followed him, stroking his back.

"Will you lie here next to me?"

It was the one pleasure he denied himself. To sleep in her bed, in her arms, would be too much like what he longed for with Bri. For many nights now he had wanted more than sex. More than the brief pleasure of release before parting.

"I have to check the perimeter," he said and grabbed his discarded clothing.

Wouldn't that just be fine if he waltzed out of here with Bri? Turned his back on the colonel and Johnny and just took off.

He had too much honor to do that. He was a member of the Corps, so he'd see this through to the end.

Bri would have to understand. He wasn't free to do as he liked.

He slipped into his skivvies and trousers in one motion, rising to his feet as he fastened the waistband. He stooped to retrieve his shirt and had it on when he reached the door. He turned back, allowing himself the pleasure of seeing her there on the bed they had just shared.

He left her to sleep and went outside, running a perimeter and checking for any sign of intruders. He made two sweeps, one close and one farther out. There was nothing but the scent of where Johnny had passed on his way back to their compound. He wondered how long before Headquarters asked him why he wasn't spending nights in his own bed. He was going to say he wasn't sleeping well, which was true. They'd probably draw more blood. Damn, he already felt like a one-man blood bank.

When he returned to the storage depot, he listened for the sound of Bri's breathing. Instead he heard a sound that stopped him. The sniffling and the choking were unmistakable. Was she crying?

Now what did he do?

He hesitated. He was no good at comforting women. He only knew one way to go about it. If he went in there, he knew what would happen. Mac blew out a breath.

"Damn it," he muttered and then marched into hostile territory.

He gathered her up in his arms and she clung to him.

"I don't deserve this," she cried. "Not after what I've done to other men."

That stopped him. Survivor's guilt, they called it. He recognized it, because he'd seen enough shrinks and knew all about how it was normal and blah, blah, blah. But looking at Bri now was like looking in a mirror.

"It's wrong, isn't it? Shouldn't I be suffering, doing some penance for Matthew?"

"It won't bring him back." That's what they had told him again and again.

She drew away. "So I just forget what I did? Just pretend it never happened?"

"If you figure out how to do that, let me know, because I've done worse."

She stared up at him.

"Besides, you didn't know your own power."

"And you didn't know what was in that building."

He used his thumbs to wipe the tears from her cheeks. "At least you can keep from doing it again. Now that you know, I mean."

"So what am I supposed to do? I can't touch them or let them touch me."

"You could have children if you wanted. I know you can."

"Not without hurting someone, and then my babies would be like me."

"Not exactly. Not as powerful, because they'd be second generation. Each generation is less potent than the previous one."

She drew away to sit on the side of the bed, head bowed and hands pressed flat on her knees. "I wanted children. But it's like having a genetic abnormality. It would be wrong to pass this on."

He released a sigh, and he realized afterward that the emptiness he felt yawning in his chest was not sympathy but sorrow. She wouldn't have children from him or anyone else, and he was certain that she would have been a great mother.

He drew her down to the mattress, lying still as she

curled against him. He stroked her shoulder and arm as her breathing went from ragged to steady.

"How do you live with it?"

He stared at the ceiling. "Wake up each morning and try to make amends. Try to fix what I can."

He lived it every damned day and it didn't get easier, but he wouldn't tell her that.

"I don't think I can ever forgive myself for what I've done," she whispered

"Maybe we shouldn't."

She lifted her head, gazed up at him with eyes streaming tears and nodded. "You're right."

Bri didn't know exactly what woke her as she startled upright in the empty bed pushed against the side of the far wall of the former storage depot. She listened while searching the dark room for any threat. Everything seemed still and calm, but her heart jackhammered.

"Johnny?" she called and then heard a roar.

There was a thump that shook the building.

Bri sprang from the bed as the door flew open and several men charged inside. She raced around the small room moving smoothly into her top speed, but an instant later the windows were blocked from outside and she found no escape. It was clear that none of the four soldiers in the room could see her. She knew now that she was moving too fast for them to perceive. But it was also clear that they had barricaded each window and the door of the supply depot before she could escape. How long could she keep her momentum up and flash about a room from which there was no egress? Would they shoot her?

The Marines held their automatic weapons ready, barring the door and only exit. She glanced at them as she passed by again. From her point of view, each stood still as a gray statue, their square jaws the most prominent feature visible below their helmets.

The adrenaline poured through her, but the room was secure, as Mac called it and she was caught like a lobster in a grocery store fish tank. Where was Mac? What had they done to Johnny? How long could she run before they saw her, shot her?

She raced on but now her legs burn with fatigue. She paused at the window to try again to force the barrier back and failed. One of the Marines swung his rifle in a slow arc in her direction. The action must have been split-second to him, but she was gone before he had time to point the barrel at her.

She kicked at the door and then considered trying to take the weapons. She grabbed one of the rifles and pulled. The Marine held on. She lifted a foot to his chest and yanked, using a tactic Mac had taught her. The weapon slipped from his grip.

Great. Now she had this heavy rifle to lug around and three more weapons to take. The metal began to burn her hands. She looked at the men's belts and saw grenades and knives and sidearms and God knew what all in all those pockets and pouches. She'd never get all the weapons, and even if she did, four Marines did not need weapons to capture one exhausted female.

Where was Mac? What had they done to Johnny?

She called to them, shouting their names, praying they would hear and come in time.

Then she realized with a sickening jolt that she wanted them to fight their own fellows for her. No, she wouldn't. If she was getting out of this, she would have to do it herself and without hurting any of these men. The rifle fell from her hands. Bri slowed. One of the three soldiers who still had his weapon. Everything sped up, the four men sprang at her and Bri sprang away, coming to her feet once more before darting from them again.

Mac had trained her to use her speed and told her about how females were said to used their gifts of attraction.

They seemed frozen again in the place she had just been, but she could see them straightening now, their movements slow but discernible as she reached top speeds. After several more minutes of running she heard more men outside. Did they have instructions not to open the doors or windows until she was captured or...

She looked at the strain on the faces of the young men sent inside to capture a vampire. This wasn't right. None of this.

Bri stopped.

One of the soldiers blocked her path. She collided with him and fell. Two Marines seized her by both arms as a third clasped her legs. Where was the fourth?

She felt a needle prick and then a rushing sensation as her mouth dropped open and her head lolled back.

Chapter 15

At eleven hundred the following morning Mac's radio crackled to life. He'd just left the medical facility, but already the command wanted him back. They said that Johnny had broken perimeter. But that didn't make any sense. Johnny was watching Bri, and Mac knew Lam wouldn't leave her unless he scented a bloodsucker, and even then Lam would come straight to him. Unless there wasn't time.

Bri.

Mac headed out of the qala. He'd find Johnny's trail or he'd find what was happening.

His phone chimed again with another text message adding to the three missed calls. The colonel wanted to see him ASAP.

Did the colonel already know about Bri?

Mac had that sick feeling in the pit of his stomach.

He acknowledged that he was obligated to report to the colonel. But some part of him had changed after the attack, and not just the furry part. Mac wasn't the good soldier any longer. He'd recognized it for a long time. Bri's coming just made him accept what his heart already knew. Mac didn't want to follow orders and he knew Johnny didn't, either.

Was it time for them to go? Past time?

He felt the tug of loyalty to the Corps pulling against his duty to his friend and to Bri.

Mac headed through the courtyard and paused at the sound of a jeep. His heart sunk. He glanced toward the adjacent wall knowing he could leap it, then his eyes trained on the surveillance camera fixed to the tree just beyond.

"Fuck," he muttered.

"MacConnelly!" It was the colonel's voice. He hadn't expected to see his commanding officer waiting for him outside headquarters. "Get your ass out here."

The moment Mac appeared the colonel started shouting. "He's off base again."

That didn't make sense. Johnny was on watch. He was guarding Bri.

"Sir, I—"

The colonel interrupted. "You said you'd watch him. You said he listens to you. Tech Support tells me you two don't even share the same quarters anymore. What the hell is going on?"

Mac stood at stiff attention. Why had Johnny left his post? "I don't know, sir."

"Clearly, you can't handle him, so I'm shutting you down. Johnny comes back into custody as soon as we catch his furry ass."

Mac lifted his gaze to meet the colonel's. Mac hesitated. He had to get to Bri.

"You are a Marine, MacConnelly. You swore to follow orders, and you are about one step away from the brig. I saw something on that video. You know what it is. So you tell me or we sweep the area with orders to kill anything that moves."

They'd catch Johnny, but Bri might get away. Was he willing to bet her life on her ability to control her unpredictable speed? Was he willing to toss Johnny back in a cage for her sake?

Mac stood before the colonel, motionless against the current that swept beneath his feet, dragging him under. He recognized the danger of this darkness and realized that if he let it swallow him up then he would be of no use to anyone. Not Johnny and certainly not Bri.

"All right, then." The colonel lifted the radio off his belt. "Lieutenant, call the MPs. We're taking MacConnelly into custody." He leaned toward Mac and glared. "And Johnny goes back in that cage, and this time he doesn't come out."

Sweat popped out on Mac's brow. Johnny hated the cage. It would kill him.

"No, sir, please. I can track him. I'll bring him back." Were there bloodsuckers near? Was that why Johnny went outside perimeter?

"We're past that. Get in." The colonel pointed with his radio to the backseat, behind his aide and driver.

Mac hesitated.

"Direct order, son. Don't be stupid."

Mac took a step backward, then turned, leaped over the fence and galloped away, hurtling through the forest at speeds no human could match. He had not gone far when he heard Johnny's roar coming from his right. He slowed. The next sound was one of feral pain. Johnny again, howling as if mortally wounded.

Mac needed to find Bri. But Johnny might be facing those bloodsuckers alone right now. He headed toward Johnny, tearing up saplings and slashing at greenery as he blazed through the woods only to come up short as he flung himself from the forest onto the jeep trail.

He glanced around trying to make sense of it. There

was a flatbed truck with two cages bolted down tight. A jeep held two large speakers on tripods and the agonized scream came again from the speaker.

Mac felt a wash of panic make his knees wobble. A diversion. They didn't want him going toward Bri.

They knew.

The minute he slowed he saw the Marines moving in behind him, closing him in a circle. He knew they couldn't stop him, but instead of rifles, they held sticks, each tipped with a metal dart. Did the colonel know that if he bit any of these men, they'd turn?

Was that exactly what he wanted?

Mac waited as they closed in, weighing his options. He wasn't getting darted in the gums. That was certain.

Colonel Lewis's jeep appeared and stopped just outside the perimeter of Marines.

"I gave you a chance to come clean, MacConnelly. We already know about her."

Her? Mac's stomach dropped.

The colonel continued on as Mac wrestled to control the urge to vomit.

"I just didn't know how long you've had her. Female vampire. That's what they tell me from the lesson we caught in the woods. You teaching her how to use her tricks, Sergeant?"

Bri was in trouble. He turned in her direction.

The howl came again from the speaker and the colonel covered his ears. "Turn that shit off."

The cry ceased, and Mac now heard only the shifting of nervous soldiers awaiting orders.

"That was Johnny during the grenade study. We tape them all. I was afraid you wouldn't follow orders. Women do cloud a man's judgment. Though she's not a woman. You know that, right?"

Mac roared, the change already on him.

"You are getting in that cage and coming in to base right now, soldier."

The pain at transformation lit through him like a flame to gasoline. His clothing shredded as he lowered his shoulder to sweep away the closest Marines and their silly pointed sticks. A moment later he bounded away but the colonel's voice followed him.

"You're too late. We got her already."

Bri came awake, drifting in and out of consciousness and finally recognizing that the bright light above her was a large, rectangular fluorescent fixture in the ceiling. She was groggy and weak. She turned her head, but felt stiff and awkward. Medical equipment stood behind her to the right. Numbers. Her blood pressure, she realized, and heart rate. On her left a metal stand held a clear plastic IV bag, but the writing on the bag was too blurry to read. With slow deliberation she turned her head to stare down at her arms, carefully arranged on either side of her hips, above the thin cotton blanket that covered her. She wore a hospital gown, blue and white.

Where was she?

Bri stared dumbly at the IV needle protruding from the skin of her right hand and secured with clear tape. The vein ached from the intruding metal. How long had it been there? How long had *she* been here?

She tried to move her hand and the throbbing ache intensified. Inside the clear tubing a thin line of dark red blood flowed. Were they giving her blood or taking it?

She tried to turn her head and her vision swam. She found her body slow and sluggish as if the world had sped up and she had slowed.

But she managed to look back at the plastic bag on the

metal stand. The IV fluid was clear. She glanced back to her arm, seeing the second IV disappearing beneath medical tape at the crease of her left elbow. Here the tube was filled with clear fluid.

They were taking her blood and replacing it with whatever was in that bag.

She reached with clumsy fingers, her muscles slow to respond to her command. Her hand halted as the circle of metal jangled against the bed rail. Bri stared at the handcuff. The skin on her wrist was puffy, red and itched. Her heart pounded; she glanced up at the machines and watched her blood pressure climb.

Bri tried and failed to sit up as tears streamed down her cheeks. She wondered if she deserved this treatment as penance for what she had done to Matthew and Jeffery.

The curtains drew back with the scrape of metal on metal, and there stood a tall, slim man in his late forties with startling blue eyes and a weathered face. This Marine had spent most of his life out of doors, she thought. His uniform looked like Mac's: the same tan color, crisp folds on the pockets and an identical belt that circled his hips. Only in place of the chevron she'd seen on Mac's sleeve, there sat an eagle with wings spread wide.

"I'm Colonel Noah Lewis," said the officer with the eagles on his shirt. "I run this show."

The officer glanced past the curtain to someone Bri could not see. She looked at the two-foot gap between the curtain's hem and the sparkling white tile floor, and she saw another pair of legs sheathed in a similar pair of creased trousers and the distinctive shiny black dress shoes. A moment later the man stepped into view and cast her a smile that clashed with the predatory glint in his eyes. He was younger, African-American, with light mocha skin and pale green eyes. He wore a white lab coat over his uniform and stepped right as the other went left.

"So, she's awake at last," he said. His voice held a very distinctive drawl, and he spoke as if she wasn't there or could not understand him.

The man's smile held charm, yet it froze her to the spot. She was afraid to even draw breath.

Bri eased back to the pillows as a chill settled in her lungs like ice crystals.

Lewis motioned toward the man in the lab coat, who loomed across the bed from him. "This is Dr. Sarr. He's been overseeing your care."

Dr. Sarr gave her a bright smile. "It's a pleasure to meet you at last, Brianna. Let me bring up the bed. Make you more comfortable. You'll feel a little dizzy. That's normal. Nothing to be concerned about. That's the anesthetic wearing off. Hopefully we won't need to sedate you again."

Again?

How many times had they sedated her so far? How long had she been here—hours, days? She realized that she had no idea. Her insides turned icy cold, and she tried to draw up her legs to roll into a ball, but they only twitched and her feet lolled to the side.

"Paralysis will also abate. Just be patient."

Is that why they call us patients? she wondered, as a wave of dizziness rolled through her. She couldn't think straight.

Dr. Sarr inched forward as if drawn and repelled all at once. "My, she is a beauty. Intel certainly got that right."

Bri jerked her hands reflexively toward her body and found them both cuffed to the raised rails.

There was a whir of a motor as the bed rose, lifting her into a semireclining position. She didn't know if it was his overzealous smile or his tone, but something about this guy sent a chill right up her neck. She shuddered and recoiled from the horror of this nightmare.

"You'll be thirsty. Let me get you some water." Sarr spun sharply away.

She'd be thirsty because they were stealing her blood. How much had they taken? Mac's words came back to her.

The only way to kill a vampire was to drain them of all their blood. They healed too fast to kill any other way.

Where they killing her now—taking all of it? But then why give her the IV?

"We know what you are, Brianna," said the Colonel. "Don't be alarmed. We aren't going to hurt you. Just running some tests."

"You can't keep me here," she whispered.

"Legally, I can, since you're a threat to national security."

"I'm not."

"Perhaps not intentionally. But I've looked into your past. There was a Mr. Matthew Solomon."

Bri hunched at the mention of her fiancé. The colonel lifted a brow and waited. When she said nothing he continued.

"And then there's Jeffery Martin. Mr. Martin is out of the hospital, by the way. He's made a miraculous recovery since your departure. I'm sure you're not surprised. But you overstayed your welcome with Mr. Solomon."

The air left Bri's lungs in a whoosh. Her skin crawled as she lay impotent—trapped. She tried and failed to draw up her legs as her breathing grew erratic.

Lewis's smile broadened at his victory.

Dr. Sarr returned now carrying a small blue plastic cup of water in two hands, as if the contents were a precious gift and then offered it to her.

Brianna lifted a hand reflexively to accept it and was

restrained by the handcuffs again. Her raw skin throbbed at the movement.

"I'll do it," said Dr. Sarr, holding the cup to her lips. He grinned at her, a foolish smile that she'd seen on the faces of many men in her lifetime. She'd even seen this stupefied expression on the faces of total strangers. Men, mostly, but women as well. She never understood it. Now she did, because Mac had explained her power. She was irresistible to them—humans.

They all found her appealing. At least now she understood why.

Delight flashed in the doctor's eyes as he continued to grin at her and slipped one hand behind her to cradle her neck.

She started to lift her head and then that little voice spoke in her head. Was she crazy? No way was she taking anything to drink from this guy.

She turned her head away.

"No?" said the doctor. "I'll set it here. You just let me know if you need anything." He hovered, keeping his gaze on Brianna as if he could not or would not take his eyes off her.

She lay on the bed, restrained and nearly naked, as she faced the two sharply dressed, confident Marines and was unable to keep her body from quivering. Her teeth tingled and her jaw clacked. She clamped down, setting her teeth to prevent them from seeing her utter terror.

Helpless, she realized. They could do whatever they liked to her and she could do nothing to stop them.

The colonel's tone was conversational and his smile genuine as she lay before him cuffed to the bed. "We need to learn more about your kind," he said.

Her kind. The words fell hard. She was not human. Not like them. She knew it, had known it for some time but still the words pierced her like thorns. She was other, outside. Bri's chin sunk to her chest and her words were a whisper. "What are you going to do with me?"

He didn't answer. She lifted her chin and met his gaze and held on as if the contact of his eyes might somehow keep her from drowning. By slow degrees the colonel's features softened, but he did not look away. Something was happening. She felt it in the tingling of her belly. Bri remained still and alert. The colonel began to speak.

"I don't know what Sergeant MacConnelly told you, but we have had some trouble with vampires. The males are nearly impossible to neutralize, though my werewolves succeeded with the two on the road, confirming they make effective bodyguards. I have a theory that they were after you."

Bri glanced away.

"Yes, I thought so. The males have proved impossible to capture. This has pressed us into the enviable position in the past of being forced to hire them."

She recalled Mac saying that she needed to look at a man to be most persuasive and so glanced at the doctor and found he was sweating in the cool room. He reached for her and then froze, his hand hovering there in midair for a moment before he redirected it to smooth over his short brown hair. After which, he shoved his wayward hands into his pockets as if to trap them. Bri turned her attention back to the colonel to find he had inched closer to her side. Dr. Sarr now stepped hastily away from her bedside, backing toward the curtains.

The colonel paid Sarr no mind, nor did he seem to note his odd behavior as he continued. "We'd much prefer to have our own unit. I dislike dealing with mercenaries. You will be our first operative and the mother of all the rest."

Bri's eyes bulged and her words were barely audible. "What?"

"Your cooperation on the first part is necessary. But not on the second, surprisingly. We can harvest your eggs or use in vitro and then implant the fertilized egg to a surrogate. Do you have a preference?"

Bri's head swam and she closed her eyes at the horror of what was happening. Whatever she deserved for her past mistakes, this was not karmic justice. In that instant she made up her mind to fight back.

She tugged at the handcuffs, feeling the burn of metal and knowing she could not escape. They had imprisoned her to this metal bed. She needed to get out of here. But how?

"I can't," she whispered.

"Oh, you can. You're young and healthy. It's a minor procedure. Surrogate might be better. You'd be free to train, and it'd be a shame to spoil your figure."

She blinked away the hot tears that rolled to her hairline and saw Dr. Sarr had reached the curtains that ringed her bed. Sweat now rolled down his face. He stepped outside her line of vision. Bri looked to Lewis to find his smile bright, as if he had just brought her flowers instead of his terrible plans. He seemed elated and slightly mad. The colonel's smile widened, euphoric now. From beyond the curtain Dr. Sarr cleared his throat. Lewis looked annoyed.

"What is it?"

"Should you be telling her that, sir?" asked Sarr.

"Telling her what?"

"Your objectives?"

The colonel scowled at Dr. Sarr, whom he could obviously see from his position, then his eyes widened. He rubbed his face with both hands. Then he glared at her. "God damn it!"

He hadn't intended to tell her anything. She'd influenced him, just as Mac had said she could. A tiny spark of hope tingled inside her. She could do this. She could get out of here.

Lewis spun and retreated, dragging the curtain closed behind him. "No one goes in there," he ordered.

"I have to remove the IV from her right arm." That was Sarr, she knew. If he looked at her, she might persuade him to let her go.

"Sedate her first. And figure out a way to sedate her from out here. Don't let her look at you."

"Yes, sir."

Her hopes withered. She couldn't influence anyone if she was unconscious. She shook her wrists against the bed rail as panic welled inside her. She glanced to the red tube where her blood drained away, and it was all she could do to keep from screaming.

"Colonel! Colonel Lewis. I have to talk to you." Her voice held a definite edge of panic.

Next came the sound of those boot heels striking the linoleum tiles as the colonel retreated. The footsteps came again and she shook her head in an effort to clear the fog that still captured from her brain.

The curtain drew open.

"Colonel." But it wasn't Lewis. It was Sarr. The doctor approached carrying a needle, his gaze fixed on the IV.

Mac raced over the uneven ground, the vegetation blurring as he reached top speeds, and still it wasn't fast enough. The colonel's words echoed in his mind. They had her already. Did they? What had they done to Johnny, because sure as shit Lam had not left his post. To get to Bri, they would have to have gone through one pissed-off werewolf.

He and Johnny were still leathernecks. *Semper Fi.* Always loyal. But now they were loyal to each other.

He jumped the trunk of a downed tree, staying low, building speed. The worry made him stomach sick. What were they doing to her?

Maybe they wouldn't even be able to catch her. She was fast. So damned fast.

Run, Bri. Run like you never ran before. Remember what I taught you.

He hoped she'd get away and that made him a traitor.

Mac had acted like those fucking rear-echelon motherfuckers, calling the shots and doing a shit job. Disobeying direct orders, he thought. Shit. He never would have believed…but he never would have thought that vampires were other than monsters. Still, if he was no longer a Marine, what the fuck was he?

Johnny was close now, he could smell him.

Mac couldn't decide if he should stay in his wolf form or switch to human. Why didn't he hear anything? No sound of struggle, no roar of fury. Just the sound of his own breathing and the pads of his feet tearing into soft earth.

He caught sight of the supply depot. The door lay hanging open, and the barricades were still braced against the windows on either side. Mac scanned the area and found him. A big black mound of fur lying on the ground. Bits of dried leaves and grass stuck to his glossy coat. Why hadn't they taken Lam in?

Mac ran past Johnny and into the depot. The furniture, boxes and supplies lay strewn about, showing signs of a struggle of some kind.

He roared for Bri and was met with silence. They'd taken her. Mac retraced his steps, checking Johnny and finding him breathing, but out. Mac retracted his gums and found no stab wound. How had they done it?

The answer to his questions came a moment later when he heard a familiar *thunk*. He knew it. Grenade launcher.

They'd left Lam as bait and were about to use on Mac the same weapon they'd used on him. Percussion grenade? he wondered, as the unfamiliar canister rolled into view.

Mac's training was to dive for cover, but instead he hoisted the nine-foot werewolf onto his back and made use of his speed, running in the opposite direction as the grenade exploded behind him in a great plume of smoke.

Gas, he realized, closing his mouth and plugging his nose with his free hand. His eyes burned and he could not see where he was running, but he stayed on his feet. To fall was to go down, and if he breathed that gas he would not get up.

Now he understood how they had stopped Johnny and how they had taken Bri.

The smoke began to clear. He could see the ground, but he kept up the pace, his lungs burning, demanding the air he withheld.

Not yet. You don't know what they used. It might still take you out.

The Marines were nearby. They'd have more gas, might be aiming at him already. He changed course, veering off as a new canister of gas exploded in the direction he had been running.

He had no choice but to breathe, drawing one long desperate breath, and he instantly felt dizzy. Johnny shifted against him and groaned. Mac patted his leg and used some of his precious oxygen to growl. Johnny relaxed and Mac charged on. He knew these woods and made for a culvert that would be good cover and difficult for Marines to reach with any equipment. Not that this would stop them for long, but he only needed to get Johnny up again.

He slid on his ass down most of the incline, happy to

disappear into the wild rhododendron bushes that lined the stream. Once at the bottom, he rolled Johnny to his back and flopped down beside him, gasping and spent.

Johnny threw a hand over his eyes and groaned. Mac rolled to one side and threw up. Lam tried to rise and fell back down. Mac grabbed him by the elbow and tugged. His gunner went still and Mac listened for signs of pursuit but heard none.

Then he called the change, gritting his teeth as his body contorted. Now he was naked, which was awkward, but at least he could speak to his friend.

Johnny turned his head in Mac's direction and groaned, panting now.

"The gas made you sick."

Johnny nodded and pinched his eyes closed.

"They used a recording of you to lure me away. By the time I realized, I was too far off to help."

Lam groaned and tried again to push himself up.

"They took her."

Johnny's head dropped back to the ground.

Just saying it out loud hurt like a body blow. What the hell were they going to do now?

"She's gone."

Johnny threw back his head and bellowed, rolled to his hands and knees, swayed dangerously and then began writing frantically. Mac squatted beside him and read.

What do with her?

It was a question he couldn't answer. "I don't know. Study her, maybe, like they are with us." Mac felt sure he would puke as the fear for her safety attacked him.

His friend held his gaze, and Mac saw sympathy in his friend's dark eyes.

"I disobeyed a direct order coming back for you both.

Lewis wants you back in a cage and me beside you. Smartest thing for you to do is take off before they find us."

Johnny wrote, *You?*

"I'm going after her."

Johnny nodded and then studied Mac's face. Finally he wrote, *I go 2.*

"No. If they catch you, then you are in that fucking cage for good. I won't have it."

My choice.

"You take orders from me, Lam. Don't forget it."

Johnny shook his head and used his fingers to pantomime walking. He was coming, too. Following him into another goddamn building, only this time what awaited them was worse than a fucking werewolf—it was the entire U.S. Marine Corps.

"Johnny, I can't stand it if something bad happens to you, something else, I mean. And I can't stand to think what they are doing to her right now."

Mac fell forward onto outstretched arms and bowed his head. He couldn't draw breath. A wave of dizziness rocked him. What if they hurt her? He covered his mouth with one hand to stifle a cry. Then he dragged his hands up over the short bristle of his hair and laced his fingers together behind his head like a captured prisoner of war. The truth struck him hard.

He loved her.

That was why he slept with her. Not to scratch her itch or because she had a cute ass or any other damned excuse he fed himself.

"Johnny, I think I'm in love with her."

Johnny held Mac's panicked stare and gave a nod.

"I have to save her," he said to Johnny.

His corporal pointed back toward base.

"Yes. After we get her, you know we'll have to go AWOL."

His friend did not hesitate but gave another slow nod. Then he extended his hand. Mac took it. When had they both stopped being soldiers and become a tribe of two?

Mac focused his energy for the change and braced as the pain swept through him like acid. They were a team again, both focused on one goal. Recapture Bri.

They were Marines. They'd improvise.

They started toward the medical center, knowing that Bri was there in the underground facility.

As they ran, Mac considered what he was doing. It was just like the night he'd ordered his Fire Teams into that building. Then, he knew he'd made a critical error. Only this time he had a chance to make it right.

Chapter 16

Bri struggled, and the metal handcuffs clanged against the stainless steel rails as she shrank away from Sarr. Her eyes fixed on the needle he carried and the clear fluid within. Sarr never looked at her and never touched her as he lifted the clear tubing.

"No, wait," she said.

He injected the liquid into a juncture in the tubing. A moment later her vein burned. An instant later her skin tingled. She tried to remove the IV but the restraints stopped her and then there was a rushing sound as everything went black.

The next thing she knew she was shivering violently, curled on her side and huddled in a tangle of sheets and thin cotton blankets. The smell of bleach and disinfectant reminded her of the nursing home where she'd once volunteered.

My God, she thought, had she hastened the deaths of any of the elderly there? No, she realized, because she had been younger then, not as dangerous as she was now that she had become a woman. That was what her nana had told her.

Her head ached, and she lifted her hands to cover her eyes. The light was too bright. It felt as if the fluorescent bulbs were burning the tissue behind her eyes. There was a steady pulse of pain that accompanied each beat of her heart. And the waves of nausea told her she was either touching metal or was too damn close to it.

Where was she?

"Mac?" she whispered.

She panted as the pain grew worse and the memories fell upon her like a pack of hungry wolves. Her capture, and then the colonel saying he'd use her eggs to create more of her kind.

He couldn't. She had to stop him. Had to escape. She lifted one hand from her eyes and peered out squinting against the ripping pain that traveled through her skull. But she could see a blurry image of the bed. A metal hospital bed that had been slightly elevated to lift her torso. A thin mattress separated her from the hated steel. Was she still in the medical facility, or had they moved her? Her eyeballs seemed to pulse with her heart, but she could make out the bedding—white cotton sheets again. She used one hand as a visor and kept the other one pressed securely to her opposite eye as she glanced down at the blue-and-white hospital gown.

Had she had surgery?

She slipped both hands over her abdomen and found no pain, no bandages, but she wasn't sure how eggs were harvested. Could they have taken one or more? She didn't know. Bri then extended her gaze beyond the bed. Even this slight movement made her stomach pitch. The sour taste in her mouth warned her to move gingerly.

Bri stilled as a realization struck her. They had not cuffed her wrists to the bed rails. She lowered her arms and endured the avalanche of pain from the blinding light.

Opposite her bed was a gray metal door with a brushed nickel latch. The white walls to either side were cinder block and lacked the customary light switch that usually sat just inside a door. A chill that had nothing to do with the thin blanket lifted the hairs all over her body. This was a prison cell.

She was alone, but she felt as if someone were watching her. Bri tried and failed to sit up. That was when she heard the whirring sound. She opened her eyes and glanced toward the door. The whirring stopped.

Bri listened. Nothing.

Then she lifted her gaze to the ceiling, squinting against the bright lights. And then she saw it. Her gaze flicked to the small black dome of plastic. A camera mounted in the corner where the walls met the ceiling. There was another behind her in the right corner.

Bri grabbed the hem of her hospital gown and tugged it down to cover her hip.

"Colonel Lewis? Are you there?"

There was a click and then a reply, slightly distorted by the speaker she could not locate.

"Yes, Brianna. How are you feeling?"

She ignored the question. Anger flared inside her, sharp as cut glass.

"You won't get away with this."

His voice came back, calm and filled with smug superiority. "Feel free to write your congressman."

"Mac will get me out of here."

The colonel's chuckle filled the room. "Werewolves are immune to your kind. He's not your puppet. He's a Marine and a damn fine one."

"He'll come."

"Extremely doubtful, since he is the one who turned you in."

"Turned…" The shock of his words hit her like a slap. She fell back to the mattress. Was it possible? Could Mac have abandoned her, or was this just a lie? "I don't believe you."

"No difference to me what you believe."

Uncertainty tugged. Had Mac betrayed her? No, she wouldn't believe it. She lifted her chin and stared at the camera. "He'll come."

"I hope you're right. Now just relax. We're prepping the OR for you."

Mac paused in the woods beside the stream to collect a rumpled, musty set of clothing from one of his drops. Lam stopped beside him and cast an impatient look as Mac tugged the sweater over the rumpled T-shirt and then zipped his pants.

The stark reality of his choice loomed large. It was a decision he had already made, but he did not have the right to make it for Johnny.

"When I go after her, it's over. You understand? I'll have to go AWOL."

Johnny gave a slow nod.

"If you come with me, we'll be on the run. All of us, and they'll never give up trying to bring us in."

Johnny's nod showed he knew this as well.

"But if you stay behind, then they won't blame you. You'll still have a chance."

Johnny growled.

Mac's head sunk. "Johnny, I got you into this mess. I ordered you into that building and I…" He couldn't finish that. He swallowed back the guilt. "But I always thought… think…that they'll find a cure. I couldn't have gone on unless I believed that. But if you go, you're stuck like this. For good, you understand? Stay here. It's your only chance."

Johnny glared.

"It's an order."

Johnny shook his head, apparently also done with taking orders. He lifted his hands as if gripping something. Bars, he realized.

"They'll lock us up. Yeah. Sure as shit."

Johnny held his position and Mac understood. "They'll lock you up either way?"

It was true. A truth they both understood.

Mac glanced away and then back to meet his friend's gaze. "If I could, I'd trade places with you."

Johnny exhaled in a long blast and then gave him a rough pat on the shoulder, hard enough to buckle most men at the knees.

"I'll never forgive myself. And I won't give up until we find a way back for you, too."

Johnny pointed at the road.

"Yeah. I just...I don't know...Johnny, I don't want to make another mistake. What if this is another bad idea? What if..." Mac hunched with his hands on his knees like a runner after a race. He blew out a breath and spoke to the ground. "If she dies or you die..."

Johnny pointed toward the medical facility.

Mac hesitated. "I can get her out. There is no reason for us both to throw everything away."

Johnny inhaled and then his head snapped up. An instant later Mac smelled it, too. The scent was sweet and metallic, like blood, but there was more, a deeper cloying fragrance of blooming jasmine and beneath that the musty stink of a carnivore.

The hairs on his neck lifted. *Vampires!*

Johnny's ears flattened back. Mac stripped from his clothing and changed to his werewolf form as Lam stood guard. Mac followed his comrade, who went after the scent on all fours, not because he had to, but because it kept his nose to the ground and his body low and out of sight. They were heading back to the place where Brianna had been taken. Before they reached the building they found what they were tracking.

Flesh eaters. Six of them.

Mac's hackles rose. Johnny dropped down into cover.

The vampires' skin was pinkish, like the skin of a newborn rabbit, but their eyes were rimmed with crimson. Their misshaped heads resembled humans but for the slit-like noses and prominent fangs that protruded over thick, liver-colored lips.

The males had found the place where Brianna had been.

He and Johnny were outnumbered three to one. To kill them, Mac needed to hold one long enough for it to bleed out. That would be challenging with two of its fellows attacking him. How long did it take to bleed to death?

Depends on the size of the hole, he decided.

"Too many," he said to Johnny.

There was no choice now. The vampires would track Bri to the medical facility and even the heavy guard would be useless, because once the flesh eaters went to top speed, the Marines would be helpless as toddlers against them. "We have to get Bri, now."

Mac ran with Johnny on his heels. How fast could a male vampire travel? He thought of Brianna, moving so quickly she disappeared, and ran faster.

Mac cut through the woods, the shorter path for someone running. If they could catch the colonel before they reached the facility he had a chance of retrieving her. After that...

Mac ran faster.

Would he have to kill his fellow soldiers to take her?

Mac felt something snapping inside himself as he recognized that he would do whatever it took to get to Bri, and he'd kill anyone who stood in his way.

"Bring her out," said a male voice.

Bri tried to relax her clenched jaw as the footsteps approached. Her bed moved. She peered through her eyelashes as they rolled her into the corridor. They paused at a locked door and were buzzed through. The bed began to roll again, into an elevator. The doors swished shut.

"She out?" asked a voice behind her.

"Not sure," came the reply.

When the doors opened she found an escort of four armed Marines.

"Secure the prisoner." The voice was deep with a Texas twang and was wholly unfamiliar. She saw the glint of handcuffs and bolted, running blindly.

"Where'd she go?" asked one of the men from the elevator.

She ran in a circle around the entranceway, pausing to try the two doors. They opened with a key card, like hotels, she realized.

"There she is."

Bri turned to face them. There was no way out. They were on her a moment later, strong hands gripping her, dragging her back to the gurney. It took the men no time at all to handcuff her to the raised bed rails and wheel her through the door. Her wrist began to burn. Blisters formed, broke and wept. But she welcomed the pain, because it helped her fight the drug that threatened to gobble her up. Bri watched to see who had the plastic key card as they swept through the next set of doors, and she noted where he kept it. Unfortunately the Marine with the key card remained behind with the other three as she continued through the open door with her original two escorts.

This corridor was wide. She passed several rooms that looked like operating theaters. She rattled against her restraints as she repeated one word—*no.*

"What'd she say?" said the one behind her.

"It's the drug," said the one at her feet. "Will you just look at her?" He grinned, his smile making him look younger, less threatening.

She recalled Mac telling her that her influence was stronger if she stared into the man's eyes. Apparently vampires and snakes had a way of mesmerizing a victim. Then, according to Mac, she only had to tell them what she wanted and they'd do it. But these were trained Marines, not weak-willed or easily influenced. Still, she saw no other hope.

Bri cleared her throat and forced a smile at the orderly. Her ears continued to buzz as if she had thrust her head into a nest of hornets.

"Could you take off these handcuffs, please?" she asked.

He gave her a "be serious" look. But she just held his gaze and gradually he reached in his pocket.

"What are you doing?" asked the one behind her.

"She wants them off."

"Yeah, and…?"

"So they're coming off."

He slipped the key in the lock and twisted it. Bri tipped her head up and glanced at the man behind her.

"I can't get away," she said to him and watched his expression soften, as if he was staring at a helpless kitten instead of a tigress.

"That's right," he said. "You can't."

"So it's all right if my wrists are free." She held her breath, expecting to be cuffed again. But both men just continued down the corridor to the last room as she tried to contain her astonishment. Large, imposing machines circled the bare stainless steel operating table. A huge light shown down on the silver surface so brightly she had to squint. Then she saw the metal stirrups fixed to the end of the table. Bri's heart rate climbed and sweat broke out on her forehead. She trembled so hard that the gurney shook.

"Easy now," said Dr. Sarr, stepping into view and smiling down on her. Seeing him in blue surgical scrubs only added to her terror. He glanced to her escorts. "Why isn't she out?"

"Maybe the dose is wrong. We figured on her weight, but she's not human."

Bri blinked as she realized how close she came to being completely helpless.

"Let's get you prepped," said Sarr.

Bri swallowed and fixed her attention to the doctor who returned holding an IV needle. He grasped her hand, turning her wrist to study her skin, searching, she suspected for a plump vein for that hollow-tipped steel needle.

He loomed and Bri tensed. If she didn't do something quickly he'd press that plunger and it would be all over.

She had no choice. To escape, she would have to become the very thing she had denied.

Chapter 17

"Dr. Sarr. I'm not quite ready for that," said Bri, eyes fixed on the terrifying needle. Her voice sounded funny and the buzzing in her ears had grown worse. "I need to speak to you."

The IV needle glinted. Bri forced her eyes up to meet the doctor's and fixed a smile as her mouth went dry as clay. His gaze locked to hers. The wrinkles on his brow eased.

"I have a schedule. Make it quick."

Her periphery still saw the needle but she looked into his eyes, seeing his pupils enlarge with each passing second.

"I don't want those Marines to hear," she whispered and pursed her lips.

Sarr ordered them out.

"Could I have some water?"

Sarr poured her a cup and hurried back to her then handed the water to her.

"Is there something you could give me to counteract the sedative?"

"That's not wise before surgery. You need to be relaxed."

"I am relaxed. Just being around you makes me relaxed.

But I'd like something to make me more alert." She kept her gaze fixed on his.

Sarr mentioned something.

"Yes, please."

It was all she could do not to pull away as he used a syringe to puncture her vein. A moment later he was injecting a clear fluid through the rubber cover and into her bloodstream. If her influence hadn't worked then it was game over.

But almost immediately she felt more alert.

"It's a mild stimulant. How are you feeling? Ready to begin?" he asked.

"Almost." She stared deeply into his watery gray eyes and wondered if she could pull this off. "You seem tense, Doctor. Why not give yourself something so you can relax?"

He turned to the counter and rummaged through drawers. "What about this?"

"Will it put you to sleep?"

"If the dose is right."

"Perfect."

She watched while he injected the drug into his bicep. The ease with which he did as she asked gave her a chill. How simple would it have been to ask him to inject a lethal dose?

"I need your exit card."

He passed it to her.

"Will this get me out?"

"I'm sure they'll stop you. There are cameras everywhere. Whoa. I need to sit down."

"Here." She patted the mattress. "Lie beside me."

Sarr scrambled up as Bri slipped off the opposite side of the gurney, her bare feet contacting the cold floor.

The doctor yawned. Bri turned to go and then asked for

his surgical scrubs. He struggled to comply, getting tangled up as his pants caught on his shoes. Thankfully his white boxers remained up. Bri helped him and received a smile in return.

"Did Travis MacConnelly really turn me in?" she asked.

"No. That was a lie. Standard procedure—turn allies against each other."

His words brought sweet relief. Mac had not betrayed her.

The doctor slipped out of his scrubs to reveal a muscular torso with some extra flab encircling his middle. She accepted his top.

He grinned at her. His words were slurred. "You're so pretty."

Bri unfastened her gown and dropped it to the floor. Sarr's gaze swept over her and he licked his lips. She stepped back and into Sarr's trousers tugging the drawstring until they fit her waist. Then she dragged on the blue V-necked top that hung on her but at least she didn't feel a breeze. She tucked the plastic key into her breast pocket. On the way out of the door she grabbed a head cover to conceal her coppery hair.

The urge to run twitched against the need to know what happened to Mac and Johnny. She glanced at the door and then to the man who might have answers to the questions that troubled her.

"How did Mac and Johnny come to be werewolves?" she asked.

"Mac was bitten."

"Accidental?"

His laughed was the kind one used as a weapon to make someone feel small. "Lewis knew. He sent the squad into that hot zone." Sarr lifted a hand to speak to her from the side of his mouth, dropping his voice in a confidential way.

"He knew about the werewolf. That was his objective. Not securing the building. Not securing the werewolf. Lewis wanted a survivor. One squad, thirteen Marines. And he got two survivors. Mission accomplished." Sarr yawned and closed his eyes.

Bri breath hissed through clenched teeth and then gave Sarr's jowly cheek a little slap. "The colonel sent them in on purpose to be butchered?"

"To face the werewolf, yes." He patted her arm clumsily and let his hand drop to the table. "I can tell you one thing, those things are vicious. I saw the surveillance tapes."

"Mac said that he attacked Johnny. Is that true?"

"Hell of a thing."

Bri's mind reeled. Mac hadn't made an error in judgment trying to take the building. He'd been sent in there like cannon fodder.

"Did Mac attack John Lam?" she asked again, feeling her opportunity at escape ticking away with the seconds.

"We haven't succeeded in generating any new ones. In vitro doesn't work. Fetuses are normal, no werewolves. Just regular little human babies, more's the pity. We've tried with both Lam's and MacConnelly's sperm. I think werewolves have to be made instead of born. That's my theory. Just can't replicate what happened to MacConnelly. But we will."

"You... Do they know that?"

The doctor frowned and shook his head. "Need to know." His eyes drifted closed. "I wonder what would happen if we mixed theirs with yours?" he muttered, dropping into a doze.

She shook him awake. "How do I get out of here?"

He explained the route and told her where she'd meet armed Marines. The stimulant was now humming in her blood like a double espresso. Her fury and the fear only added to the mix. She knew she could run fast. But she'd have to pause at doors to unlock them, and there she would be vulnerable.

Time to go.

Brianna took the surgical mask from around Sarr's thick neck and secured it over her face. Then she tucked her hair into the blue cap and headed through the door. All Dr. Sarr told her spun in her mind like a cyclone.

She made it out of the operating wing without discovery and slipped unnoticed into the adjoining corridor past the signs indicating the recovery room and the pre-op area. She glided past the nurses' station at normal speed, keeping her head down and her feet moving. Bri used Dr. Sarr's key to slip out of the secure area and ran right into Colonel Lewis. He apologized and stooped to retrieve her key card. She didn't wait for him to hand it to her but snatched it from him as she broke into a run that transitioned to a full-out dash. The nurses in the corridor seemed to slow and came to a standstill as she streaked past.

With luck she'd be out of this damned building before they could sound the alarm.

Then where?

Bri paused to let herself out of the medical building and then bolted across the yard on bare feet, losing her cap. She could see the ten-foot perimeter fence, the razor wire rolled on the top, glistening with spikes. She'd have to jump it. She could. She knew it. But her gaze fixed on the razor wire and fear washed her cold.

Her panic was roaring inside her, making her movements spastic. Was the stimulant wearing off or was the sedative growing stronger? Whatever the reason, she saw the Marines pouring from the buildings like red ants, their movements sluggish, but discernible. She was slowing down. She could hear their shouts now. See them pointing—at her.

She'd never make the fence before they cut off her escape. Bri sprinted forward, but her legs grew heavier with each step. She leapt and hit the fence midway, clinging to the chain-links like a gibbon monkey. The metal seared her flesh. She reached and pulled, scaling the fence. Below her the wire shook as men climbed after her.

She'd never have another chance. She felt it in her marrow. Her hands burned, blistered, and still she clung.

You'll heal. Keep going.

McConnelly and Lam approached the perimeter fence that ringed the medical facility and headquarters. The evening air had turned cold, but warmth still clung to the damp earth. Above them the sky was a midnight-blue carpet casting the trees in dark silhouette.

It was hardest to see at this time, when the light had faded, yet the sky was still too bright to see with his night vision. Colors faded to black.

They stared across the stretch of open ground before the medical facility, which squatted like a toadstool with much of its structure belowground.

What were they doing to her right now?

A moment later they heard the siren and saw Bri running across the open yard toward the fencing. He could see her clearly, despite the fact that the spotlight had not yet found her. She wore pale hospital scrubs, like oversized pajamas, and her wild red hair flowed out behind her as she galloped across the ground barefooted. She was moving fast, but nowhere near her super vampire speed. Bri ran and they chased—a dozen Marines charging after her. He watched her awkward gait. Something was wrong with her. They wouldn't catch her before she reached the fence.

But they'd reach her before she cleared it. Their bullets wouldn't kill her. She'd heal no matter how many bullets they put in her, unless she bled out.

Mac forgot the plan. He forgot every blessed thing except getting to Bri as he streaked to the fence, determined to tear it down with his claws.

A sharp sting of pain ripped through her upper arm and Bri lost her grip. Her opposite hand reflexively squeezed tighter, taking her weight, until she recovered enough to lift her left arm again, reaching to clutch the hated metal wire once more. Her palms burned as if the metal were molten hot, but she clung, ,tenacious as a barnacle, knowing that to release her grip was to fall back into the hands of that maniac Lewis and his evil doctor, Sarr.

She caught movement beyond the fence and trained her gaze on the creature, recognizing him instantly. Huge, gray and running on all fours. Mac! He bolted straight at her on the opposite side of the fence. Behind him, some fifty yards back, Johnny followed, as always.

Bri clung as Mac reared up on his hind legs and slashed at the barrier that separated them. The metal links popped open with a ringing sound as his nails sliced through steal. No wonder his squad had stood no chance against the werewolf.

Behind her came the shouts of men and an instant later the pop of gunfire. Bullets sparked on the metal beside her head, and she dropped to the ground as the fence buckled and Mac leaped through. He gripped her upper arms and dragged her to her feet. Before she could run through the gaping hole, he lifted her and ducked out the way he had come. Bullets whizzed past them, and she knew from the way Mac arched that more than one shot had found his exposed back. But he crouched around her, protecting her from the flying bits of lead.

As bullets drummed against his hide, he didn't slow, just kept running over uneven ground, shielding her from harm as he carried her closer to the line of trees and the protection of the forest. Johnny passed them, running into fire as they fled. He moved so fast he was a blur of black fur, but she heard him howl a challenge to anyone foolish enough to try to follow his sergeant. She looped her arms even more tightly around Mac's neck and clung. An instant later a ripping pain lanced through her arm as if she'd been stung by a hornet. Her arm dropped from Mac's strong neck as the pain changed to a burning. A glance told her she'd been hit again because blood now ran from her upper and lower arm and stained the front of her scrubs. Mac looked down at her, spotted the wound and placed one hand on her head, covering her further as he increased his speed.

Behind them the gunfire continued amid Johnny's roar. She knew Johnny held back their pursuers, gaining them precious minutes.

She and Mac reached the woods and Mac slowed, stopped and then howled. The sound shivered over her skin and iced her blood. Mac dropped to a knee and turned the way they had come. He set her gently on the mossy ground and looked toward the compound behind them.

"Go get him!" she shouted to be heard above the din.

Mac ran back toward Johnny. She was alone. Bri stood on shaky legs. Her skin flashed hot from the blood and cold from the night air. The palms of her hands looked as if she had been branded, but even as she stared the red welts and burns faded. She gingerly held her left wrist with her right hand, supporting her injuries and taking a more careful look. The blood that had poured like water from a pitcher, now oozed from blackish wounds. There were two holes for each bullet. Entrance and exit, she realized and she also realized the bullet had shattered at least one bone in her upper arm. That was likely why she felt nauseous. Her stomach pitched and kicked. Bri folded and lost the contents of her stomach. The dizziness came in waves as she stood with her forehead resting on the trunk of a tree. At last she could open her eyes. The gunfire had stopped.

"Mac? Johnny!" Bri straightened and instinctively moved toward the two men who had protected her and risked everything to get her out. What would they do to them?

Bri made it half the distance to the open ground beyond the trees when Mac leaped into view. Johnny dove into sight behind him, and they both landed gracefully amid the undergrowth. She could see them perfectly in black and white, and she knew they could see her just as clearly. But still Bri gasped when their glowing predatory eyes fixed on her. Together in their wolf forms, they were a formidable pair.

She stared in awe, taking in the differences. Johnny's coat was pure black and Mac's the mixture of gray, white and black hair that she thought a more traditional color for a wolf. They looked neither man nor wolf, but some corruption of both, and the combination unsettled her.

Mac's gums were black and he had the upright musculature and carriage of a man, but the fur, face and eyes of a wolf. The claws that jutted from his fingers did not belong on a wolf, but more resembled something from a horror movie.

Bri was used to seeing Johnny like this but not Mac. He had seldom shown her this second self. Then as now, he had little choice.

He was terrible and fearsome and she was so happy to see him that she threw herself into Mac's arms, hugging him fiercely. His hand cupped her head and he let her cling for a moment before setting her on her feet. She stood staring at Mac and looked to Johnny, who shifted from side to side, his eyes on her.

"Thank you for coming for me." She held Mac's hand and then reached toward Johnny. "Thank you, Johnny."

Johnny looked at the hand she extended and then took it in both of his, bringing it to his cheek for just a moment before releasing her. If Johnny had resented her at first, he had apparently changed his mind and now meant to protect her. She did not know if it was for Mac's sake or for her own, but she was grateful.

"Are you both all right?"

They nodded. Mac clasped her injured arm. His nostrils flared as he sniffed at her wound. She trusted him. She trusted both of them. So she offered her injured arm for their inspection.

"It hardly hurts now," she whispered, noticing the holes now scabbing, the blood drying. "Healing, so fast."

It was the most serious injury she'd ever sustained, and the bone did not even hurt now.

Johnny cocked his head toward the compound and then signed something to Mac. Johnny took the lead.

She fell into step with them, and for the first time since her capture she felt safe.

After a few minutes the sounds of shouts and curses died away. But they were back there. She knew it, because the colonel would not give up his prizes so easily. And what would happen to Johnny and Mac now?

She felt shaky again as she realized what this rescue would cost them. Did they understand what they had just done? The weight of their sacrifice dragged at her. She didn't deserve such loyalty. All she had ever done her entire life was use and hurt people. Why would they help her?

Chapter 18

Bri looked around them and saw that her night vision had begun to pick up color. It was nearly morning. Mac slowed to a walk. How far had he run with her in his arms?

The silence of the forest enveloped her like a cloak and she could hear nothing but her own heartbeat and Mac's labored breathing.

The fur that blanketed his face did not quite cover the upper and lower canines that jutted dangerously in opposite directions. She wasn't used to seeing him like this, and she thought it would take some getting used to. But this was part of him. Just like her powers were a part of her. Welcome or not, they just were.

Her excellent eyesight made it possible to see his restless eyes and the way he rubbed one hand over the other in an anxious motion.

Bri stepped forward and stroked him from shoulder to elbow. He tensed but allowed it.

"It's soft, your coat."

Mac glanced behind her. She turned to follow the direction of his fixed stare, listening for Johnny.

"Is he angry with me because of this?" she asked.

Mac shook his head and lifted a hand to point. A moment later she heard the approach of something tearing through the undergrowth. She knew it was Johnny, because Mac waited with a casual ease that should have reassured, but Bri still found herself inching closer to Mac and taking hold of his thick, muscular arm. It was hard to forget the first time she saw Johnny. The night of her arrival. The night he'd tried to kill her.

Mac glanced at her and then back in the direction of the noise as Johnny broke from cover and then made a graceful stop. Only his heavy breathing and the lolling pink tongue indicated that he had exerted himself.

Johnny had scouted in front, and now he and Mac engaged in a series of hand gestures that Bri did not understand. It occurred to her that they should both learn sign language and then realized they had invented one of their own.

"Is it clear?" Bri asked.

Johnny huffed and nodded.

"I never would have gotten out without you two."

Johnny grinned and then looked to Mac who motioned in the direction that Bri surmised they would be traveling.

"Wait. I need to tell you something. Something Dr. Sarr told me."

At the mention of the good doctor, Johnny's entire body went ridged and a low growl emanated from his throat. The hairs on his body lifted until they stood out making him look even more deadly.

"Yes," she said. "I feel exactly that way. But I remembered what you taught me, Mac, and tried my persuasion on Sarr. He was very easy to control. At my suggestion he injected himself with a sedative and gave me a key card."

Mac and Johnny now both more resembled owls as their eyes went big and round as they exchanged a look.

"It's how I got out."

Mac recalled telling Bri just that the same night he had assured her that her talents would not sway him and that her energy draw would not weaken him. He had told her purely for his own self-interest. Telling her the truth had been the simplest way to get what he wanted—her.

Only he wasn't really immune to her. Not really. But it wasn't the magic or her power that drew him. It was something much more alluring—her spirit, her empathy, her kindness toward Johnny and her optimism that things could be better.

Now he was willing to risk all their necks for hers. Brianna Vittori was the one female in the world who could understand him. What it was like to be different, outside. And she could understand what it was like to have hurt the ones you love, because she had done the exact same thing. And something else, something he couldn't do for himself. She had forgiven him for the critical error that brought death to his squad.

He loved her for all that and more. Mac had acknowledged the truth when he realized he'd lost her, but he his heart had known far before that.

She was speaking again. Something about making humans do what she told them. He tried to focus on her words while listening for any sign that the colonel or the vampires he and Johnny had seen had found them. They needed to move.

Bri shook her head. "It feels weird to say that— 'humans'—because it forces me to admit that I'm not one of them anymore, at least not completely." She laced her fingers together and then twisted her hands one against the other as she stared up at Mac. Her gaze did not hold the accusation he deserved but something he thought might be anxiety.

"I have to tell you something I found out about how you two were turned."

The moment she said the word *turned* Johnny set his teeth with a snap and Mac spun away. This was a topic they did not speak of—ever. In all the months since their return, he had never told Johnny how sorry he was for doing this to him. He had tried to show him day after day, but to say it aloud? No. Mac squeezed his eyes shut and thought he might be sick.

She began speaking again. *No. No. He did not want to hear this.* It took all his restraint not to clamp his hands over his ears like a child to shut out what came next.

Bri touched Mac's shoulder, her fingers threading through the hair that covered his back. "Sarr told me that Lewis knew there was a werewolf in there and he sent you in anyway. No, not anyway. He sent you in *specifically because* there *was* a werewolf in there."

He spun to face her now, his lips curled back to show the long white teeth capable of tearing her to ribbons. She drew back her hand and clamped it over her throat. But she did not run. Bravery, he wondered, or trust? How could she know the hatred blazing through him was not for her but for Colonel Lewis?

Bri turned to Johnny, extending her hand and stroking his upper arm. "Johnny?"

He motioned for her to continue. Mac braced for her next words. Could it be true? Had his commanding officer known what was in that building?

Bri nodded and cleared her throat, her gaze darting between them as they loomed like twin nightmares.

Her voice was tight and trembled when she spoke. "Lewis knew the werewolf was there and he sent your squad. He didn't expect you to capture that building or clear the roof or whatever he told you to do."

Mac stood stupefied by her words as his version of reality collided with this new one.

Bri continued her voice a dirge. "Sarr said that the objective was to have at least one survivor. Instead, Lewis got two."

Mac stumbled back as if she'd punched.

Could it be true?

The solid surface of a tree trunk was all that kept him standing as the dizziness flooded through him. Half of him was relieved because it made it easier to go. The other half was mad as hell at being used.

He glanced to Johnny to see how he was taking it and saw his Lam's eyes narrowed as he turned in the direction they had come. Mac knew his gunner's intention was murder, so he moved to stop him and a scuffle ensued that sent Bri retreating behind a sturdy tree. Mac held Johnny. Johnny broke free. Mac caught him again. They thrashed and tumbled, but Mac never lifted a finger or fang and neither did Lam until Johnny raised a hand to call a halt.

Bri knew her words were triggering something dangerous. But instead of retreating as anyone with sense might have done, she waited until the two werewolves had ceased their struggle and then continued on in a rush as if speed might somehow help in the delivery of her words.

"It was Lewis. Not you. *His* decision. Not yours. None of this was your fault."

Mac's heartbeat thundered in his ears so loudly that he feared he could not trust his hearing. It was like a windstorm roared within him as the forest all about sat still and calm.

"There's one more thing."

Mac didn't think he could stand one more thing. He

shook his head and pointed at the trail. They needed to move. He needed to move.

Bri held her ground and launched in as he reached for her, intending to carry her if she would not walk.

"Sarr said that Lewis planned to lock up Johnny either way."

Her words brought him up short.

"But worse, terrible." She covered her hand with her mouth and drew a long breath through her nose. Then she shivered as if trying to toss something vile from her skin and he and Johnny stood rooted like the trees that surrounded them.

What had they done to her? Mac flexed his claws and lowered his chin, wishing for a chance to pay Dr. Sarr and Colonel Lewis back for all their attention.

"Lewis had plans for me, too. He wanted to harvest my eggs and breed his own vampires. I escaped from the operating room."

Mac forgot he could not speak. His words came out as a howl of outrage, an explosion of fury.

Bri didn't cringe or brace, she just continued on. "And they harvested your sperm as well. Johnny's, too. They've already tried to impregnate women with them. Sarr said the fetuses were normal. Do you know what that means? Mac, your children will be normal. You can have them, lots of them."

The two Marines looked at each other in stunned silence. The horror of being attacked had been hard. Knowing it was his fault had been agony. Now Bri had added the knowledge that he had been attacked twice. Once by the werewolf and once by a man he had respected. The treachery of Lewis's action seeped into his skin like poison until he burned from within. The government they had sworn to protect had betrayed them.

And there was fallout: he and Lam might have children out there very soon. Normal children. He squeezed his eyes shut as the relief and sadness gripped him.

When he opened his eyes, there was no doubt, no more uncertainty. Mac believed Brianna's words and felt in his heart they were true. It all made perfect sense. Mac had to get them away.

Mac didn't remember setting off. But he found himself carrying Bri again, loping over uneven ground with Johnny at his heels.

His feet moved methodically and he scented the air for any spoor that indicated threat. But his mind stuttered and wobbled as he tried to absorb what Brianna had told him. He'd been set up, tricked, betrayed because he followed orders.

Semper Fi. Always Faithful.

But how could he be when those he trusted had betrayed that loyalty?

Before he had turned wolf, he had never disobeyed an order. Now he didn't know how to follow one. So what was he now if not a Marine? *A monster, that's what. And a man.*

He'd heard it said that there were no ex-Marines. No retired Marines, no former Marines. Once a devil dog, always a devil dog.

Was it true? Because his world had now shrunk to include only two people: Bri and Johnny.

Protecting them no longer ran in two opposite courses. They all needed to escape this place and the commander who did not understand the Code.

Duty, Honor, Country. Lewis had no honor, and so Mac held him no allegiance. He still loved his country and was still willing to make the ultimate sacrifice to protect her from all enemies. But he wouldn't be used like a zoo animal. No, that he would not do.

Mac was still a Marine. It was Lewis who wasn't. He didn't deserve to be. And Mac would make it his personal mission to see he was held accountable.

My God, they've taken our sperm and used it, too.

For now, Mac ran. They didn't stop. That was the thing about his second form—he could run tirelessly. When Mac did draw to a halt, it was because he had reached his first objective—an isolated home with a female occupant who hung her laundry on a long line.

He set Bri on her feet, and she stretched and rolled her neck as if stiff and sore from being jostled for hours. She could run faster than either of them, but to do that was to leave their protection. And she stayed, making her choice to trust him. He promised himself to be worthy of that trust.

He had to tell her about the vampires they had scented. She needed to know that they faced two threats.

But for now he was mute. He motioned to the little square of grass cut into the forest by human hands. The lawn was dotted with weeds and scattered with a collection of discarded and rusting automobiles in various stages of disassembly. Between the white Thunderbird on blocks and the unidentifiable truck seats lay the clothesline. He pointed, and she understood what he wanted. She crept into the yard. He watched from cover, ready to protect her if she was sighted, but knowing it would be far better for the homeowners to catch a glimpse of her than him.

She began by removing an old comforter from the line and laying it beside her on the grass. Into this she tossed a pair of men's jeans, a wrinkled white T-shirt and an old blue-and-gray plaid flannel with elbows worn so thin he could nearly see through them. She turned to go, then glanced at her green scrubs and added a few more items to the pile. Then she looked toward the house as she bundled them all in the bed covering and returned so fast that he lost sight of her for a moment. An instant later she was beside him, extending the offering, but he didn't take them. Instead he lifted her and the bundle and set off at a run. This time Johnny took point, pausing only to check the air for any scent of the vampires.

At first Mac had no direction. His objective was only to put as much distance as possible between them and the colonel and to stay in the cover of the forest. But as he ran, he began to consider options and formulate a plan. He knew the colonel would set up a perimeter. He needed to be outside it and in a vehicle large enough to carry two people and a nine-foot werewolf.

Mac knew that the colonel would anticipate his objective and therefore watch the motor pool. Mac needed his move to be unpredictable. He considered and dismissed several possibilities before he finally settled on a strategic risk—the local ghost town, Bodie. It was isolated, but several of the area businesses drove tourists up there. Most of the tour companies had vans or small buses. He thought the drivers might not be too careful about the keys, but it would be easy to take them by force, if necessary.

The trouble was the location. It was exposed with no good cover for miles in any direction. Lewis would expect him to stay in the forest. That was why he needed to leave it. Mac did not trust his intuition. That was why his breath caught and his skin tingled. He glanced from Bri to Johnny praying he was doing the right thing.

Could they stay ahead of the vampires? His preference was to take on those bloodsuckers one at a time and not fight them on open ground.

He'd tested the theory that a werewolf bite was the only kind of wound that a vampire could not heal. Was it also true that only a vampire's fangs could pierce a werewolf's thick hide and that their venom was lethal?

Mac feared he might soon find out.

As the night slipped quietly into morning, they crossed a road and continued into the woods on the opposite side. The light glimmering through the trees told him they were on a course paralleling the river. At midmorning the sky had clouded over as they skirted well around the town of Bridgeport in the Toiyabe National Forest. By late afternoon the rain swept in, muddying the river and making the unpaved roads a quagmire.

Good, Mac thought. That will slow down the search. Then Bri began to shiver. The warmth of his arms was no longer enough to protect her. She needed a fire. He motioned to Johnny, who understood and took off on a recon. Johnny found an abandoned miner's cabin that looked to have been forgotten since the 1849 rush. The roof had collapsed on one side, and the remaining portion was thick with moss, but it was dry inside because the miner had set the cabin into the sloping hillside. The subterranean back third was protected and dry. The stone fireplace chimney had fallen, but the hearth remained and the gaping roof would vent the smoke, while the rain would make it invisible. Once inside, Mac saw that someone had more recently used this shelter and left behind several articles, including a rusty lantern half full with fuel oil, aluminum pots and pans, candles and a stack of dry wood tucked against the earthen wall on the backed dirt floor, along with kindling and newspapers from the 1980s.

Johnny left them to search for something to eat. Mac knew he could run down anything on two legs, with the possible exception of Bri, and he felt sure Johnny would not come back empty-handed.

Mac began the fire by splashing kerosene on the newspaper and using an iron spike and a stone to throw sparks. Bri huddled, watching, and Mac noted that her toes where all white from frostbite. He needed to get her warm.

By the time he had a flame started her jaw was clacking like a set of chattering teeth.

He retrieved the bundle of clothing to find that the comforter had kept them reasonably dry. He offered Bri the female things she had gathered, motioning for her to get dressed. Then he called the change, enduring the shift and then lifted a bare foot into the denim jeans still warm from Bri's touch. After much tugging, he found the pants too snug, the flannel too loose and the wrinkled white tee just right. He untucked the tee so it covered the fact that he couldn't fasten the top rivet of the jeans and left the flannel unbuttoned, flapping over his ass so Johnny wouldn't make fun of how tight the jeans were. He hadn't worn civilian clothes in so long, he wasn't sure how they were supposed to fit.

When he turned, it was to find Bri still in her wet clothing, clutching the ones he'd given her and staring at him.

"That bad?" he asked, wiping the sweat from his brow with the soft flannel of his sleeve.

"No, no. You look fine. I'm just not used to seeing you in real clothes."

Mac wasn't either, but he supposed he'd have to get used to it.

"How are the bullet wounds?" asked Mac.

Bri lifted her pale arm and touched the flawless skin at her forearm and then bicep. "Perfect," she said, the astonishment evident in her voice. "You'd never even know."

"Fast healer."

She lowered her arm. "What about you?"

He lifted the shirts to show her his back, which looked

perfect, though the ache was still there from the bruising underneath.

Her smile was weak, pained.

He motioned a finger at her clothing. "Get out of those."

She quickly stripped out of her sodden surgeon's outfit.

Mac felt his skin flush at the sight of her, but Bri was quick to drag on a pair of jeans that swam on her and a woman's purple turtleneck that was wet in only a few places.

"I wish I'd taken socks."

He glanced down at her dirty bare feet and set both pots under the stream of water running from the holes in the roof, determined to offer her hot water. Outside the rain poured down in gray sheets.

Soon he had the water heating, and Brianna was no longer shivering.

Bri dipped a finger in the water and grinned. "Warm enough for a bath. How long do you think Johnny will be gone?"

Long enough, thought Mac.

Chapter 19

"I was so frightened," Bri said, sinking easily into his arms.

He gathered her up, comforted by the floral fragrance of her skin and her small body, molded perfectly to his. He wanted this, wanted her, but not just for an hour or a night. No, that would not be enough. Would a lifetime be enough?

He didn't think so.

Bri drew away and dragged off the turtleneck. Mac tore a patch from the hem of his stolen T-shirt and dipped it into the warm water. He used the wet cloth to bathe her stomach and chest. Driving off the chill and washing her clean of the mud that splattered her arms and face. As the water ran in rivulets down her pale skin, she dropped her jeans. He knelt at her feet, bathing first one slim leg and then the next. She sat on the comforter as he washed her feet, admiring the perfect toes and fit of her foot in his large hand. Her skin was no longer unnaturally white. Now they glowed pink with good health and warmth.

"They're still tingling," she said.

He wanted her entire body to tingle. He offered the

flannel, and Bri dried what the fire's heat had not. Then she stretched out on the comforter and waited for him to come to her.

"We don't have a condom," she said.

"I can work around that."

She grinned as he started at her toes, nibbling and licking up her calves to her knees. She made a sound of satisfaction and settled back as he stroked her inner thigh with feathery caresses. Her hips were satin smooth as he slid his hands up to the soft skin of her belly, his hand the scouts for his mouth. He dipped his tongue into her navel, and she writhed beneath him. He cupped her breasts, stroking the soft mounds as he dropped kisses straight up the center of her body then veered along the fragrant ridge of her collarbone. The yielding tissue was trapped between his mouth and the bone beneath. At her throat he felt the bob of her Adam's apple as she swallowed and then the purr as she gave her approval of his caresses. The outer shell of her ear tasted sweet as nectar. Mac reached between her legs to stroke her there and found her body already wet with need. She wrapped her hands around his neck and pulled. He allowed her to bring his mouth to hers. He wasn't sorry, for she gave him a kiss of fire and promise that stiffened his already hard body.

She moved her hands over his chest with quick, needy strokes that trailed down his torso and to the skin of his abdomen, which twitched at her caress. Finally she grasped the root of his need. Her eager fingers wrapped about him and she tugged, allowing her fingers to slide over him with just the right amount of friction.

He was so grateful to have her safe and here in his arms, so grateful for the rain that sheltered them and to Johnny, who gave them these few stolen moments of privacy. He drew her hands away and sunk between her legs, grasping the two round cheeks of her pear-shaped bottom and lowering his mouth to her clitoris.

Bri moaned and writhed. He sucked as she lifted to meet his mouth and he licked her as she bucked against him. Her breathing grew erratic. Small needy mewling sounds came from her throat as he increased the speed of his kisses. The now familiar shimmer of gold rose from her skin and became a brilliant aurora of light. She placed her feet solidly on the ground and lifted to meet his ministrations. Her stomach tightened and he recognized the sounds she made. She was close, so close. The urge to thrust into her welcoming body roared like a living thing, but he pushed it back. There was no protection, and Bri did not want a baby.

A baby... He had once wanted to fill a house with kids and dogs and rabbits and any critter his kids dragged home. Now he only wanted her.

She came against his mouth in a sweet flood of sound and moisture. When her body stopped trembling and she relaxed back to the earth, Mac scaled her slim body and gathered her against him. They both needed sleep. But Bri was not done with him.

She wriggled from his grasp and sunk down to take him in her mouth. She used her hands to toy with his balls as her tongue danced along the ridge of engorged flesh, stroking him from stem to stern. Sweet Lord, the sensation of her mouth on his body. He groaned and threaded his hand through her hair, encouraging her with a gentle pressure on her head.

He drew her away just as the need grew too strong. But she wrapped her eager fingers about him and brought him the rest of the way home. He came in a sweet rush of pleasure and liquid. Bri held him a moment longer, then drew away to crossed to the heating water and gingerly retrieved the cloth, returning to wash him clean.

The lay together in each other's arms, dozing. Sometime before Johnny returned, Mac slipped into his clothing and helped Bri into hers. He nestled with her beside the fire and drifted toward sleep.

"I love you," he whispered.

He thought he felt her stiffen, but then she relaxed and he dozed.

The birdsong woke him before dawn and they found Johnny roasting a shank of elk for Mac and cattails for Bri.

They ate and washed, and he changed to his werewolf form before they were off again. Bri was unusually quiet all morning, which Mac attributed to worry and fatigue. He and Johnny remained watchful for pursuit by either Lewis or the six male vampires they had sighted.

Last night's rain and the morning fog condensed on the needles and leaves, dripping down onto them as the sky lightened in slow degrees.

By sunrise they reached the higher elevations and left the timberline, crossing into open country. Mac knew the chance they were taking. In broad daylight with nothing but the rocks and sage to hide them, Mac felt as exposed as a miner with the seat torn out of his britches.

In the afternoon Bri asked to run and he agreed, provided she stay close. She kept up easily, vanishing and then reappearing up the trail. Somehow they reached their destination without seeing anyone, though that did not necessarily mean they were not seen. He hoped he had guessed right, that the very thing that made this course most dangerous for them would also make it the least likely place the colonel would search and a place the vampires would not wish to journey, for they had good reason not to be seen in daylight. The open ground would also provide no opportunity for the bloodsuckers to come at them unawares. Unless, he reminded himself, they came at them fast. Not even he could see a vampire moving at high speed. But Bri could. He'd need to count on her for that.

They crested a high rise of exposed rock and strawlike grasses and sighted their destination.

Below, the defunct stamp mill clung to the hillside like a big, ugly wart. The ore-crushing plant was by far the largest structure but was by no means the only surviving building. Despite boom and bust and several fires, much of the town remained, with wide spaces between buildings like the gaps between the teeth in an old man's mouth.

The dirt road wound down the valley and threaded through the town that once bustled with miners, gamblers and businesses at the peak of the California Rush. He'd taken the tour. "Bad men from Bodie," they'd called them, and with three killings a day they'd earned their reputation. Now managed by the California State Parks system, the desolate heap attracted curiosity seekers, history buffs and two werewolves escorting a female vampire.

They needed to get to the cover of the buildings before the tourists arrived, so they cut straight past the mill. Mac kept alert for attack from within the hulking three-story structure with wooden trestle, which once held the track from which the ore cars ran from the mountain to the top floor of the stamping plant. Mac recalled that the plant once crushed stone into dust to extract the ore. Inside, he recalled, lay rusting pistons, flywheels, camshafts, and other equipment. Could Bri sense all that iron? Was that why she leaned away as he descended the mountain where the building perched?

They made it past the stamp mill without incident. Mac felt a mixture of relief and unease at reaching the relative cover of a sagging shed and tilting house that seemed to be losing the battle with the winter's heavy snows. Beyond, a bellows with dry, rotted leather and fallen timber told that the blacksmith's shop had given up to collapse. Before them the town of Bodie waited.

Mac instinctively moved toward cover, checking the interior of a charred outbuilding and finding nothing but dirt, weeds and piles of gravel. He called a halt.

He glanced at Johnny and found the familiar look of agitation. His gunner felt it, too. The town was too quiet.

Mac stared down the empty road to the series of ramshackle buildings, and a chill stole down his spine. What was it that set him on edge?

He listened to the creek and groan of the wind whistling through the abandoned buildings but found no threat. The smell of dust and decay clung to his nostrils, but it was the decay of dry rot and moldering wallpaper and charred wood. Not the sweet, sickly stench of vampires.

What, then?

He could see nothing that threatened. Yet both he and Johnny were crouching in the dead grass, uneasy as steers in a slaughterhouse.

He listened and surveyed their surroundings. The wind and snow had scoured all paint from the planking, leaving the entire place the universal gray of driftwood. Portions of the wooden walkway stretched beneath overhangs beside the false fronts of a few buildings.

Bri hunched down beside him, her gaze flashing from the empty town below them and then back to him.

And then he realized what made his insides swirl like water down a drain. He had not realized how much this stretch of century-old wreckage resembled the rows of buildings recently abandoned by the Afghani outside of Kabul. Now daylight streamed down upon the town. Back then he had seen the world through infrared goggles. But it felt exactly the same as the night he had led his men to their doom. Then as now he did not know what awaited him inside. Then as now he needed to secure a building for the safety of others.

Which building should he choose? Mac gazed from one to the next, knowing he must find cover but fearing another mistake.

Bri again offered Mac the rumpled clothing that she had stolen for him. This time he accepted them.

He left her with Johnny for only as long as it took to call back his human form because he couldn't bear for her to see him writhe and contort again. The transformation bathed him in sweat and left him sick to his stomach, but he knew the weakness would not last. Besides, in werewolf form, he couldn't sit behind the wheel of the vehicle he planned to steal.

He dressed quickly and returned to Lam and Bri.

"We have to get down to the center of town. The tour guides leave their vehicles in that lot and walk." He pointed and she followed the direction of his raised finger.

Mac stared down a sagging row of buildings. "The church. We can see approach from both sides and it's near the parking area." He glanced at Johnny. "That sound right to you?"

Johnny's ears went back. His corporal was still uneasy with his squad leader asking his opinion. Well, things had changed. Mac waited. Lam hesitated before nodding his agreement.

Mac glanced at the sky. "Park offices should open soon, and they'll unlock the gates. First tour probably left Bridgeport by now. We better go."

The feeling of unease grew as he approached the abandoned town. He could hear nothing but their footsteps as he took point, leaving Johnny to guard their backs. He couldn't tell if he was sensing danger or just reliving it. His senses were all tangled like a ball of barbed wire. He couldn't trust them. He couldn't trust himself.

Mac made a quick march through town, avoiding the roads but walking in a beeline from the stamp mill past two foundations and across Main Street. They hurried over one wooden walkway past the false front that looked straight out of a John Huston movie. The peeling sign announced the establishment had once been Sam Leon's Bar. From there they cut past the sawmill, the circular blade visible through the bowing boards and missing timbers. When they reached the church—Methodist, according to the State Parks sign—Mac was relieved to see it secured with only a flimsy wire mesh fence across the entrance. He peeled it back with ease and entered first, turning immediately right. His training caused him to hug the wall. A moment later Johnny was nudging Bri out of the door as he hugged the wall on the opposite side of the doorway. The quiet yawned. He scanned the empty room. Dust coated the wide floorboards and the pews. Midway down the row against the right wall, a cast-iron stove still squatted. Rusty with age, it must have once been a welcome relief from the snow and cold of the Sierra Nevada Mountains. The altar had gone, but the commandments remained painted on the wall above the raised dais. *Thou shalt not kill.* Mac wondered if he'd get through the day without breaking that one again.

Johnny returned the wire fence to place so it almost looked undisturbed. Mac motioned and Johnny crossed down the center of the pews, his feet raising dust and leaving unnatural prints on the floor. Mac signaled to Bri to follow him then turned toward the door, backing after them.

Johnny reached the front of the church and looked out the small door to the right of the dais. Then he motioned for Bri, who came at his bidding and waited where he indicated. With luck they could go out that door after the tourists left their van and before they toured past the church. Then Johnny joined Mac at one of the long segmented windows that gave them a view of the road and the parking area.

"Can Lewis track us?" she asked.

"He doesn't know where to look."

"They could use dogs or something. Helicopters, maybe."

They'd use both, he knew.

Johnny cocked his head and glanced to Mac. He heard it, too.

"The van," said Mac.

The sound reached her ears, a low hum of an engine and the bounce of struts on uneven ground. The first tour group had arrived.

"What if they see Johnny?" she whispered.

"We'll wait until they clear the vehicle and then we'll go."

Bri stooped on the pew below the window, crouching now to peek out of the glass pane rippled with age and streaked with grime. The white van rolled into view. A magnetic sticker on the door advertised *Gold Rush Ghost Tours, Badmen from Bodie*. The van swung in perpendicular to the warehouse, pulling up to the hitching post in the same place as older tire tracks. The gears creaked as the driver shifted and stopped. Then he exited to the dirt square designated for parking. He was dressed in a wide-brimmed cowboy hat and period clothing, including red suspenders that stretched over his faded cotton work shirt.

"Okay, folks, here we are. This way for a brief overview and a story of a public lynching that happened back in the day."

The van door slid open and a teenage boy unfolded first. His ball cap advertised he was an Angels fan. Behind him came a pretty blonde woman, followed by a tall man who quickly gathered her elbow as if fearful a ghost might spirit her away. The woman checked her camera as he stretched his back. A heavy middle-aged couple groaned and heaved their way from the back of the van and then joined the teen, who ignored them.

Mac stood beside the window looking at the group. Johnny held the opposite side of the frame. He was so big he did not need the pew to gain a view from the window.

What came next happened so fast Bri did not even have time to scream. Below them six male vampires rushed in. Each captured one member of the tour group. Bri pointed and fell back. Mac caught her and set her on her feet. Mac and Johnny looked at her, scrambling backward with one hand clamped over her mouth and the other pointing to the window and looked again. Couldn't they see?

She knew the moment the vampires became visible to them. Johnny growled and Mac tensed but the vampires already had hold of their victims.

A scream came from the parking lot, high and thready. Bri leap back to the pew. She saw them, the vampires each with their teeth clamped on the exposed neck of a tourist. They held them from behind as blood poured from the exposed wound at their necks. This was no sensual puncture and romantic draw of the force of life, but a ripping of vessels and a slurping of the hot gush of blood. Bri could not look away. She stared in horror as one after another of the tour group went slack and were discarded in the dust with the rest of the rotting, decaying town.

Mac acted first, surging toward her and gathering her

against his side as he rushed to the side door. Johnny ran past them and leaped out. He rolled to his feet in the yellow grass that dotted the backyard. Mac tossed her like a football to Johnny, who snatched her from the air and threw her over his shoulder.

The world blurred as Johnny ran. She caught glimpses of Mac beside them. There, then gone. A door slid open and they rushed inside a building. Mac drew the door shut.

Johnny set her on her feet, and she saw Mac throw off his two shirts as he shifted into his silver werewolf form. Instantly she felt sick. A glance around told her why. They'd retreated to the stamp mill. All about her, rusting iron machinery seemed to pulse with lethal energy. She stared at the lattice of iron cam shafts and tappets, power wheels that once spun, driving the iron stamp shoes down to crush stone to dust. She swayed.

"Too much metal," she whispered.

Mac glanced back at her, pointed to the long rows of metal pistons and then to the door.

She understood. Mac had chosen the one place they might have an advantage over their attackers. All the iron that affected her would also affect them. That did make sense. Her stomach pitched. Johnny slid the door back a crack and peeked out.

"He can't see anything," she said. "Because they move too fast for you to see. I should be lookout."

Both werewolves exchanged a glance.

"They're coming," she whispered. "I feel them. God, I hope the metal weakens them the way it weakens me."

Johnny left the door to stand back to back with his squad leader. She saw the vampires rush through the door but Mac and Johnny did not. They still turned their heads from side to side, searching for the invisible.

The fear poured through Bri like an exploding geyser

as she left them to charge the first vampire. This one she knew. This was the same thing that had nearly caught her at her apartment. But since that day she had learned how to run and how to fight. Thanks to Mac.

She was past her guardians before they could move. As she charged she felt herself changing. Not just speeding up but preparing for battle in a way that was new. Her teeth grew in an instant so they jutted past her gums. Her fingers stretched into claws, horrible talons as she assumed her second form, the one she had taken only once and never even tried to show Mac, for if he saw her like this could he ever love her? And despite her knowledge that she could never have a life with Mac, she still wanted his love.

Bri slashed at the first vampire, taking him by surprise. Her blow cut across his neck and blood sprayed her face. Was it the blood he had just stolen from those poor people? He fell to the ground and Johnny grabbed him, clamping on to his neck like a pit bull as he used his strong arms to twist. The snapping of the creature's spine sent a shudder through Bri. Johnny jerked his neck, leaving a raw tear over the jugular and blood vessels of its neck. Two vampires grabbed her but Mac was there. He didn't stare at her in horror or shrink from the sight of her. Instead, he latched on to the closest creature and tore open its throat with his jaws. Bri's stomach heaved and she fell to her knees, only to be lifted by her hair by a third attacker. Two held her now and dragged her toward the exit. The remaining two vampires engaged Mac and Johnny, staying clear of their jaws and long reach while delaying them.

Bri twisted and snapped her fearsome teeth but could not break free. She clawed at their arms, tearing flesh to ribbons. Johnny lunged at the legs of his opponent and managed to grab hold. A swipe of his claws opened the vampire's chest. A moment later the creature was airborne as Johnny tossed him into the stamping mill. At the contact with the iron mortar box the vampire screamed, writhed and twisted, trying to escape the wide stretch of metal even as his flesh seared, sizzling like meat in a hot skillet. He bled from his wounds, growing weaker with each passing moment. He fell still as Mac managed to get hold of his attacker. Bri's captors dragged her toward the door as she heard the screams behind her. Was that his opponent or Mac?

Chapter 20

Mac gutted the vampire and then used his claws to tear something vital away. Johnny's opponent struggled weakly on the top of the stamp press. The two remaining vampires dragged Bri toward the exit as he and Johnny bounded after them.

The vampires released Bri to face them. It was a mistake. She bit the shoulder of the closest one, lacerating the thing's muscle and exposing the blue pulsing blood vessels that threaded beneath its stark white collarbone.

The creature howled and slapped her, sending her to the ground. Johnny leaped and landed on the vampire's chest. There was no escaping Johnny's jaws that latched hold of its throat and held on as its blood drained away.

Mac charged the remaining vampire, but before he could reach it, the male vanished. Mac turned in a circle expecting it to come at him from behind but the seconds ticked by and nothing happened.

Bri rose to her feet, a large welt now marring her perfect skin. The creature she had been had vanished, the gaping jaws receding to the straight white teeth that brightened her smile.

For a moment there she had looked like the males except her skin had never turned to that bruised mottled color. Had she known she had a second form?

"It's gone," she said looking out toward the door and pointing at the air.

He glanced at the empty space beyond to the horizon and then fixed his gaze on her. He used his index finger to circle his face and then pointed at her lifting his hands into claws. He was sure she understood his question because she glanced away and her pretty face flushed clear down to her neck.

"I don't know. It only happened once before. We had a break-in and…I don't really know how I do it. It just sort of is. When I'm really, really angry I can feel it coming. When I saw it attacking you, I…"

Mac squeezed her shoulder and nodded his understanding. Then he and Johnny checked the other five vampires. Their wounds did not heal. Methodically Mac moved from one corpse to the next to be certain they had all bled out. In death their skin turned an even more hideous plum color, and their cloudy eyes turned opaque and white as marble.

Johnny climbed up on the stamping press to check the last body and Mac saw it move. Johnny growled and lifted his claws.

Bri felt something cold touch her neck. A heartbeat later it began to burn. She turned and found herself captured against a hard male body. One hand grasped her hair, the other held the long silver blade to her throat.

She opened her mouth to scream but no sound came.

"Hold tight," came the whispered order from behind her captor.

Bri recognized the voice. It was Lewis.

Her gaze darted to Mac and then Johnny, but they were watching the stamp press where a vampire, who was still alive, held their attention. From the change in his posture, Mac seemed to sense disaster first.

Johnny and Mac turned in unison as the Marines poured into the large open room of the stamp mill like ants, their boot heels drumming on the thick wood planking.

And here it was, Bri realized, Mac's decision coming to him in the worst possible way. To rescue her, he would have to attack his fellow Marines.

"One move and I slit her throat," said Lewis to Mac. "It's iron, Sergeant. Just a twist and the wound stays open."

Mac held his position as his gaze flicked from one Marine to the next. His breathing showed his upset and the locking of his long dangerous jaws. Finally his gaze swung back to Lewis.

"Get down from there," the colonel barked.

Both Johnny and Mac eased off the large iron block. Behind them smoke rose from the vampire's burning body.

"Check them," said Lewis. "See if any are still alive."

Several of the Marines fanned out, moving from one vampire to the next and then dragging them into a line at Lewis's order. Two of the men climbed up to check the final vampire still on the mortar box.

Johnny shook his head. Lewis saw the gesture and smiled.

"Missed one, did you? I hope so. I need a male and female to insure the next generation. Be stronger if both parents are vampire. You both did well in your second engagement. I knew you could do it. Been at each other for centuries, according to MI." Lewis stepped forward. Mac and Johnny followed him with their eyes. "I wonder how long sperm lives after the body dies." Lewis turned to the assistant flanking him. "Call Dr. Sarr. Get him up here in a chopper, ASAP. And bring body bags and ice. Lots of ice."

The metal touching Bri's throat seared her skin and she set her jaw to keep from whimpering. She was scared down to her toes, but she couldn't call her second form. Why did it only come when she was angry? Now, when she needed to change, it eluded her.

"Captain," barked Lewis. "Check the bodies."

The Marine moved down the line performing some ghastly version of an inspection of dead vampires. He stepped from one body to the next, nudging them with his foot.

Lewis watched his progress. "Look at those wounds. Spectacular."

One of the Marines on the pressing mill called out, "This one's still breathing."

"Breathing?" said Lewis's aide. "I thought vampires didn't breathe."

Lewis gave him a suffering look. "Breathe, fart, working kidneys. They even die of old age. That undead crap is bullshit. These things aren't human, but they *are* alive." He snapped an order. "Drag him down."

The two men on the press handed down the limp, smoking form of the living vampire to another Marine, who dragged him before the colonel.

Mac growled and the colonel glanced his way, the grin of supremacy broadening on his face. "Got one."

Mac shook his head. Lewis held his gaze and that was why he did not notice that the vampire's body no longer smoked. The wound that Johnny had given him bled, but his burns healed fast.

Lewis squatted before the inert form as he spoke to his aide. "Bring in the steel cage and lock up my wolves. No more liberty for you two."

The aide spun away barking orders. Bri leaned against the man behind her trying to put some distance between her neck and the burning blade. But the soldier just pressed harder.

"It burns," she whispered.

"Hold still," he growled.

She breathed in short little pants against the pain, dropping her gaze to the ground. That was when she saw the vampire's eyes pop open, meeting hers. For what seemed an eternity he held her gaze, those cloudy, dead eyes on hers. Then, in a move so fast that she was certain only she could see it, the vampire was on his feet and behind Lewis. It took one vicious bite from the side of the colonel's throat. Bri heard the vampire's teeth click shut. Blood sprayed from Lewis's neck as he dropped to his knees. Men moved in slow motion now as the vampire charged her. He knocked the blade from the Marine holding her and kicked him backward. Bri imagined the Marine must look to the others as if he was suddenly flying. The vampire grabbed her wrist and dragged her out of the stamp mill. He ran her past the Humvees and jeeps, dashing up the road with her in tow.

He was taking her to the others. She knew it, and she knew Mac could not stop him. If she was to escape, it would be her fight.

Bri wound up and punched the vampire in the stomach as hard as she could and heard a satisfying *oooff* sound as the air left his lungs. Her feet touched the ground and she hit him again, this time in the face with the heel of her hand. He staggered, recovered and reached for her again.

"You don't belong with them. You're one of us."

She hit him in his bleeding shoulder.

He covered the wound with his opposite hand and glared at her.

"We'll come back." His words were not threat, but promise.

"And I won't be here."

Her grandmother had evaded them for years. She could, too. But for how long now that they knew of her existence?

"We will find you."

When she spoke her words were not threat or bravado, but also a promise. "And when you do, I'll kill you."

She meant it. Mac had been correct. Given the right circumstances, anyone could kill.

The vampire stepped back and then back again before turning to race away. She watched him crest the hilltop an instant later and then disappear. Behind her came the sounds of gunfire.

She turned to see Marines fleeing the stamp mill as yellow smoke poured from the interior. The men outside quickly donned their gas masks.

But Johnny and Mac were still inside.

Mac and Johnny hit the floor the instant the first canister went off. The gas did not smell like the caustic smoke designed to send men fleeing from buildings and right into enemy fire.

The gray smoke billowed out and Mac knew that it was something to either kill them or render them unconscious.

Mac's lungs burned. He could not hold his breath much longer. Through the haze Johnny motioned toward the back. They both knew they had no choice. The Marines outside would fight, and he and Johnny would defend themselves. *My God,* Mac thought, *how many will we have to kill to escape?*

He had to get out and find Brianna before that thing took her where he'd never find her. He recognized then that he would make any sacrifice to have her. He would even give his life for hers. He had to survive this, had to live to save her so he could tell her that what he wanted most in this life was her.

Something moved before him. Who was stupid enough to enter a building consumed with gas?

Then he saw her. Brianna crouched, low feeling her way through the swirling smoke—a gas mask fixed on her head—as she swept the ground for them. She'd come back for him. He was elated and furious in equal measures.

"Mac!" Her words were muffled by the plastic shield that covered her face.

He grabbed her ankle and she gave a yip of fright then sank to her knees offering two masks. They didn't fit over their faces.

Mac forced his change, writhing on the floor as his bones and tendons collapsed into his human form. The moment he went still, Bri slapped the mask over his face. Ten seconds later he was holding the mask on Johnny, who had fallen to his back.

"I'll get one of those Hummer thingies." Bri pointed and disappeared before his eyes.

Mac tore the breathing tube from the mask and shoved it into Johnny's mouth then pinched his nostrils shut. Johnny roused slowly, his eyes tearing as he blinked up at him and shook his head as if fighting off the lethargy that stalked him.

The crash brought Mac to his feet. Bri had taken out the closed barn door. Red lights glowed in the toxic mist as Mac lifted Johnny and ran with him to the backseat of the Humvee and then tore the wooden door from the grill. Bri shoved over as he climbed into the driver's seat, naked, the vinyl hot on his bare butt cheeks.

"Go, Bri. We'll be right behind you."

She hesitated a moment, pressing her lips together. Then she nodded and vanished an instant later.

He decided to break out through the side of the stamp mill, hoping the plants were as dry-rotted and weak as they appeared. He knew that once he tore free, he'd have only seconds to avoid whatever obstacles lay beyond.

The side of the stamp mill exploded in splintering wood as they crashed through. Mac turned hard left before he saw the circle of jeeps that ringed the buildings. He aimed between the closest two and floored it. The Humvee swept the two smaller jeeps aside with a crash and the screech of twisting metal. Then they were bumping over rough ground. He'd gotten out without killing anyone. It was a miracle.

At least he didn't have to worry about IEDs out here. He steered for the town and fishtailed onto the wide dirt road, roaring past the Marines who guarded the entry by veering around their portable plastic roadblock. Next he passed the abandoned van surrounded by the dead tourists scattered in dark pools upon the ground.

His rearview mirror told him two things. The Marines were on his ass, and Johnny was still out.

Mac tore off his mask at the same time Bri reappeared in the passenger seat. Mac startled and gripped the wheel.

"Holy shit. You can jump into a moving car?"

"It moves slower than I do," she said and swung the door closed.

Mac motioned to the rear seat. "Check him."

Bri scrambled into the back and hoisted Johnny's massive head onto her lap and began patting his slack cheek as she called his name. Mac focused on gaining top speed in their vehicle. If they could stay ahead of pursuit until Johnny regained consciousness, maybe he wouldn't have to kill anyone.

"How did you get away?" Mac asked.

"I used what you taught me and punched him in the stomach." She slapped the heel of her right hand and grinned.

"That's my girl."

He focused on the road and getting Bri and Johnny to safety. Johnny needed to be able to run. The Marines were good, but they'd never be able to track a vampire and two werewolves once they got to cover.

In the backseat Johnny groaned and pulled the breathing tube from his mouth. He coughed and choked while Bri rubbed his hairy back and murmured encouragement.

"Careful. He wakes up hard."

"No, he's fine. Aren't you, John."

When Johnny straightened, he hit his head on the roof. Mac caught his eyes in the mirror.

"You guys ready to run?"

Johnny nodded and Bri's eyes went wide before she gave a nervous series of nods.

They descended from the high deserted plains with the Marines following close behind. Once below the tree line Mac knew they were in territory where the humans could not follow. He swerved from the road and zigzagged through the sage and tufts of yellow grass. Even the Humvee couldn't climb the incline of rock that stretched before them. But he and Johnny could.

"Can you climb this?" he asked Bri.

"Better. I can jump it."

He scrambled out from behind the wheel and then helped Bri. She took a moment to let her gaze sweep over his nude form before she hurried after Johnny, who had already reached the incline. Behind them vehicles screeched and men shouted orders. In a few minutes the din they made faded away. Mac shifted and followed Johnny. Bri had vanished, but not too far, he hoped. There were at least two males still out there. Johnny ran and Mac followed. Before they'd reached cover Mac heard the helicopters. Take cover or run? he wondered.

"Bri! Get to those trees." He pointed to the timberline several miles below them.

Her voice came from far off. "Okay."

"Meet us there."

She appeared, giving him a view of her already at the tree line, and then she vanished. He and Johnny charged one of the birds. The helicopter spotted them when they still were five hundred yards out. It started firing at one hundred. The high-caliber rounds did not break his skin, but they knocked him around, as if he was the sparring partner of some heavyweight champion.

Johnny went down and Mac helped him rise. They made too damned big targets. Just fifty feet to the trees and then they'd vanish just like Bri.

They reached cover. Above them the treetops exploded as branches were cut to ribbons by the gunfire.

They hadn't gone far when Bri appeared carrying running shoes, shorts and a turtleneck. Mac noted she now wore dirty white tennis shoes. Mac accepted the clothing with a questioning look.

"Backpackers," she said thumbing over her shoulder. "A few miles that way."

"Stay close now. Those vampires might be hanging around."

Her eyes went wide, and he realized she hadn't thought of that.

They moved quickly through the forest and did not stop until evening. There was no sound of pursuit. He still didn't have a vehicle, but now he thought that staying in deep cover was best. They could travel east to Nevada or all the way up the Sierras into the Cascades. With luck they would reach Canada without ever leaving the woods. They couldn't put a roadblock in the forest. Their first night's camp, he did not risk a fire.

Bri stood a little way off, hands folded before her and a troubled expression on her face. She seemed worried. Was it the vampires, the Marines or had she heard him say that he loved her?

Mac intended to find out.

Johnny curled up to sleep and Mac took the first watch. Bri must have been exhausted, but she came to sit beside him, her back to the downed log and her knees drawn up to her chest.

"You came back for me," he whispered.

She made a humming sound of agreement. He looped an arm around her shoulders and pulled her close.

"Mac, stop." She cut him off and slipped from beneath his arm, rising to her feet.

He followed feeling a sense of approaching disaster from her tight expression and the way she would not meet his gaze. It was bad.

She crossed one arm over her middle and pressed the opposite hand to her mouth, as if she was trying not to be sick. The dread grew in him. His flesh began to tingle.

"Mac, you've taught me how to take care of myself. It's time for me to go. Past time, really."

The shock rendered him momentarily speechless, when he found his voice it was thin and strained. "No. We're staying together."

"I can't. I'm not going to hurt one more person I care about."

"Please, Bri. I love you."

"I know you do, and that's precisely why I have to go."

"That doesn't make any sense."

"My being her, my staying. I'm keeping you from what you want, Mac."

He gave her a look of utter confusion.

Her chin sank to her chest. "I've thought a lot about this, about what will happen next. Even if we get away, even if there were no vampires chasing me and the military didn't want to put you and Johnny in a cage, what kind of a life would we have?"

"We'd be together."

"What about your family?"

He looked away.

"Are you going to bring me home to meet the folks? Your mother, your younger brother. He'll fall in love with me. You know that, right? He'll be crazy with jealousy and try to spend every waking minute taking me from you. What about your father? You said he has a bad heart. How much of my company can he stand?"

"I'll tell them about you. I'll make them understand."

If he chose her, he'd lose them. The truth hung about them like smoke, how much it would cost to love her.

"Even if you picked me, sooner or later you'd grow to resent me."

"Never. Bri, I love you. We will make it work."

"You deserve a life filled with love, and children. And those children deserve doting grandparents and holidays with their big loving family. You can have that Mac, have it all. I can't. They'd be hunted and they'd be killers. Just like me." She lifted her gaze to meet his, her eyes pleading. "A family. That's what you said you wanted. I'm giving you that—by leaving."

"Is this because you don't love me or because you do?"

He waited with his heart pounding in his throat.

"I love you. And that's why I'm going."

Bri knew the moment that Mac recognized what would

happen next because the color washed from his face. He opened his arms. But she would not let him touch her because if he got hold of her, he might not let go. But even worse, she might not have the strength to leave.

"Bri, no," Mac said, already reaching for her. "I can protect you."

Yes, he could protect her and he would never leave her. Just like her father would not leave her mother even to save his own life.

Her power would not kill him, not in the way her mother's had killed her father. It would be a different kind of death, one that stole away each person he loved. She saw it all repeating. His devotion and her willingness to take everything he offered because she could not imagine her life without him.

She gave him a smile that hurt right down to her heart.

"I can protect you, too, Travis. Take care of Johnny." Bri blew him a kiss and then ran. He dove at her, but she was too fast. In an instant she had left them behind. She didn't look back, because she knew what she would see, Mac changing and moving too slowly to catch her. Mac howling as she put a mile between them and then two.

As she ran, she ignored the crushing sensation in her lungs and the quavering ache that vibrated from her beating heart. Was this why her mother stayed, to keep from feeling this terrible pain? Was this what her grandmother had wanted, for her to protect the ones she loved?

"Did I do it, Nana? Did I keep my humanity?"

Brianna reached the paved road and continued along in her bounding run, galloping up the miles with no destination except away. Away from Mac. Away from Johnny. Away from the life Mac offered—a life of sweetness and sorrow.

She wondered if he would ever forgive her. Wondered if

she'd ever forget him. Did her mother still love her father from her place in that other world? Did her mother ever think of her daughter?

Bri wished she could have gone with her to the Fairyland instead of being condemned to a life apart from the rest of humanity.

The road stretched out before her, long and lonely and dark. But she ran it because she had no other choice.

Chapter 21

Mac followed Bri's trail, with Johnny on his heels, until well into the moonrise. But she'd taken the highway, knowing, he supposed, that Johnny could not follow.

He had to find somewhere safe for Johnny. Then he could go after Bri. But even if he found her, how could he convince her that he wanted a life with her?

Mac suffered the change as Johnny watched glumly. Once in human form he told Johnny what he planned to do. Johnny agreed to wait but he wasn't happy.

Two hours later Mac had found Bri's old apartment. Her scent hung about the place, but it was an old scent. But then he saw something move inside the upper apartment and went to investigate.

By sunrise he pulled the compact car to the shoulder closest to the place he had left Johnny. He exited the vehicle dressed in an assortment of clothing from Bri's grandmother, slip-on shoes, black sweatpants and a sky-blue turtleneck that fit a little too well.

Johnny stood waiting then lifted his head at the car's arrival.

"Bri's grandmother's, according to the registration. Keys were in the apartment."

Johnny waited.

"No sign of her. But she had company. Another one. I killed it."

Johnny drew a long breath and blew it out. Mac knew it was his concern come to fruition, that he would find himself outnumbered because he had asked Lam to stay behind.

"Just one. I handled it. Also got some money and a few sacks of food. Her grandmother kept a well-stocked cupboard."

Johnny motioned for paper. Mac rummaged in the glove box and came up with a stubby pencil and the back of a receipt for an oil change. He handed them to Johnny. The pencil disappeared into his hand as he scrawled across the page.

Followed her trail. Lost it. She's gone.

Mac felt his heart drying up inside him. Johnny wrote, his handwriting all but illegible. *What now?*

Mac wondered the same thing. "I'm not giving up."

Mac combed their trail again and found no trace of her. He backtracked and followed every lead to a dead end. After three months of seeking Brianna, fall had arrived and he was still wondering what he and Johnny should do.

The summer months had been lush and the cover excellent. Now with the seasons changing again, he'd found a series of cottages on a lake far to the north but still in California. They seemed to be used only in the summer. He and Johnny established a residence in one in early September. He left Johnny to search for Bri but found no sign. Then he visited his family, careful to avoid the military surveillance. He spoke only with his dad, told him everything and arranged a way to get in touch. Then he returned West, taking a job with a local lumber mill clearing trees from private land. He was at a job site on 314 acres, working on a tree he'd just dropped, when a small, mud-spattered pickup pulled up and out stepped Paul Scofield, Mac's drill instructor from basic training.

The Marines sent the right man to confront him, likely one of the only men whom Mac still respected. Scofield was a tough old leatherneck, but every man under him knew his aim was to give them the skills necessary to stay alive.

Mac let his chain saw idle. It wasn't an automatic weapon. But it would do in a pinch.

"MacConnelly," said Scofield as he slammed the driver's-side door of the mud-streaked black pickup, which was not standard issue.

The DI looked thinner in civilian clothing, and his bald head was not covered with his familiar headgear but a cap advertising the brand of truck he drove.

"Drill Sergeant." Mac started to snap a salute and then stopped himself.

"You look as comfortable with that chain saw as you did with your M-4."

"Less recoil," he said and waited.

"They want you back, son. Both of you."

Mac said nothing to this. He knew Johnny was nearby, listening. Waiting for a signal from him.

"They asked me to tell you that Lewis and Sarr went off the farm. They never had clearance for any of it. I know what they did to you, son. And I know it was outside the orders of their superiors. Colonel Strangelove and Dr. Mengele, there, were out of bounds. *Way* out of bounds, and I'm sorry for what happened to you and Lam."

Suddenly Mac's throat felt tight and he had the urge to tell Scofield how betrayed he felt. Then he shook himself and held on to his anger. That, at least, had never let him down.

"You better go," Mac said.

"They replaced him with a man they think you can trust. He's overseeing the operation now and he is on board with helping fix Private Lam's, uh, issues."

"I don't trust anyone but Johnny."

"That wasn't their first choice, since he's still on a UA."

Unauthorized Absence. Mac knew that was a lesser term for what they were—AWOL.

"What asswipe do they think I'd trust enough to come back in?"

Scofield scratched beneath his cap. "That asswipe would be me."

The two men stared at each other.

"It will be different, MacConnelly. You have my word. You'll be in the loop on everything because I'm appointing you my second in command."

"I'm only a sergeant."

"Not if you come in, you're not."

"I'm trying to find someone."

"Yes. Brianna Vittori. We found her, but we thought you might like to be the one to ask her to come in."

Mac switched off his chain saw but his heartbeat seemed to be revving at the same speed. "You found her?"

Mac sat in the helo beside Maj. Paul Scofield and listened intently as he reviewed their intel on Brianna Vittori.

Below them the tops of the aspens shone a brilliant gold in the October sunlight.

Bri's new place lay in a remote area in the mountains outside Taos, New Mexico. Off the grid, solar powered and heated by woodstove. She had no neighbors and had moved twice since Mac had seen her last.

"She spends four hours each afternoon in a cubicle at the public library working online helping nonprofits with grant preparation, project planning and the creation of skilled volunteer programs," said Scofield.

Mac smiled at this as he realized that she'd managed to find a way to help people even as she avoided them.

"Small income, but she gets by. Does all her banking online. That's how we track her. She rides a motorcycle which she could easily abandon if attacked."

"I don't want her to see the helo," said Mac.

"We'll drop you and wait for your signal."

"I appreciate that."

The bird touched down and Mac disembarked holding a map and a cell phone.

"Good luck, Captain," said Scofield, using Mac's new rank.

His throat felt suddenly dry. What if she wouldn't come back?

Bri took the last quarter mile on her motorcycle slow. October's cold had gilded the aspens and the cottonwoods a lovely red, but the afternoons were still sunny and warm.

Bri pulled to a stop and cut the engine. She had already lowered the kickstand of her bike and removed her helmet when she noticed her front door lay open.

She stepped away from the motorcycle knowing she was faster on foot, faster than anything human and everything half human that she'd met so far. She'd already outrun the vampires twice.

"Who's there?" she called as she eased backward, letting her power tingle through her like a shower of sparks. She was ready to run. Ready to disappear again.

Something moved from the darkness beyond her door. A man stepped out.

The heels of his shoes slapped loudly upon the large stone step. She stared at the familiar blood stripe on the royal-blue trousers above the shiny black shoes and the midnight-blue coat of a Marine's dress blues. He held his white cap, clamped under one arm by the shiny black brim, perpendicular to the midnight-blue belt that cinched his trim waist. Fixed in the center of the belt's buckle was the gold emblem of the Marines, the anchor, eagle and globe. As he moved into the sunlight of the yard she saw the flash of his gold buttons and two parallel silver bars on his shoulder. Bri took another step away, but the possibilities kept her from running. Could it be?

Mac!

She recognized him now beneath the pressed midnight-blue jacket festooned with bars of color across his left chest. The instant his blue eyes met hers she felt that familiar rush of excitement and the tingling awareness that only happened with Travis MacConnelly. It was all she could do not to rush into his arms.

Oh, nothing had changed in three months, except now she wanted him even more. Somehow she held herself back.

"Bri." He replaced his hat to his head, the brim now shielding his pale eyes against the bright afternoon sunshine and then extended a hand toward her. "I'm alone. Don't run again. Please."

She swallowed back the emotion that choked her. It took all her willpower not to rush into his arms. Her eyes drank in the sight of him as she trembled with the sheer joy of seeing him safe and whole.

"How's Johnny?" she asked, her voice a whisper.

His brows tented, disappearing beneath the brim of his hat. "The same."

She nodded her understanding, absorbing the sorrow that the news brought to her bruised heart.

He kept one hand out like a blind man feeling his way along as he inched toward her. She watched his approach. Each step brought an new urgency to her pounding heart.

"How did you find me?" she asked.

"Military intelligence. They've had you pinned for two months."

She glanced over her shoulder at the empty road. Her escape.

"Don't," he said, his voice tinged with anguish.

When she turned back it was to find him too close. Her skin tingled and she knew she should go, but she couldn't make herself do it. Instead, she stood there gobbling up the sight of him. She could see the blue of his eyes now and the intensity of his stare. If she let him grab her there would be no escape. How she wanted to let him.

"Stop," she ordered.

He did, holding up his hands in surrender. "Okay. Just don't run."

She agreed to this with a slow nod. "I've only been here two months."

"A little more. Boulder, Colorado. Then here."

Her jaw dropped. It was true, then.

"But if they knew, then why wait?"

"Because now I'm in charge of the unit that studies vampires."

She didn't understand. "You're what?"

"The brass had no idea what Lewis was doing, which isn't really surprising considering the stupidity of those rear-echelon motherfuckers."

She glanced about to check if they were really alone. Something about him was very different than when they had parted, and it wasn't just the shiny shoes and new badges on his chest. There were circles under his eyes and a weariness that clung to him like a heavy cloak.

"Bri, I've missed you," he whispered.

She absorbed the sharp thrust of pain in her heart at his words. She didn't respond in kind. What was the use?

"I want to take you back with me. Major Scofield has a position for you."

She stiffened. "Who?"

"My commanding officer. He's a good man. I trust him, Bri. What's more, Johnny trusts him."

Johnny didn't trust anyone but Mac and with good reason. Her heart tugged at her and she wanted so much to believe everything he said.

"Johnny trusts him?"

Mac touched his tongue to his upper lip and nodded. His eyes earnest and his expression hopeful. "The whole operation has changed. They court-martialed that rat fuck Sarr and six others."

That was welcome news. Still, it changed nothing.

"Do you remember saying that I couldn't have the life I deserved if you stayed?"

She flushed.

"And you were right. Because if you stay, my life will be more than I deserve."

She opened her mouth to object but he lifted a hand and she fell silent.

"It won't be the life I envisioned. That's true. But it will be different only because it will be so much better. I can't picture a future that doesn't include you. Bri, I'm miserable without you. If you want to protect me from loss and sorrow, you have to stay with me."

Had the last few months been as terrible for him as they had been for her? Yes, she realized, seeing the truth in his sad, tired eyes. And she knew he was right. They needed to be together.

"What about your family?" she asked.

"I told my parents everything, about me, about you, about us."

"You what?" Astonishment rolled through her. Was he even allowed to tell them this?

"They are waiting to meet you in Taos. I flew them out."

"But it's dangerous. I—"

He held up a hand. "Princess, you keep thinking of what I'll give up, but the only thing I can't give up is you. It's time to forgive ourselves. It's time to take what life offers— the love and loving." He removed his cap and tossed it to the ground before capturing her hand. Then he dropped to one knee in the dust beside his cap and fished in his pocket, then drew out a black velvet box, which he flicked open and extended to her.

"Brianna Vittori, I love you. Please, be my wife."

Inside the folds of ivory fabric nestled a pale green ring. The band had been inset with diamonds.

"Yes," she whispered, extending her hand, accepting the forgiveness he offered with the love.

Her hand trembled as Mac slipped the ring over her knuckle. She waited for it to burn. But it never came.

"It's jade and diamonds. No metal."

Bri stared down at the beautiful ring. "It feels just right."

She cradled her left hand over her heart and then extended her arms to her fiancé. He pulled her close. She rose on her tiptoes to hug him, pressing her cheek against his. Bri locked her hands about his neck as Mac swept her off her feet and carried her in a slow circle. She was breathless with joy and dizzy with hope when he set her back on solid ground and gave her a long, languid kiss.

Mac laced his fingers through her thick hair, gazing down at her. "I love you, Bri. And I always will."

She wiped the tears away and gave him a trembling

smile. The lump in her throat was so big she didn't know how she spoke past it.

"I was terrified that I'd keep you from happiness."

"That can only happen if you leave me." He gave her hand a squeeze. "Don't ever do that again, Bri. Promise me."

"No, never again," she promised.

He kissed her again. When they broke apart he was grinning and looked years younger. "Ready to meet my parents?"

"Is any woman ever ready for that? What do they think about me?"

"Curious, of course. Bri, I showed them what I am. They know I will not be leading an ordinary life."

"You…"

He nodded.

"Where are we going?"

"Taos first. They're waiting there. Then on to Oahu."

"Hawaii?"

"Yes. Deep cover for Johnny, a defensible position and a specialized research facility for us."

"Hawaii?"

They exchanged grins.

She clung to his elbow. "I'm ready."

Bri stooped and retrieved Mac's hat, dusted it off and offered it to him. He set it expertly on his head, then lifted a phone from his pocket and spoke into the unit. A moment later she heard a loud *womp-womp-womp* that vibrated through her chest.

"What's that?" she asked, covering her ears as she turned toward the sound to see a large military helicopter sweep in from the east.

"Our ride," he shouted. "Unless you'd rather run?"

She shook her head as the dust rose all around her. "No. No more running for me."

The helicopter touched down and Mac assisted her into the compartment. As she took her seat beside Mac, she felt her grandmother smiling down on her for Bri knew that she had found forgiveness and love. That was the best way to keep one's humanity.

* * * * *